Clare Darcy

F
D

First published in the United States of America in 1973 by the Walker Publishing Company, Inc.

Published simultaneously in Canada by Fitzhenry & Whiteside, Limited, Toronto.

ISBN: 0-8027-0408-5

Library of Congress Catalog Card Number: 72-95767

Printed in the United States of America

Lydia
or Love in Town

Also by Clare Darcy:

CECILY
GEORGINA

To C.L.D.

CUPITT, OPENING THE FRONT DOOR at Great Hayland on a warm May morning, suffered a shock at sight of the gentleman standing before him— a shock so severe, in fact, that the magisterial calm cultivated over fifty years of service came near to deserting him entirely.

"My lord!" he gasped. "Oh, dear! Oh, my gracious! Why, we never expected—Your lordship never wrote—"

At first glance, there would have appeared to be little in the figure before him to cast even an elderly butler into such affliction. The Fourth Viscount Northover, who until some seven months previous had rejoiced in no more impressive title than that of Captain of Dragoon Guards, was a young man still, not quite thirty-four, and one, moreover, whom Cupitt had found totally disinclined to stand upon his new dignity on the brief visits he had earlier made to Great Hayland. He had a trim, powerful figure, considerably above medium height, a face which, although of too swarthy and aquiline a cast to be called handsome, had a certain appearance of careless distinction, and satirical dark eyes set beneath brows as black as his hair, which he wore in the severe style known as the Stanhope crop.

He greeted Cupitt in his usual offhand manner, cocked a quizzical eyebrow at the butler's failure to budge from his panic-stricken position in the doorway, and uttered an equable enquiry as to whether there were some particular reason why he might not enter his own house.

"No, my lord! Certainly not!" Cupitt stammered, stepping back and allowing the Viscount to walk inside. "It was only the shock—the surprise of seeing you so unexpectedly—"

The Viscount, who had had experience in many quarters of the world with the universal look of a Guilty Conscience lurking behind the dignified façade of an upright servant, cast a speculative and somewhat amused glance about him as he stepped through the doorway, but saw nothing that might immediately account for Cupitt's odd behaviour.

It was true that a critical eye might have found much to cavil at in the appearance of the hall, where the furniture stood gloomily swathed in holland covers, and tarnished gilt, faded brocade, and peeling paint gave evidence of a shocking state of neglect. Lord Northover, however, was not shocked. He was well aware that his great-uncle, the Third Viscount, had been far too clutchfisted to spend a groat on keeping up an estate where he had never resided and which he had valued purely from the point of view of the income that it had brought to him. And he himself, having every intention of disposing of this Berkshire property which had come into the family barely thirty years before, and which lay in a quite different part of the country from his principal seat, had not troubled himself over the restoration of the house, but had been content to leave it as it had been in his great-uncle's day, under the care of a pair of elderly servants.

He was aware, therefore, that it was not the state of the house that was responsible for Cupitt's present perturbation. Neither, he guessed, was it possible that petty pilfering had set that guilty look on the butler's ruddy face, for the Third Viscount Northover, he knew, had been totally disinclined to hire servants capable of making off with even the smallest part of his substance.

The matter intrigued him only for a moment, however, and he would have dismissed it from his mind entirely as he handed his curly-brimmed beaver and York tan gloves to Cupitt, assuring him meanwhile that he had stopped off only to have a look in at the place on his way to London, had not Cupitt himself brought it into the open.

"My lord, if you please—" said Cupitt, in an agitated voice. "If you will but allow me to explain—"

"Yes?" Northover paused. "What is it, Cupitt?"

But Cupitt seemed to find it less than easy to come so directly to the point.

"You must believe, my lord," he said almost tearfully, "that I would never in the world have done it if I had had the least expectation of your lordship's arrival—or that your lordship was even in this part of the country—"

"Done what?" demanded Northover. "Cut line, Cupitt! What the devil have you been up to?"

Thus adjured, Cupitt made a desperate attempt and gathered his resolution. "My lord," he plunged into his confession, a look of the deepest mortification upon his face, "I regret to be obliged to inform you that you will find a—a young female in the library!"

The Viscount's black brows went up slightly. "Really, Cupitt?" he said gravely. "At your age? You astonish me! And what has Mrs. Cupitt to say to this?"

The colour surged back into Cupitt's face. "My lord!" he said, affronted. "You quite mistake the matter! I should not dream of engaging in such—such—" He saw the gleam of a smile lurking in Northover's ordinarily rather cynical eyes and drew himself up, on his dignity again. "Your lordship may find the matter a subject for amusement," he went on, rather stiffly. "I assure you that it is not so to me. The fact is that I have been induced by—by past attachment to commit an act which I must anticipate you will take the most serious view of. I cannot think how I—But there it is!" he said, despair overcoming him once more. "In short, my lord, there are persons unknown to you staying in this house!"

The Viscount, who was beginning to find the matter increasingly interesting, maintained a creditable calm in the face of this disclosure.

"Indeed?" he said. "I hope you won't consider it uncivil of me to enquire who they may be?"

"No, my lord." Cupitt resigned himself, sighed heavily, and said, "Mrs. Leyland, Miss Leyland, and Mr. Leyland —and Mrs. Leyland's maid, Miss Winch. From America, my lord."

"From America? Have you ever *been* to America, Cupitt?"

"No, my lord."

"Then how—?"

"Mrs. Leyland, my lord," Cupitt explained unhappily, "is the former Miss Tresselt."

9

The Viscount considered this statement. "I gather," he remarked presently, "that that fact is expected to explain the matter to me, but I confess I am still in the dark. No doubt it is lamentably dull-witted of me—"

"The Tresselts, my lord," Cupitt said, in the same hopeless tone, "are—were the former owners of this estate. I daresay you may not recall, but this house was in their family from the time it was built, in the reign of Queen Anne, until some thirty years ago, when Mr. Gerald Tresselt was obliged, owing to financial reverses, to see it pass into your great-uncle's hands. You may not recall, either, that I began my service here as a lad some fifty years ago, when the Tresselts were still in possession."

"I see! Or do I?" Northover again considered. "Deuce take it, Cupitt, I can well imagine your former Miss Tresselt's wishing to *see* the place, but—staying here, with her entire family, it appears?"

Cupitt nodded gloomily. "Yes, my lord. Her grandson and granddaughter, at any rate. Not too plump in the pocket, I fear, if I may so express myself. They are on their way to London from Bristol, and—and I believe Mrs. Leyland fancied it a good idea, for purposes of both sentiment *and* economy—"

The Viscount could control his risibilities no longer, and gave vent to a shout of laughter. "In short, she bullied you into taking her in here!" he said. "My poor Cupitt, what a termagant she must be! Assuredly, I must meet her! In the library, you said?"

"No, my lord. It is *Miss* Leyland who is in the library," Cupitt said, looking doubtful at this totally unexpected reaction to his news. "Mrs. Leyland and the young gentleman, I believe, have gone for a stroll about the grounds."

"Then I shall have to postpone the pleasure and settle for *Miss* Leyland for the moment," Northover said, and strode off purposefully in the direction of the library.

Cupitt, left alone, trotted off apprehensively to the housekeeper's room to seek counsel of his wife, a round, ruddy woman, cut in the same mould as himself, whom he found engaged in a comfortable chat with Miss Winch. The dire news he had to impart to them, however, swiftly put an end to this conversation. Mrs. Cupitt fell back in her chair with a hollow exclamation that she was sure she felt one of her spasms coming on, while Miss Winch attempted instant succour with the aid of a vinaigrette fetched from her capacious reticule, at the same time adjuring her old acquaintance not to be so henwitted as to go off on her now.

"This is no time for the vapours, Martha Cupitt!" she said tartly. "We are in the suds, and must keep our wits about us. Drat the man! What possessed him to turn up when he was least wanted! What sort of creature is he, Mr. Cupitt? Cutting up stiff over the business—is he, now?"

"No, no." Cupitt sank down helplessly into the nearest chair, turning a bewildered face on Miss Winch's homely one. "As a matter of fact, he—he laughed when I told him!"

"Laughed?" Miss Winch shook her head, between amazement and disapproval. "Not queer in his attic, is he?"

"Lord Northover! Oh, no—no, indeed!" Cupitt said, shocked. "He appears to have an excellent understanding—though I am not, of course, well acquainted with him. He never visited here in the old lord's day, you see."

"He didn't? Why didn't he?" enquired Miss Winch, whose discourse was nothing if not direct. "He was the heir—wasn't he?"

"The heir? Oh, dear me, no!" Cupitt said. "That would have been Mr. Matthew Brome, the old lord's son. I knew *him* very well. But he was killed in a carriage accident only two months before the old lord died, and his son with him, so that it was Captain Christopher Brome, his lordship's great-nephew, who inherited. I knew *him* only by reputation," he concluded heavily.

"Well?" said Miss Winch. "And what sort of reputation has he?" Mrs. Cupitt groaned, and Miss Winch transferred her gaze to her. "Bad, is it?" she demanded.

Mrs. Cupitt nodded, with tragic emphasis. "You wouldn't credit the stories they tell, Amelia!"

"Women?"

Mrs. Cupitt, looking somewhat shocked at this frankness, managed a prim little nod. "The *first* one," she confided—"well, he wasn't twenty yet, they say, and her a married woman!—so *that* was when they sent him off to the Army. But from all accounts he was no better there—got himself into every sort of scrape and scandal, till I've heard it said the old lord swore he wouldn't so much as have him in the house."

"Now, Martha!" Cupitt said uneasily. "That's only gossip, you know. You'd best hold your tongue."

"Gossip, is it?" Mrs. Cupitt kindled at the aspersion. "And didn't Sarah McNish hear with her own ears Lady Sealsfield say she hoped Sir Peter wouldn't call on him if he came into the neighbourhood, for she wouldn't have *her* daughters exposed to the conversation of such a man?"

"Lady Sealsfield," said Cupitt, with unexpected spirit, "is a platter-faced old harridan. And I noticed Sir Peter *did* call when his lordship was here last—ay, and invited him up to the Manor as well, and pestering the soul out of him to tell him about Waterloo and the Peninsula—"

Miss Winch, who had listened to this interchange with increasing impatience, interrupted at this point to remark, "Ay, that's all very well, but it has nothing to say to the pickle we are in *now*. What are we to do, Mr. Cupitt? Had I best go and try to catch Madam and Mr. Bayard before they come into the house? And much good *that* would do!" she answered her own question. "Eh, the fat's in the fire now, and no mistake! I warned Madam how it would be, but when once she takes a notion into her head—!"

"She was always a—a very persuasive lady," poor Cupitt said, his head in his hands. "I can remember when she was no more than sixteen and not even out, she coaxed me into carrying letters to young Sir Harry Brinley at Crossflats—I very nearly got the sack over *that*! Ay, she had every spark in the neighbourhood at her beck and call—and to think that, in the end, she threw herself away on no better than a Brigade-Major in a Line Regiment, and went off to America to live among the savages—"

"Savages!" Miss Winch interrupted him, bridling. "I'll have you know, Mr. Cupitt, that Madam lived in as great a house as this one ever was, with all the furniture and carpets brought from France, and so many servants underfoot that you tumbled over them! Major Leyland did very well for himself in America, I can tell you, and was considered one of the first gentlemen in Louisiana when he died. It was only afterwards that we fell on hard times, for Madam's son, Mr. Henry, cared for nothing but his horses and his books, and let it all slip away from him, so that when he died there was nothing left but a nasty, damp plantation off in the midst of nowhere. And Madam is quite as bad as he was," she added darkly, "for she's no more sense than a baby when it comes to managing, and spent every penny she could lay her hands on in New Orleans, tricking herself and Miss Lydia out in the latest fashions, before they ever stepped on the boat to come over here. And now she must give way to one of her starts and stop off here to see the old place—and only look what's come of it! You'll be lucky if you and Martha don't lose your places on the head of this day's work, Mr. Cupitt!"

Cupitt was inclined to agree. He said dismally that he had best be getting back to his post, in case he might be needed there—to say nothing of the fact, he added, that it hardly seemed right to leave Miss Leyland in the library alone with a man of Lord Northover's reputation.

But, somewhat to his surprise, Miss Winch merely shrugged up her shoulders at this expression of anxiety. Miss Lydia, she said, was well able to take care of herself—a remark which drew a shocked protest from Mrs. Cupitt.

"Oh, no! How can you say so, Amelia? Didn't you tell us yourself, she has been living for four years completely retired in the country? And she can't be more than twenty—"

"True," Miss Winch agreed, imperturbably. "But that don't make a ha'porth of difference, Martha, my dear. She has the sense for the whole family—what there is of it to go round, that is—and as for her looking out for your pre-

cious Lord Northover, he'd best look out for *her*, instead!"
A slight, unaccustomed smile briefly lit her wintry face. "Ay,
let him look out for *her*," she repeated. "She can handle
him, or any other man alive, I dare swear, but as for his
handling *her*—that's another kettle of fish entirely. For she's
neither to lead nor to drive, as the saying goes, and what
he will make of her I'm blessed if I know!"

THE MASTER OF THE HOUSE, AT that precise moment, might have been somewhat inclined to agree with these words.

Opening the library door, on parting with Cupitt, he had found himself facing, not the dowdy, bashful young provincial he had expected, but a young lady with a decided air of fashion, dressed in a thin chemise gown of apricot muslin with short, puffed sleeves, which his experienced eye immediately recognised as being in the latest French mode. She was seated at the top of a pair of library steps with a book in her hand, looking perfectly at home, and, glancing up as he strolled into the room, addressed him at once in a rich alto voice.

"Well, I call *this* pretty cool!" she said.

The Viscount, finding himself the object of a direct and somewhat accusing gaze, paused and gave her back a look of considerable amusement.

"I beg your pardon?" he said.

"I should think you might!" Miss Leyland remarked, rising from her perch and descending from it to show him at full length a tall, slender, elegant figure, perfectly in accord with an almost classically cut face which was redeemed from the coldness usually associated with this type of beauty by the ripe colour of the lips and the riot of black curls modishly confined by an apricot ribbon above it. "Walking into a man's house as if you owned it!" she continued, with some severity. "I wonder where you can have learned your manners, sir!"

The Viscount was privately wondering where she had learned *hers*, for, though he had been acquainted with most of the audacious beauties of the past dozen Seasons, he could not recall one who would have greeted him with exactly this combination of nonchalance and candour.

"Shocking, isn't it?" he agreed, preserving a grave face.

"The point is, though, that I am—er—particularly well acquainted with the owner."

"That," Miss Leyland observed forthrightly, "is *not* an excuse. I suggest that you leave at once and return when Lord Northover is in residence."

She appeared to believe that he would follow her advice, for she moved to a chair and sat down in it with her book, looking up rather speculatively after a moment, as she saw that he had not moved, to remark to him, "I daresay you would not particularly care for me to send for someone to *escort* you out?"

"Frankly, I don't think you would find anyone who could," he retorted. "At any rate, I have an idea that I have quite as much right as you to be in this house. If Northover is not in residence, what are *you* doing here?"

"That is none of your affair," she said largely.

"It might be, if I happened to be Northover."

"But you are not—" She broke off, her eyes narrowing suddenly as she regarded him. "Oh!" she said. "You *are* Northover! Let me tell you that I regard *that* as completely unfair!"

"Not at all," he said, the smile he had been endeavouring to repress appearing upon his lips. "It was you who began it, you know, by accusing me of the most abominable rag-manners. In mere self-defence, I could not lower myself further in your opinion by being ill-bred enough to contradict your assumption."

She regarded him darkly. "Slippery, as well!" she pronounced. "*And* extravagant. How could you have expected me to imagine that you were Northover when you came strolling in here in that dapper-dog rig? From the looks of your house, you ought to be in rags. But I daresay that is *some* people's idea of economy—to let their house go to rack while they spend their last penny on a well-tailored coat!"

"I am glad," Northover returned, glancing down at his sleeve, "that my coat, at least, meets with your approval, Miss Leyland."

"Well, actually, it does," she conceded. "I wish you will

16

be good enough to give your tailor's name and direction to my brother when he comes in, for he swears that no Frenchman can make a well-fitting coat, and, after seeing you, I am inclined to believe it."

"You and your brother have been travelling in France, Miss Leyland?"

"Oh, no!"

"But your gown—?"

"New Orleans," she explained, looking with a critically approving gaze at the narrow silk braid with which the high waist and hem of the apricot gown were decorated. "Of course, direct from Paris—*not*," she confessed, "that I can afford it any more than you can afford that coat." She regarded him speculatively once more. "I daresay you are wondering what we are doing here," she observed. "You have been talking to Cupitt, of course, since you know my name. What did he tell you?"

"Only that your—grandmother, is it?—had formerly lived in this house before going to America, and that he had been induced to allow her and her party to spend the night here—or were you perhaps planning on a longer stay?" he broke off to enquire politely.

"Well, we *should* have liked to stop over until tomorrow," she acknowledged, not at all disconcerted by this thrust. "But I expect that is out of the question now, since *you* have arrived in this totally disgruntling way. You really should have given poor Cupitt notice, you know! How was he to imagine that you would behave so unceremoniously as to turn up here without the least warning? It is not at all the thing to do in your position—is it?"

Northover, who was beginning to enjoy the conversation, said that he supposed it was not, but explained that, having been used to occupy his exalted position for less than a year, he was no doubt somewhat remiss in fulfilling all the obligations owing to his rank.

"You don't mind if I sit down?" he added, moving towards a chair. "Unless, of course, that too would not suit your notions of propriety—?"

17

"Well, it is *your* house, so I suppose you may do as you like," she conceded handsomely. "Would you like me to ring for some refreshment?"

"If you please," he said, maintaining his gravity with even more of an effort.

But the quiver of a telltale muscle at the corner of his mouth as she rose to pull the bell-rope beside the mantel gave him away to her observant eyes, and a sudden ripple of laughter rose to her own lips.

"Abominable—isn't it?" she agreed. "To be playing the hostess in *your* house! But, you see, I am feeling very lady-of-the-manorish today. Grandmama's family have lived here since the beginning of time, and she has told me so much about it that I believe I could walk through it blindfolded. It is all exactly as she described it—though I must say I never expected to find it in such bad loaf. However," she added kindly, "I daresay you are as hungry as a church-mouse, in spite of your title, and have no funds to set things in better order."

The Viscount, whose inheritance had included, in addition to Great Hayland, one of the most extensive properties in Derbyshire, did not see fit to enlighten Miss Leyland concerning her misapprehension, but devoted himself instead to interrogating Cupitt, who appeared in the doorway at that moment, as to the refreshments it might be possible for the house to provide.

These, it developed, were neither numerous nor elaborate, but Cupitt was able to inform him that a tolerable sherry and some Queen-cakes baked that morning by Mrs. Cupitt would be forthcoming. He appeared quite non-plussed by the sight of his master seated in amicable conversation with Miss Leyland, and confided in amazement to Mrs. Cupitt and Miss Winch, when he repaired to the kitchen for the Queen-cakes, that the young lady had seemed quite as unperturbed as his lordship by the very awkward situation in which she found herself.

Upon this, Miss Winch unfolded her rather forbidding lips in a slight smile. "Lord bless you, Mr. Cupitt, if you think

18

a little thing like *this* is enough to overset Miss Lydia," she said tolerantly, "it's plain to see you don't know her yet!"

Cupitt, rather dazed, admitted that he did not, and wondered, as he departed with his laden tray, if all American young ladies were as unreserved as Miss Leyland, or whether it was only this particular one who was so unconcerned with the conventions.

He found her, on his re-entry into the library, regaling Lord Northover with an account of her former life in America.

"We are land-poor, you see," she remarked, as Cupitt set the tray down upon a heavy oak table. "I expect poor Papa had the worst judgement, when it came to business, of any man in the world, for he *would* buy Belmaison, which is nothing but a dismal swamp, fit only for snakes and mosquitoes. Of course no one was so bird-witted as to offer to take it off our hands when he died, so there we were set down for four long years, with no hope of escape, until my Great-aunt Letty, Grandmama's sister, was so obliging as to die here in England and leave her her jewels. Of course we have no idea as yet how much they will bring, but at least we have got to England on our expectations, where Grandmama says there is not the least doubt that I shall soon be able to make an advantageous marriage that will set us all up famously."

Unfortunately for Cupitt, he was obliged at this point to leave the room, so that he heard no more of Miss Leyland's past history or future plans; but Lord Northover, privileged to continue the conversation, was moved to interrupt here to enquire why this laudable plan could not have been carried out on Miss Leyland's home grounds.

"I have been in America myself, you see," he explained, "and it appears to me that you might find gentlemen there who are quite as wealthy and susceptible as any in this country."

"Oh, yes!" she agreed. "It was Grandmama's idea that we come to England—not merely because it will be more convenient in taking up her inheritance, but also because she has been longing for years to settle here once more. She *cannot* like America, you see. Even when Papa was alive, and we were still well enough off to visit New Orleans for several months each year, she disliked it, and if she could have persuaded him to return here, I am sure she would have done so."

"I see. And her plan now is that it is you who are to repair the family fortunes?"

"Yes, for Bayard—my brother—is exactly like Papa, with not the least notion of how to go on. Grandmama thinks he would do very well in the Army, however, if someone were so obliging as to buy his commission in a cavalry regiment."

"The obliging 'someone,' of course, being your future husband?"

"Well, it certainly seems as if he might—don't you think so?" she enquired. "If one were tremendously rich, it would be a mere bagatelle!" She added, "Of course, there is Sir Basil Rowthorn, Great-aunt Letty's husband—"

"What—the Nabob? Are you connected with him? He is as rich as Croesus, by all accounts."

"Yes, but he has never seemed in the least inclined to do anything for us. However, that *may* have been merely because he did not know us. Now that we shall be able to go to London and meet him, it may put our relationship on quite a different footing."

The Viscount, regarding with a connoisseur's eye the slender, elegant figure and enchanting face of the young lady before him, agreed that it might, and enquired whether, in that case, the need for an immediate search for a wealthy husband might diminish.

"Well, I suppose so," she said, considering the matter. "But I don't *think* it is particularly likely that Sir Basil will actually do anything for us. My great-aunt was his second wife, you see, and he has a great-nephew and a great-niece on his first wife's side as well, who I should imagine have been turning him up sweet for years. So I expect, in the end, it will have to be the husband." She looked at him with a suddenly interested expression upon her face. "I daresay that *you*, being a peer, are well acquainted in *ton* circles," she said, "so if you have any advice for me, I should be very glad to hear it. Of course, Grandmama was a famous belle in her day, but that was years ago, and I expect things have changed a great deal since then and *her* ideas will be considered quite gothic."

"Not if yours bear any relation to them," Northover assured her, a gleam in his dark eyes.

She surveyed him, arrested. "Oh!" she said. "Do you think I am *fast*? To be sitting here talking to you alone, I mean?"

"Let us say—unconventional," Northover emended it. "And—if you care for my opinion—delightful. I abominate missish females."

She shrugged her shoulders, her composure not at all disturbed by the frankness of the compliment. "That is all very well," she said candidly, "but I shall get nothing by pleasing *you*, you know."

Northover gave a crack of sardonic laughter. "You are in the right on that point, my dear," he said. "I am not a marrying man."

"Well, it cannot signify to me if you are or are not, since you are not rich," she said decidedly. "Grandmama has warned me not to be taken in by a title alone, for she says there are peers who have not a feather to fly with, and it seems, from the look of this house, that you must certainly be one of them. But I daresay there are dozens of others who are quite affluent?"

"Oh, dozens!" he agreed. "But if I were you, Miss Leyland, I shouldn't set my cap at men who were quite above my touch. A girl without a fortune can hardly hope for one of the greatest prizes on the Marriage Mart, you know. If you will heed a word of the advice you sought from me, you will not look for rank and title along with the fortune you are so frank in saying you must have."

Her chin went up slightly. "In other words," she said,

"you don't think I could do it—marry *both* wealth and title, that is. What a very poor opinion you must have formed of me, my lord!"

"Not of you—of my own sort," he said cynically. "You will find plenty of us to dangle after a pretty face, but few to offer marriage, except where there are family and fortune to make up the balance."

"Well, of course, one will get nowhere if one is poor-spirited enough to give up before one has even made the attempt!" she said. She broke off to add, at the sound of footsteps in the hall, "But here are Grandmama and Bayard now. You *will* be civil to them—will you not? Grandmama—Bayard—" she addressed the newcomers as they stepped into the room, "this is Lord Northover. He has dropped in from nowhere and intends to send us packing at once—that is, unless one of you is clever enough to talk him out of the idea!"

THE TWO PERSONS AT WHOM THIS rather startling statement was flung stopped short upon the threshold, regarding the Viscount out of what appeared to him to be identical pairs of very dark blue eyes.

There, however, the similarity ended, for one pair belonged to an aquiline-featured, rather startlingly raven-haired lady of some sixty years, attired in a modish bronze-green walking-dress and carrying a Chinese sunshade, and the other to a tall young gentleman in a slate-blue coat, who bore a striking resemblance to Miss Leyland. Northover, rising, greeted both with an imperturbability quite unimpaired by Miss Leyland's blunt charge, and invited them to be seated and partake of the refreshments that Cupitt had provided.

"Miss Leyland has been telling me something of the circumstances that have brought you here, ma'am," he went on, addressing himself to the lady. "An unexpected pleasure, I assure you! I only regret that it is not in my power to offer you more adequate hospitality."

Mrs. Leyland, accepting his invitation to be seated with aplomb, regarded him with approving eyes.

"How very kind of you!" she said graciously. "But then I knew how it must be, once you were acquainted with the circumstances! Poor Cupitt was cast into such a taking when we arrived, but I assured him he was making a piece of work over nothing, for no one—*no one!*—could be so marble-hearted as to dispute the propriety of my wishing to revisit the scenes of my girlhood." She regarded the Viscount interestedly as he handed her a glass of sherry. "I knew your father—no, I daresay it must have been your grandfather," she said. "A most disagreeable man, as I remember him."

Northover laughed. "I imagine it is my great-uncle to whom you are referring, ma'am, and I entirely agree with you," he said.

He poured a glass of wine for young Mr. Leyland, who

seemed to find the sudden appearance of the owner of the house no more disturbing than did his grandmother, and only smiled at him lazily as he sat down and stretched his long legs comfortably before him. He was a tall young man, almost a head taller than his sister, whose senior he might have been by a year or two, and he had the same air of unself-conscious assurance that Miss Leyland herself possessed, without, however, her vivacity of manner. Northover, observing the brief glances that occasionally passed between the two, realised that in their case the usual bond between brother and sister had been reinforced to such an extent—probably, he thought, by those four years of isolation on a remote Louisiana plantation—that each knew almost without the necessity for words what the other was thinking.

He guessed Miss Leyland to be the leader of the pair—which explained her feeling that it was she who must manage to provide for her brother, rather than the more usual alternative of the latter's undertaking to look after her. Looking after Miss Leyland, in fact, the Viscount decided, would be an exercise in futility, for it was apparent that she was a young lady of great resourcefulness. It was, he reflected, the very devil that the circumstance of her being a guest under his roof precluded his initiating what he was sure would be one of the most interesting flirtations it had been his privilege to indulge in over a dozen years.

That it might have required some address on his part to inaugurate such a flirtation he was well aware, for Miss Leyland, he thought, showed no sign of considering him as anything but a somewhat troublesome and probably—since she had applied to him for advice—respectably avuncular figure.

In this latter notion, however, he was not entirely correct. Miss Leyland, critically surveying the bronzed countenance on which years of campaigning and not infrequent bouts of dissipation had carved somewhat harsher lines than his actual years might have accounted for, had indeed dismissed him as being beyond the age to take her interest; but she was far from considering him in an avuncular light. As a mat-

24

ter of fact, the thought had immediately entered her mind that her host—except for the fact that he seemed to possess rather too much levity of disposition to take himself seriously in the role—might have stood very well as a model for the Byronic heroes who had enlivened her solitude and Bayard's at Belmaison. His penetrating dark eyes and indefinably reckless air, she considered, gave him very much a "corsairish" appearance, and the elegance of the cut of his olive-green coat and fawn-coloured buckskins could not conceal the powerful muscles that rippled beneath them.

As he had guessed, however, she was far from feeling an inclination to carry on a flirtation with him, and was more disposed merely to make use of him in learning more of the world of fashion which she desired to enter. Her brother, on the other hand, discovering in the course of the conversation that the Viscount had been a soldier for more than a dozen years, and had been engaged in most of the Duke of Wellington's campaigns, immediately lost his air of tolerant detachment and began to ply him with eager questions. Had he been at Salamanca? At Waterloo? Had he ever seen Napoleon himself? What was the Duke like? Was it true that he was the greater commander of the two?

Northover, who had been accustomed for years to this sort of catechism flung at him by ardent young subalterns, handled it with the ease of long practice, winning the approval of Mrs. Leyland by refusing to pronounce Napoleon either a monster or a hero.

"Quite a vulgar little man, by all I have been able to learn," she gave it as her opinion, "with a habit of setting up his brothers and sisters as pinchbeck royalty that I cannot but consider as excessively bad *ton*." She glanced about the room in which she sat, where the windows looked out upon an unkempt lawn and the gilt grilles enclosing the book-shelves showed the tarnish of long neglect, and said, with a disapproving shake of her head, "I hope I shall not find such sad changes in London as I have done here; but indeed it appears to me, from what I have seen since setting foot in England, that that dreadful war has had quite a *devastating* effect upon Society. When I remember this house as it used to be—!" She fixed Northover with an eye quite as accusing as her granddaughter's had been and observed, "I cannot but think that persons who take advantage of the difficulties in which distinguished families may find themselves to purchase their estates have an obligation at least to keep them in respectable repair!"

"Oh, what does it signify, Grandmama?" Bayard said impatiently. "Besides, Lord Northover has told you that he has been serving abroad until only recently, so how should he have known how things were going on here?"

"He knows now," said Mrs. Leyland, with awful incontrovertibility, which, however, quite failed to quell the Viscount. He remarked instead, with a wicked glance at Lydia, that Miss Leyland had already informed him of her plans for entering the no doubt sadly decayed but still exclusive world of London Society, and enquired whether Mrs. Leyland had connexions at present living in England who could be of service to her to that end.

"Oh, as to *that*," replied Mrs. Leyland, with undiminished assurance, "I daresay I shall be able to find out *someone* who is willing to sponsor us. I was acquainted with *hundreds* of people when I was a girl here, and there are always cousins, you know. It is so much in their interest not to have a set of relations on the town who are quite outside of Society that they are usually only too happy to put one in the way of entering into fashionable circles. Would you happen to know, for example, my dear sir, if Lady Fowlie is still alive? We quite loathed each other when we were girls, but, after all, she *is* my first cousin and married to a baronet, which is exactly the rank for her to fret excessively at the idea of having relations setting themselves up in London whom no one feels obliged to receive!"

"I am afraid," said Northover, reflecting with some amusement that it was easy to see whence Miss Leyland's peculiar notions of propriety derived, "that I can give you no information on that head, ma'am. I am unfortunately not acquainted with the lady."

"Well, it is of no consequence." Mrs. Leyland shrugged, dismissing Lady Fowlie without regret. "There are the Whitefords, as well, who are connected with my mother's family—and then there is Lucinda Pettingill, who is only a very distant connexion, but was my bosom-bow when we were girls. She married Sir Henry Aimer after I went to America—"

The look of amusement deepened on Northover's face. "Good God, are you acquainted with Lady Aimer?" he asked. "Now *there*, ma'am, is someone who can be of real service to you, if you can but induce her to take you up. She knows everyone, and goes everywhere—but I should warn you that she has no great reputation for amiability."

"Oh no, I expect she has not," Mrs. Leyland said tranquilly. "She had always a waspish tongue. I shall certainly look her up."

"Berkeley Square," Northover said helpfully, advising her further, with a gleam of unholy amusement in his eyes, "You might find it useful to request her to furnish you as well with an introduction to her daughter, Lady Gilmour. She entertains widely and, as she has a marriageable daughter of her own, may be able to be of more assistance than Lady Aimer in bringing Miss Leyland into company with a somewhat younger set, more suitable for her purposes."

Miss Leyland, who had not failed to observe the glint in his lordship's eyes and the slight emphasis he had placed upon his last words, regarded him suspiciously.

"Are you hoaxing us, Northover?" she demanded. "I don't like the look in your eye!"

"Not in the least. You will have everything to gain from Lady Gilmour's taking you up. She married within the past twelvemonth a gentleman of the first rank, after having been left a widow a few years before, and has every intention, I believe, of making a great stir in Society with her new consequence. Under her aegis you may meet all the most eligible peers in London and take your pick among 'em."

"I do not consider, my lord," Mrs. Leyland remarked, an expression of some hauteur upon her face, "that it is quite

27

proper for you to speak in such terms to my grand-daughter—as if she were on the catch for a husband, to use the vulgar phrase. Naturally she will wish to be introduced to the company of eligible gentlemen—"

She was interrupted at this point by Miss Leyland, who said to her frankly, "Oh, it is of no use your trying to wrap it up in clean linen, Grandmama. I have already told him what our situation is, and that I *must* have a rich husband."

"A confidence which I am highly honoured to have received," said Northover, with a slight bow, "but may I advise you further, Miss Leyland, not to be so devastatingly truthful with *every* gentleman you meet? We are an abominably sensitive lot, you know, and are apt to shy away from the bargain if we are allowed to see that it is only our purses, and not ourselves, that are in demand."

"Well, of course," Mrs. Leyland put in, superbly, "my granddaughter will not marry *any* gentleman for whom she does not feel the proper regard. But it is *quite* as easy for a girl to fall in love with a gentleman of rank and wealth as with a nobody! I am sure if I had known as much at *her* age as I know now, I should have been a marchioness. But my mama was a very unworldly woman, who gave me no proper advice at all, and as a result I ran off with a mere Brigade-Major—something that I am *determined* shall never happen to Lydia."

Northover, with a commendable command of his countenance, agreed that such a contingency was indeed to be avoided at all costs, and Mrs. Leyland then relented in her disapproval sufficiently to spend an agreeable quarter hour in conversation with him concerning the present state of those now elderly members of the *ton* whom she remembered from her girlhood. At the end of this period his lordship arose to take his leave, saying that he must speak with Cupitt before he departed.

As his instructions to that anxious functionary contained no hint of censure over his having so far overstepped his authority as to allow the Leylands to remain overnight at Great Hayland, Cupitt was cast into such a fervour of relief and gratitude that he nobly offered to have the entire party out of the house before another hour had gone by; but this drew an entirely negative response from the Viscount. Mrs. Leyland and her young relations, he said, were to remain as his guests for as long as it suited them, and the Cupitts were to show them every attention in their power. This statement so much staggered Cupitt that he returned to Mrs. Cupitt and Miss Winch, after seeing his lordship off, with the freely expressed opinion that either his master was the easiest touch he had ever known or the Leylands a party of magicians.

Miss Winch smiled slightly, showing no surprise at the Viscount's unaccountable complaisance.

"Well, I told you how it would be," she said. "Between Madam and Miss Lydia, I wouldn't lay a groat on the chances of any man, lord or no, holding out against them. But you needn't fret yourself, Mr. Cupitt, for we won't be stopping here long, I'll be bound. Madam has other fish to fry, and if I know her, we'll be off to London in the morning. And then," she concluded, with a certain martial air of scenting future triumphs as yet unsuspected by the less knowing, "*then*, Mr. Cupitt, mark my words—*then* you'll begin to see action!"

IT DEVELOPED THAT MISS WINCH'S prediction was correct in at least one respect: the following morning found the Leylands on their way to London.

On arriving there, Mrs. Leyland instructed the chaise to set them down at Grillon's Hotel, where she proceeded to direct her grandson to engage a set of excellent rooms. The appearance of the party, travelling in the first style and displaying the latest mode in their attire, procured them a degree of attention at this exclusive hostelry which must have been sadly abated had it become known that barely enough remained in their common purse to pay the post-charges.

"Not that it signifies, of course," Mrs. Leyland remarked, surveying with equanimity the small heap of coins that now represented her total fortune. "Tomorrow morning we shall call upon Sir Basil's man of business, Mr. Peeke, and I have no doubt that he will be obliging enough to advance us any trifling sums we may have need of before I am put in possession of the money that can be realised from the sale of poor Letty's jewels."

Her granddaughter and grandson were too well used to living under a system of economy in which the morrow's necessities were no part of the present day's cares to evince any opposition to this plan. In point of fact, they were able, the next morning, fully to approve their grandmother's project to have the hackney-coach that was to convey them to Mr. Peeke's office first drive them about the town so that they might have a glimpse of the sights of London. Mrs. Leyland was eager to set eyes once more on the scenes that had been so familiar to her forty years earlier, and her granddaughter and grandson were equally interested in seeing the streets and edifices of which they had heard and read so much.

The excursion, however, was not an unmitigated success.

Mrs. Leyland, though in transports to find herself driving by the fashionable shops in Bond Street once more, yet lamented the passing of old landmarks; and Lydia and Bayard, whose knowledge of town life had been drawn from their visits to New Orleans, missed the colour and softness of the American South in this bustling, noisy metropolis. Lydia, indeed, her ears assailed by the ceaseless rumble of traffic on the cobblestones, and assaulted by the raucous cries of vendors of coals, rat-traps, silver-sand, and doormats, gave it as her opinion that Londoners must all have been deafened long since, which accounted for their addressing one another in such piercing voices.

But to this Mrs. Leyland would not agree.

"No, no," she said decidedly. "It is *your* accent that is deficient, my love. If I have told you and Bayard once, I have told you a hundred times that it will not do for you to drawl your words here as Louisianans do."

Lydia, who was looking thoughtfully at a modish hat of satin-straw, trimmed with puffs of ribbon, in a milliner's window, said encouragingly, "Nonsense, Grandmama! Lord Northover said he found my accent charming."

"I daresay he would," Mrs. Leyland remarked with asperity. "Winch has told me that, according to the Cupitts, he has a shocking reputation, and no doubt is perfectly used to insinuating himself into the good graces of unwary young females by fulsome and *quite* insincere compliments."

Lydia turned her head, opening her eyes wide. "Is *that* what he was doing?" she enquired innocently. "Good gracious, and I had not the least notion—"

Bayard grinned. "Coming it a little too strong, Lyddy!" he said. "Is that the tone you mean to try on the London beaux? I don't advise it; it don't suit you in the least."

"No, I don't think it does," she agreed, considering the matter with a critical air. "All the same, Northover *did* advise me to try for a little more *maidenly reserve*."

Her brother's eye caught hers; she broke into a gurgle, and Bayard into a shout, of laughter. Mrs. Leyland looked at Lydia disapprovingly.

"Yes, it is all very well for you to laugh, but on *that* point Lord Northover was *quite* correct," she said. "I can't think where you have learned such unbecomingly frank manners, my love! Not from *me*, certainly—and your poor papa, whatever his faults may have been, had the most polished of addresses. But I daresay it comes of his having allowed you to read any book you fancied out of his library—some of which I am sure were not at *all* suitable for a young girl's eyes."

"*And* of his having carried her to New Orleans so often, and allowed her to flirt outrageously with every man who came in company with her before she had ever put her hair up," Bayard said cheerfully. "You'd best give it up, Grandmama. Lyddy cut her eye-teeth on men's hearts; she knows exactly how to handle them. Do you remember that Russian baron who wanted to marry her when she was fifteen? Said she was *La Reine des Coeurs*, in the most execrable French imaginable—"

"Abominable! *The Queen of Hearts*! A chit of her age!" Mrs. Leyland said. "Your papa found it very amusing, but I am sure I did not! The man must have been all of forty!"

"Yes, but very plump in the pocket, Papa always said," Bayard remarked. "I'll tell you what, Lyddy—*I* think you would better have remained at home and set up your search for a husband in New Orleans. Scores of plump purses there, you know, and you might choose your nationality—Spanish, French, German—"

"Do *not* be talking so, you wicked boy!" Mrs. Leyland chided him. "You encourage her unbecoming language by your own! I vow I have never seen such exasperating children—but so it has always been, since you were in shortcoats! Your poor mama was used to say that it was always double mischief with the two of you, for one never misbehaved but he pulled the other into it as well. But here we are, I daresay!" she ended these reminiscences suddenly, as the hackney stopped before a row of respectable-looking buildings in the City. "Come now, the pair of you! *Do* try for a little conduct!"

She allowed herself to be assisted from the carriage by Bayard, and waited with an air of unruffled calm while he attempted to persuade the driver, in the most good-humoured of tones, that the sum of money still remaining in his possession was sufficient to defray the expense of the rather extended journey they had just made in his vehicle. The driver, however, was adamant in requiring the full amount he had originally demanded, and Mrs. Leyland was finally moved to summon one of Mr. Peeke's junior clerks, who had been peering interestedly from a window at the altercation going forward outside, and dispatch him to his employer with an imperious request that he pay the charges due. The clerk, who was rather dubious of accepting this commission, soon reappeared with the necessary sum and an altered air of great civility, and invited the Leylands to step inside, where Mr. Peeke, he said, would be glad to see them at once.

Mr. Peeke, in fact—a small, neat gentleman of some fifty-odd years—had himself by this time hurried out to usher them personally upstairs to his office, assuring them meanwhile of his eagerness to be of service to them. When he had seen them comfortably seated in his private room, he sat down himself behind his desk and, placing the tips of his fingers together, made a civil enquiry concerning their journey.

"Very tedious," Mrs. Leyland dismissed the topic summarily. "Perhaps you will be so good, Mr. Peeke, as to come to the point at once, for we have a great deal to do if we are to establish ourselves properly in town before the Season is far under way, and have no time to waste upon details. If you will merely inform me to what amount my sister's bequest will come, and when I may receive possession of it—"

Mr. Peeke blinked, but made a quick recovery and said that, regretfully, he could not answer the first part of her question categorically, as the amount must depend on what the jewels would bring, in the event she wished to sell them.

"Of course I wish to sell them!" Mrs. Leyland said, staring

at him. "My good man, if I did not, I should not have a feather to fly with! Now do *not*," she begged, as she saw him pick up a sheaf of papers from his desk, "go into niggling details, but merely tell me if I shall be able to realise enough to hire a house in a fashionable neighbourhood for the Season and maintain myself and my grandchildren there in good style. That is *all* I am interested in, for I am sure that, if Sir Basil Rowthorn entrusts you with *his* affairs, you are perfectly capable of seeing to everything else yourself."

Mr. Peeke appeared somewhat overwhelmed by this tribute to his competence, but almost immediately displayed his acuity as an observer of human nature by taking Mrs. Leyland at her word and assuring her that Lady Rowthorn's bequest was sufficient to allow her to follow, within reason, the programme she had just outlined.

"You must understand, of course," he added, "that the bequest does not extend to any jewels that might be considered as family heirlooms, but includes only those personal tokens of his regard which Sir Basil—"

He was interrupted by an expressive exclamation from Mrs. Leyland. "*Family* heirlooms! My good man, there ʼs no family; are you not aware of that? ʼʼ Sir Basil knows who his grandfather was, it is as much as he can tell you. He is the veriest mushroom, and if his father had not had the good fortune to find himself in India at a providential moment, with diamonds apparently dropping out of the trees into his lap, I daresay he would count himself happy to find employment as your clerk." She appeared struck by a new idea at that moment, and added, "Though I expect he would be considered somewhat superannuated for such a post *now*. Good heavens, he must be all of eighty by this time, for he was years older than poor Letty when he married her."

Mr. Peeke agreed that Sir Basil was indeed hard upon his eightieth birthday. He spoke somewhat absently, however; he was looking thoughtfully at Lydia and Bayard, and appeared to be turning some new notion over in his mind. Before Mrs. Leyland could speak again he had addressed her abruptly.

"My dear Mrs. Leyland, may I speak frankly to you?"

She eyed him a trifle warily. "Upon what subject? You are *not* going to tell me, I hope, that there is some obstacle in the way of my receiving this inheritance?"

"Not in the least. It has merely occurred to me—" Mr. Peeke suddenly threw caution to the winds and said, lowering his voice conspiratorially, "My dear ma'am, you must be aware that this bequest from Lady Rowthorn is a mere bagatelle compared to what might come—not to yourself, of course, but to your grandson, if Sir Basil were to make him his heir! Sir Basil is, as you have remarked, superannuated, and in failing health, and, as there are no nearer relations—"

He paused, a prim smile unexpectedly appearing upon his face as he observed the arrested expression in Mrs. Leyland's eyes.

"Go on!" she commanded. "No nearer relations—except, as I understand, for a great-nephew and a great-niece of his *first* wife's. Are you trying to tell me that *they* have been such jingle-brains as not to have already put themselves in Sir Basil's good graces to the extent that he intends to leave his fortune to *them*?"

The smile widened on Mr. Peeke's face. "They have *attempted* to do so—oh yes, I should be deceiving you, ma'am, if I did not admit *that*!" he said. "But whether they have succeeded is another matter. Indeed, as Sir Basil's man of business—in the strictest confidence, of course—I can assure you that the thing is still hanging fire. He is not, if I may say so, greatly taken with either young Mr. Pentony or his sister, and as for Lady Pentony, their mother—an estimable lady, but of a somewhat talkative and lachrymose disposition—I believe he has expressed himself in such uncomplimentary terms concerning her that she no longer dares to call upon him."

"Indeed!" said Mrs. Leyland, favouring him again with her penetrating stare. "And what is *your* interest in this, Mr. Peeke? Why should *you* care a button whether it is these Pentonys who inherit from Sir Basil or my grandson?"

Mr. Peeke coughed genteelly. "My dear ma'am," he con-.

fessed, "I will tell you frankly that the notion of doing so never entered my head until you were so good, a few moments ago, as to indicate that you were willing to honour me with your confidence by placing your affairs entirely in my hands. You will not have given the matter your consideration, of course, but if you will do so now, you must realise that it is extremely profitable to me to have the management of such an extensive property as Sir Basil Rowthorn's. Now if it were to fall to Mr. Pentony upon his demise, I am most certain that it would immediately be taken out of my hands."

"I see! Whereas, if my grandson were to inherit—"

"Exactly." Mr. Peeke regarded the tips of his fingers, which he had once more joined together, with demureness. "May I suggest," he said, "that we might be of—er—mutual assistance to each other, my dear ma'am? I have very little influence, I will confess, over the decision Sir Basil will make in regard to the disposal of his fortune, but I have gleaned a certain knowledge of his character over the years, and may be able to advise you as to the—er—tactics that might be most successful in obtaining his good will."

"I never heard of such impudence!" Mrs. Leyland declared with some hauteur, but then continued briskly, without giving Mr. Peeke time in which to frame an apology, "However, beggars can't be choosers. Bayard, my dear—I daresay you would be very happy to have Mr. Peeke manage your affairs, would you not?"

Lydia, anticipating her brother's rather lazily amused nod of assent, burst into an irrepressible ripple of laughter. "Grandmama, you are too absurd!" she said. "Sir Basil does not know us—nor, it would appear, from the way he has completely ignored the letter you wrote him announcing that we were coming to England, does he wish to know us."

"Ah," Mr. Peeke put in eagerly, "but you must not be deterred by *that*, Miss Leyland! Sir Basil—if I may so express myself—is somewhat eccentric in his habits. In point of fact, he receives no one these days but a certain—er—set of his intimates—and very odd creatures they are, to be sure!" he added, permitting himself a slight titter. "He has taken quite a disgust of Society, you see, which I understand is the result of his having failed many years ago to attain the entrée into its more exalted circles to which he felt he was entitled by his wealth and his marriage to a young lady—your sister, ma'am," he said, bowing to Mrs. Leyland —"of excellent family. This did not come to pass, however—owing to some extent, I believe, to Lady Rowthorn's preferring the country and refusing to exert herself in the world of Society."

"Good heavens! What a ninny!" Mrs. Leyland said, with marked disapproval. "What a vexing thing it is that Letty should not have had *my* opportunities and I hers! But I still do not see, my good man, what all this has to say to my grandson's chances of inheriting Sir Basil's fortune."

Mr. Peeke's prim smile appeared once more. "Let me put it to you in this way, ma'am," he said. "Sir Basil has, I believe, suffered a second disappointment in the fact that neither Mr. nor Miss Pentony—though both are well-looking, genteelly educated young persons—has had a marked success in that world of the *ton* to which he himself aspired in his younger days. You may be aware that the family of his first wife, with whom they are connected, was quite undistinguished, and that the greatest honour achieved by their father was a knighthood, bestowed upon him when he was an official of the city of Nottingham. I do not say," he acknowledged, "that Mr. and Miss Pentony have not attained the entrée into a more elevated stratum of Society than *that* on the strength of their somewhat dubious expectations from Sir Basil, but Sir Basil chooses to sneer at the fact that they do not move in the first circles—"

He paused, seeing that Miss Leyland was observing him with an appreciative gleam in her eyes.

"Why, Mr. Peeke," she accused him, "what a totally Machiavellian plot you are hatching! You think that if *we*—my brother and I—can succeed in making a great splash in Society, poor Sir Basil will be so completely overcome—"

"I believe he would be highly gratified, Miss Leyland," Mr. Peeke said, twinkling at her in unexpected responsiveness. "Dear me, you are a very acute young lady, I see! I have no doubt that, in spite of your lack of fortune, you will succeed in making a very good thing of your—if I may say so!—undeniable beauty and excellent background in London this Season, to the extent that it must come to Sir Basil's ears. Perhaps even an engagement to a gentleman of rank—"

"Disgraceful!" said Lydia severely, adding pensively, "I daresay it would require a great deal of money to carry out such a scheme—perhaps more than Great-aunt Letty's bequest would come to?"

Mr. Peeke bowed gallantly. "You must allow me to be your banker, Miss Leyland," he said. "Upon—speculation, shall we say? I am sure, if your brother should be named in Sir Basil's will, I should have no difficulty in obtaining repayment."

"And if he is not, you will be gapped!" Lydia said frankly. "However, that is your affair, and if you are *quite* determined to behave in such an utterly unscrupulous way toward poor Mr. and Miss Pentony—"

"Lydia, do give over!" Mrs. Leyland said reprovingly. "There is nothing in the least unbecoming in Mr. Peeke's kind offer to assist you to make yourself agreeable to your great-uncle! Perhaps we should call upon him this very morning—"

"I rather think—if you will permit me—not," Mr. Peeke said firmly. "Sir Basil is at present recovering from a severe attack of the gout, which has left his temper—never, I may say, an even one—quite exacerbated. I cannot believe that your visit would be welcomed under such circumstances; indeed, I am of the opinion that you would do better to wait to bring yourselves to his notice until you have made an entrée into Society."

As none of the Leylands was in the least eager to make Sir Basil's acquaintance, this suggestion was agreed to without demur, and a conversation of greater interest to them was then entered into on the subject of the house and servants which they would require for the Season. Here Mr.

Peeke promptly showed his mettle, for he declared that, if Mrs. Leyland would but leave the arrangements in his hands, he would engage to have them settled within the week in an elegantly furnished house in an excellent neighbourhood, with a capable staff—complete from housekeeper to footman—to go with it.

"Green Street, I believe," he said, considering the matter. "Yes, yes, by the greatest stroke of fortune I shall be able to settle you there, for Lady Woodforde and her daughter, whom I have the honour of numbering among my clients, have been obliged to go into the country for several months for reasons of health. Then you will wish, of course, to set up your carriage—a barouche, I think, for landaulets have gone sadly out of fashion. And a hack, no doubt, for Mr. Leyland—"

Bayard, however, interrupted here to say that that was a matter which he would prefer to take into his own hands, for he was eager to look in at Tattersall's himself and inspect some of the sweet-going bargains he had seen advertised in the columns of the *Morning Post*. Mr. Peeke made no objection to this, and in a short time, agreement having been reached on all points, the Leylands took their leave—having first been provided, owing to Mrs. Leyland's remembrance of their impoverished state, with an advance against her inheritance which would enable her to cope with present necessities.

 ON A BRIGHT MORNING IN EARLY June, several days after this interview had taken place, a sporting curricle drawn by four perfectly matched greys halted before my Lord Gilmour's town-house in St. James's Square and Lord Northover, who followed the currently fashionable practice of driving with a diminutive Tiger perched up behind in place of an adult groom, tossed the reins to the undersized but intelligent-looking stripling who filled this post and strode up the steps to the door. He was admitted into the hall by a magnificent butler, who, having received the Viscount's hat and gloves, which he immediately, with an air of ineffable hauteur, consigned into the care of a powdered and liveried footman, unbent sufficiently to inform their owner that her ladyship was expecting him, and thereupon conducted him up the crimson-carpeted stairway to a small saloon, all yellow satin and gilded mirrors. A lady who had been standing before a pair of windows overlooking the square quickly came forward to greet him.

"Kit! I made sure it was you!" she exclaimed. "I peeped from behind the blinds like a schoolgirl! Where *did* you find those splendid greys? Ned will be green with envy!"

Northover, taking both Lady Gilmour's outstretched hands in his own, gave them a friendly clasp, dropped a kiss lightly upon her cheek, and surveyed the splendour about him with frank dislike.

"Good God, it's like living in a jewel-box!" he said. "Did Ned know you were doing this? I think not!" He sat down beside her, at her invitation, on a sofa resting on crocodile legs inlaid with silver. "As for the greys, they're Laycock's breakdowns—eight hundred pounds, and dog-cheap at the price, but tell Ned he shan't have them from me for twice the sum. How *is* Ned, by the bye? I haven't seen him since Brussels."

"Nor have you seen me—though I gather you don't care

41

about *that*, from that very *coolish* greeting!" the lady said, her brows lifting slightly. She was past the age—as she was well aware—at which a pout might have appeared attractive, but if she had been a dozen years younger there could have been no doubt that she would have made use of one.

This was not to say that she could not still vie with her daughter—an acknowledged beauty, whom she was bringing out that Season—at almost all points. Sir Thomas Lawrence had begged to paint them together, declaring that each made a perfect foil for the other—Lady Gilmour tall, slender, and fair, with a dazzling complexion and hair which, with some assistance to nature, was still the colour of a new-minted guinea; Miss Beaudoin delicate and dark, with a clear olive colouring and great liquid brown eyes. But Lady Gilmour, though scarcely noted for prudence in any other respect, was very wise when it came to her own looks, and as a result it was her ladyship's portrait alone that hung over the mantelpiece in the Crimson Saloon, untroubled by odious comparisons with a younger beauty.

The same careful consideration had caused her to choose this morning a half-dress of deep gold, veiled by a tunic of amber muslin, which made the room in which she sat appear as if it had been designed for the express purpose of providing a background for her beauty. Northover, eyeing her appreciatively, said, "*Was* I coolish? I'd say I was overcome!"

"Fiddle!"

"Perhaps. But you seem to forget, my dear, that Ned's a friend of mine—and a deuced good friend, if it comes to that!"

"Does that matter? I thought all was fair in—"

Northover laughed. "Don't come the Bath miss on *me*, Trix! Finish your quotation! *In love and war*? What very odd ideas you females have of men, to be sure! Of course it was fair while you were married to Beaudoin. He was old enough to be your father, and as ramshackle an old court-card as ever I came across into the bargain, and if he had any notion, when he got himself riveted to you, that either of you was about to set up as a pattern-saint, it escaped *my* notice! But Ned's a different case. I told you when you married him that you were making your choice, my dear."

"I had no choice!" Lady Gilmour said, rather pettishly. "*You* never offered to marry me!"

Northover grinned. "And you wouldn't have accepted me if I had—not before my great-uncle and both my cousins were so obliging as to stick their spoons in the wall and leave me heir to a title and property as good as Ned's. Now *don't* pitch me any Banbury tales, love; you know it's the truth as well as I do. You were determined to make a good match *this* time!"

"And why shouldn't I have been?" Lady Gilmour demanded. "After *years* of odious pinching and scraping, trying to keep up an appearance, at least, that we weren't always outrunning the bailiff—" She waved her hand to indicate the room. "So you needn't wonder at *this*! I told Ned when I married him that I was bored to death with being poor, and had every intention of making a stir in Society."

"Well, he's rich enough to stand the nonsense, and he's such an easy-going fellow that I daresay he won't mind," Northover said, a satirical look on his dark face. "You may think yourself very well off that I didn't marry you, Trix, for the first thing I'd do, if I had, would be to pitch all this"—he glanced around at the overornamented room—"out the window."

"It is in the very *latest* fashion!" Lady Gilmour defended herself indignantly, and then, catching the look in his eyes, relaxed and said, "Oh, very well! You are roasting me, as usual, you provoking creature! Now *don't* let us come to cuffs with each other, but tell me instead what you have been doing since you left the Army, and all the latest crim. con. stories—"

"Why you should couple *those* two items has me in a puzzle," the Viscount said, with a great assumption of virtue. "Besides, I've been far too busy to get into mischief. Taking up the reins from my great-uncle's hands has worn me down more than following the Duke all through Portugal and Spain ever did."

She surveyed him skeptically. "I must say you don't *look* worn to a thread," she said. "Are you too exhausted to show your face at my dress-party tomorrow evening? I'd have sent you a card, but I had no notion that you were coming to town until I met you yesterday in Bond Street. You *might* have let me know!"

"Of course I'll come," he said, ignoring her last words. "Whom am I to meet? Have you snabbled the Regent, or at least a Royal Duke or two?"

"Oh, I expect York will look in," she conceded, without a great deal of enthusiasm. "But I shall not mind in the least if he does not, for I have been obliged by Mama to invite a set of distant connexions from America whom I should be mortified to death to introduce to him! You *know* how unpresentable provincials are! But it seems that Mama and Mrs. Leyland were bosom-pieces when they were girls, and so she is determined to do what she can to bring her and her granddaughter into fashion."

The Viscount, who had crossed one leg, clad in the tightly fitting biscuit pantaloons that were the approved townwear for gentlemen of the *ton*, over the other, examined the tip of a gleaming Hessian boot and enquired in an innocent voice, "Have you met them as yet—your provincials?"

"No, for, as kind Providence would have it, they were out when Mama insisted on dragging me to call upon them." Struck by something in the tone of his question, she asked, "Why? Have *you* met them?"

"Oh, yes!"

"But where? Mama says they are but just come to town, and have been nowhere as yet—"

She was interrupted by the opening of the door and the entrance of a young lady wearing a pretty China-blue walking-dress and a chip-hat tied under her chin with blue ribbons. She was accompanied by a much older lady, of a square, stout figure, with her quivering dewlaps and magnificent dark eyes rather startlingly complemented by a splendid full-poke bonnet of puce silk, trimmed with drapings of thread-net.

"Mama, see whom I found on the doorstep as I came in," the younger lady began gaily, and then, observing the Viscount, broke off to exclaim in some confusion, "Oh—Captain Brome—I mean—Lord Northover, of course! I did not see you! I beg your pardon!"

Northover rose, and stood looking approvingly at the lovely little face before him.

"Well, Minna!" he said, taking the small gloved hand which she shyly offered him. "So you've managed to grow into a young lady while my back was turned! Lady Aimer—"

He moved from her to the older lady, who stared him up and down frankly before she gave him her hand.

"You look like a town dandy, Northover!" she said. "That rig don't become you half so well as your regimentals. Well, and I daresay you are finding it a dead bore, eh?—being a respectable member of the *ton*, instead of careering all over Europe and America raising riot and rumpus, like the hell-born babe you are?"

Northover laughed. "Now I know why I am so fond of you, Lady Aimer," he said, kissing her hand with an air of great gallantry. "You always have such flattering things to say of me."

"I don't flatter, and you wouldn't like me any the better for it if I did," her ladyship said bluntly, as she plumped herself down in a winged armchair. "And I'll open my budget to you even further, Northover, now that I've begun—I don't want you running tame in this house, dangling after Beatrix and causing trouble between her and Gilmour. This isn't Brussels or Madrid, and she isn't Beaudoin's widow, or even Beaudoin's wife, any longer."

Lady Gilmour gave a tinkling little laugh. "Dear Mama, *must* you be quite so outspoken before Minna?" she said. "At any rate, I assure you it is perfectly unnecessary! Kit has the greatest sense of his obligation to his friendship with Ned; he has only now been telling me so! I do not believe

45

he would even have called here today if I had not met him in Bond Street yesterday and pressed him to do so."

Lady Aimer's hard eyes surveyed Northover in a not unfriendly manner. "Well, that doesn't surprise me over-much," she said. "You may be a loose-screw, Northover, but you're not a scoundrel. The thing of it is, I've had such a time of it putting this girl of mine into a position where I don't need to lie awake nights worrying because she's in the briars from one cause or another that I don't intend to have my peace cut up again by you or any other man! We made a great mistake with Beaudoin; I'd be the first to admit that—though, lord! how was I to know he'd turn out to be such a hedgebird, with his name and fortune? But we've made no mistake with Gilmour, and there'll be no havey-cavey business to set his back up, if *I* have anything to say about it!"

Lady Gilmour, shrugging resignedly at her mother's blunt speaking—a trait for which that lady was famous—gave up the attempt to silence her and said to her daughter, "Minna dear, had you not better run upstairs? You need not stand upon ceremony with Lord Northover, and Phipson is waiting to help you to try on your gown for tomorrow evening, now that that odious Celeste has at last had it sent round."

Miss Beaudoin docilely rose and, murmuring her excuses, left the room, upon which Lady Aimer said downrightly to her daughter, "Upon my word, Beatrix, you are a positive dragon when it comes to that girl! She is not in the school-room any longer, you know. It will do her no harm to hear a little plain talk. You can't keep her wrapped in cotton-wool forever!"

Lady Gilmour gave a rather angry little laugh. "Oh, dear Mama, allow me to know my own business when it comes to Minna!" she said. "*You* may not credit it, but there are still men who prefer to marry innocence and simplicity—yes, and men of the first rank and consequence, let me tell you! Lord Harlbury, for one, seems not in the least repelled by the idea of a bride who knows no more of the world than Minna does, and you will grant that he is a far greater catch than *I* snared at her age, for all my having been so much more up to snuff than she is!"

"Yes—*if* she catches him!" Lady Aimer retorted witheringly. "I shouldn't be too sure of landing *that* fish if I was you, my girl, for, in the first place, it's not what Harlbury likes or don't like that will settle the business in the end, but what his mama likes! A handsomer piece of nature than that boy I never clapped eyes on—I'll give you that; he's a very Adonis! But if he makes a move that his mother hasn't first given him permission to make, *I* wasn't by when he did it."

"Nonsense!" Lady Gilmour said, looking none too well pleased by this unflattering estimate of Lord Harlbury's character. "Merely because he is the soul of amiability and consideration—*both* of them attributes that should make him an excellent husband—"

Lady Aimer gave a crack of laughter. "To say nothing of his having a round forty thousand a year and an earldom; don't forget *that!*" she said. "No, no, Trix—you'd best set your sights a *leetle* lower, my dear. Not but what Minna isn't as pretty a girl as you'll see on display at Almack's this Season, but her fortune is nothing at all unless Gilmour takes a fancy to do something for her. And you haven't so many years in your dish yet that he can't expect to get children of his own by you, so it's not likely he'll come down handsome for her at *their* expense!"

Northover, who had been listening imperturbably to the dispute, enquired at this point if he ought to be acquainted with this paragon.

"Oh, I shouldn't think so; he is half a dozen years, at least, younger than you," Lady Gilmour said, "and has never been much on the town. I believe he is addicted to country pursuits and to—to scientific farming—"

"I fancy he has been pointed out to me in the Park," Northover said gravely. "A young genius—is he?"

"*I* should not say his understanding was more than moderate," Lady Aimer said. "But that is neither here nor there, for I cannot think that Beatrix's scheme has any great chance

47

of success." She gave another bark of laughter and said, "If you are so fond of matchmaking, my dear, I wish you will set your mind to finding a husband for your poor little cousin from America, Erminia Leyland's girl. Lord! I thought I should drop when Erminia told me she wishes me to obtain vouchers for Almack's for her, since she has her heart fixed on her marrying into the *ton*! She's a well-looking girl, according to Erminia—though I haven't seen her myself to decide upon that—but as poor as a church-mouse, and you know what deplorable figures these provincials cut—no ease of manner, no air of fashion, and dressed as if they'd bought made-up clothes in Cranbourne Alley!"

"Kit says he has met them," Lady Gilmour said, "and I wish you will not call them *cousins*, Mama! You have told me yourself that there is only the slightest of connexions."

Lady Aimer ignored this, turning to the Viscount. "Ay, I recollect now—old Northover owned Great Hayland, did he not? Erminia spoke of having stopped to have a look at it. Lord! it is forty years since I've set eyes on it, but it was used to be a mad, gay place when I was a girl, with Erminia and Letty and Gerald to set the pace—What did you make of her?" she broke off to ask abruptly.

"Of Mrs. Leyland?"

"Of the girl."

Northover considered. "Why, she is—quite unusual, ma'am," he assured her, after a moment.

"Humph!" said Lady Aimer. "A dowdy, I expect?"

"I should not call her so."

"Well, I will give Erminia credit for being rigged out in prime style herself," Lady Aimer granted, "but even *she* can't make a silk purse out of a sow's ear, and I daresay the girl hasn't the least notion of how to go on in a ball-room, or even of how to behave properly when she is in company."

"Yet you foist her upon *me*!" Lady Gilmour said tragically.

"Well, she has to learn somewhere—doesn't she?" her mother demanded practically. "And with Erminia to teach her she'll come along fast, if she isn't a ninny. *Is* she a ninny?" she asked Northover.

The Viscount's eyes glinted. "I believe I shall leave you to make up your own mind on that point, ma'am," he said.

"As bad as that—is it? Well, I should have known it!" her ladyship said philosophically. "We must set our sights on some respectable widower who is hanging out for a healthy young wife to mother his brood, or a half-pay officer, Trix. And even *that* may be above her touch, if she turns out to be a Homely Joan or one of those May-poles they seem to breed in America!"

 **LORD NORTHOVER, ARRIVING EARLY**
in St. James's Square on the following
evening with the express purpose of
being present at Miss Lydia Leyland's entry into Society, was privileged to behold the faces of both Lady
Gilmour and her mama when that
young lady swam into their ken. Miss
Leyland wore for the occasion an
Indian mull muslin gown far re-
moved from any suspicion of provincial dowdiness; her
dark hair, cropped and curled in front and twisted up behind
into a high Grecian knot, was dressed in the latest mode;
and the diaphanous gown and the length of silver net which
draped her shoulders *à la Ariane* did nothing to conceal the
elegant lines of her figure and the gracefulness of her carriage as she mounted the grand staircase between her
grandmother and her brother and sustained an introduction
to Lord and Lady Gilmour.

The Viscount noted that Lord Gilmour, though not, as he
himself expressed it in his bluff, good-humoured way, much
in the petticoat-line, gave her a most appreciative glance,
while Lady Gilmour, her eyes narrowing slightly at this new
beauty suddenly appearing upon the London scene, had difficulty in concealing her incredulity on learning that *this* was
the "poor little cousin" who must consider herself fortunate
to find a worthy middle-aged widower content to take her
as housekeeper and spouse.

A fan rapped sharply on Northover's arm. He looked down
to see Lady Aimer's pugnacious face thrust up at him.

"You are a humbug, Northover!" she said.

"A humbug, Lady Aimer?"

"You know very well what I mean, you rogue! That girl.
You said she was—unusual."

"Is she not?"

"Unusual! A diamond of the first water! Look at Trix; she's
as blue as megrim! Lord, she never could endure to see a

woman handsomer than she was herself! And, to make it worse, the chit's as self-possessed as if she'd been reared at Chatsworth or Woburn, instead of in a swamp full of savages and mosquitoes! The boy's a well-looking lad, too," she added, looking with approval at young Bayard Leyland, impeccable in blue dress-coat and satin knee-breeches, as he bowed over Lady Gilmour's hand. "Resembles her, don't he? The two of 'em together make a handsome picture."

That she was not the only person who thought so was evident from the shyly admiring expression upon Miss Beaudoin's face as she, in turn, was introduced to her cousins from America. Miss Beaudoin, herself demurely lovely in a white sarsnet gown, its tiny puff sleeves trimmed with seed pearls, was too much accustomed to being cast into the shade by her mama to be envious of the advent of a new beauty who might be expected to steal more than one of her own admirers from her; and, as a matter of fact, she had spared only a cursory glance and one of her gentle smiles for her new rival. Her gaze was riveted, instead, upon Bayard. Really, Northover thought, amused, the cub *did* make a romantic picture, with his dark hair brushed *au coup de vent* in careless locks over his forehead, his handsome face with its air of composed detachment, and his intense dark-blue eyes. And not sixpence to scratch himself with! If Minna were to cast sheep's eyes in that direction, she would be in for a pretty rating from her mama, he thought ironically.

He was the recipient of a friendly nod from Mrs. Leyland, resplendent in garnet satin and a Spartan diadem, and of a dazzling smile from Miss Leyland as they passed on into the ball-room, but Bayard halted for a more extended greeting.

"I say," he remarked reverently, his eyes upon Miss Beaudoin, "what a *devilish* pretty girl, sir! Is she—is she much sought after?"

"Moderately so, I believe," Northover replied. "She is indeed a little beauty—but her fortune is nonexistent, which makes a great many eligible gentlemen quite impervious to her charms."

"What a set of gudgeons!" Bayard said scornfully. "As if that signified!"

"It may not signify to you, but I assure you that it does to Lady Gilmour," Northover said dryly. "*That* bird is above your touch, halfling. Her mama is looking out for a plumper purse than yours."

Bayard reddened slightly. "You are very good to warn me, sir," he said, with a stiffness quite at variance with the usual lazy good-humour of his manner, and moved away, to be seized upon at once by Lady Aimer, who was apparently bent upon making herself known without delay to her young relation.

Northover strolled on into the ball-room, where he found, not at all to his surprise, that Miss Leyland's hand had already been claimed for the set of country dances that was forming. He watched her as she went down the dance, observing with approval that she performed her part in it with all the aplomb of a young lady to whom the glitter of a fashionable ball-room, with its high, pilastered walls, silk-hung windows, and hundreds of candles in gleaming chandeliers, was the merest commonplace. Her partner, he saw, was Sir Carsbie Chant, a well-known figure in *ton* circles, for not only was he the possessor of an enormous fortune, but he aspired, in spite of having reached middle life, to the leadership of the most extravagant wing of the dandy-set. His narrow shoulders were broadened by an absurd amount of buckram padding set into a wasp-waisted, bottle-green coat of Nugee's cut; his thin legs were encased in exquisite black satin knee-breeches and striped silk stockings; and his sallow, self-important countenance was propped above a towering neckcloth tied in the style known as the *Sentimentale*.

But, in spite of the singularity of his appearance, Miss Leyland, Northover conceded, had made a notable first conquest. Sir Carsbie was an intimate of the Regent's and an

53

accepted connoisseur of female beauty, and it was certain that the cachet of his approval, so immediately bestowed upon Miss Leyland, would inspire other gentlemen to seek the honour of leading her out for subsequent dances.

Meanwhile, Lord Gilmour, presently released from the necessity of greeting his arriving guests, came to seek out Northover and drag him off to exchange Army reminiscences over iced champagne, and it was some little time before the two returned to the ball-room. When they arrived there a quadrille was in progress, and Northover, propping his shoulders against the wall beside a sofa on which a pair of dowagers sat gossiping, listened with amusement to the astonished comments of one of these ladies on the facility with which Miss Leyland, now partnered with a young baronet, performed even the most difficult of the steps.

"Where she can have learned them, I cannot conceive," she remarked, "for I have been assured that she has only just arrived from America, where she lived *quite* out of society. I am sure my Louisa has spent *hours* with her dancing-master without obtaining sufficient proficiency in the *grande ronde* and the *pas de zéphyr* to feel herself capable of standing up for the quadrille with any gentleman who is a master of those steps." She added in a lowered voice, behind her fan, "However, I must say that I should *never* allow Louisa to appear in such a gown as Miss Leyland is wearing. Entirely too *French*, my dear, if you wish my opinion, and I am quite certain, too, that she must have dampened her petticoat to make it cling so—a custom of which I thoroughly disapprove!"

"And I," virtuously agreed her friend. "I hear that Lady Aimer intends to ask one of the Patronesses of Almack's to procure vouchers to the Assembly Rooms for the girl, and poor Lady Sefton is so good-natured that I daresay she may allow herself to be imposed upon to do so. But she is not here tonight, I believe, and, although I have seen both Lady Jersey and the Countess Lieven, I doubt if even Lady Aimer will be bold enough to ask either of *them* to sponsor a girl from the backwoods of America!"

"At any rate," said the first lady, with some satisfaction, "since Miss Leyland has not yet been approved by the Patronesses, she cannot dance the waltz at a London ball —which means, my dear, that she must resign herself to being a wallflower at least for this next while, for no gentleman will be foolish enough to ask her to stand up with him!"

"If, indeed, she has any idea of how to perform the steps!" the second lady tittered—and then broke off, apparently stunned by the sight of what was occurring before her on the ball-room floor.

Northover himself muttered, "Oh, the devil!"—and took a step forward, but it was too late. Miss Leyland, finding herself relinquished, partnerless, into her grandmother's hands as the musicians struck up the opening measures of a waltz, had glanced around, seen her brother standing nearby, and beckoned to him; the next moment the two had swept off together to the center of the floor, the lady's draperies flowing seductively about her, her partner's arm lightly encircling her waist, the two moving together with such effortless precision and grace that the shocked murmur which had arisen at sight of what Northover was sure was an unconscious audacity was quickly augmented by an even more audible murmur of admiration.

It was, in fact, quite evident to anyone looking on that not only were brother and sister superbly matched partners, but that they must have waltzed together so frequently that each was responsive to the slightest movement the other made. As if by mutual agreement, they introduced several graceful variations in the basic steps of the dance, and these were so smoothly and exquisitely performed that the couples around them involuntarily halted to watch, so that in the space of a few minutes the Leylands were almost alone upon the floor. Northover felt a tug on his sleeve, and looked down at Lady Aimer's despairing face.

"Can't you *do* something?" she demanded of him. "I've spoken to Gilmour; all I can get from *him* is, 'Dashed fine, by Jupiter!' And Lady Jersey looking on, and the Countess Lieven! I could *flay* myself for not having warned Erminia that the girl must on no account waltz in public until she has been approved by the Patronesses of Almack's!" She glanced with some asperity across the ball-room at Lady Gilmour, who, although standing in conversation with several gentlemen, was quite evidently missing nothing of what was going forward on the floor. "I vow, Beatrix is actually enjoying this!" she said tartly. "How she can be such a widgeon as not to realise that it cannot add to *our* consequence to have the girl ruin herself—"

"Oh, I doubt if it will come to that!" Northover said, with a slight smile. "To tell you the truth, I am enjoying it, too!" She gave an angry exclamation and he said soothingly, "Never mind, ma'am. I'll engage to give Miss Leyland the opportunity to right herself—and, if my impression of her is to be trusted, she is quite capable of doing so, with only a hint to set her in the right direction."

Lady Aimer, still fuming, looked skeptical, and, after a sharp admonition to him not to make the chit any more conspicuous by paying attentions to her himself, went off to find Mrs. Leyland and apprise her of the solecism she had allowed her granddaughter to commit. Northover, left alone, went back to his appreciative contemplation of the two young Leylands' performance, but as the music wound to a close he took care to change his position so that, when the final notes sounded, he was standing near enough to them that a half dozen rapid steps brought him to their side.

"Now, children," he said amiably, as the two, who appeared somewhat surprised to find themselves almost alone upon the floor, turned identically questioning eyes upon him, "you are to listen most carefully to what I say! You are in disgrace, Miss Leyland, because you have presumed to break one of the canons of London Society—no young lady is to dance the waltz until the Patronesses of Almack's have set the seal of their approval upon her doing so. I shall now introduce you to two of those ladies—Lady Jersey and the Russian ambassador's wife, Countess Lieven—both of whom have been observing you as you flouted their authority. Therefore, if you do not wish your first appearance in Society to be your last, you will manage somehow to propitiate their wrath—"

He paused, looking sternly down into Lydia's face, where an expression of startled incomprehension had been replaced, as he spoke, by a look of pure amused mischief.

"I mean what I say, you abominable little gypsy!" he said severely. "*Will* you be serious!"

She tucked her hand into his arm. "Oh, you may trust me!" she said confidentially. "What shall it be? Tears and remorse? Shall I beat my breast and promise amendment of my ways? I warn you, that is definitely *not* one of my better acts."

Bayard grinned at Northover's exasperated face. "Never mind, sir! She'll contrive to rub through," he said cheerfully. "She's *not* such a goosecap as she sounds, you know."

"Well, you *said* I was to be propitiating!" Lydia said, in an injured tone, and then, as they approached the group in which Lady Jersey and the Countess stood, composed her countenance swiftly into an expression of enchantingly rueful contrition. Northover made the introductions, which were acknowledged by the two ladies with the most arctic of bows. But they had no time in which to make clear their opinion of what they evidently considered Northover's outrageous audacity in bringing Miss Leyland up to them before that young lady herself had rallied to his support.

Fixing the most beguiling of smiles upon Lady Jersey, she said in a rush, in her rich alto voice, "Oh dear, and I had *so* looked forward to meeting you! Dear ma'am, have I quite sunk myself beneath reproach? If I had had the least idea I was running counter to your wishes, I should have stabbed myself with the nearest convenient implement—I daresay there *are* fruit knives in the supper-room?—before I permitted my brother to lead me out on to the floor."

Lady Jersey, who had herself a very volatile sense of humour, could not prevent herself from laughing, though she said nothing, but merely glanced with slightly lifted brows at the Countess Lieven. That lady, who was accounted, along with Mrs. Drummond Burrell, as among the haughtiest of the Patronesses, appeared unmoved by Miss Leyland's appeal, which, her manner seemed to indicate, while it might be accepted by such a light-minded madcap as Sally Jersey, did nothing to lessen the impression in *her* mind that Miss Leyland was a hoydenish provincial, whose lack of *savoir faire* she would do nothing to countenance.

Her expression changed markedly, however, when Lydia, as if in comprehension of her attitude, turned to address her prettily in fluent French, with an impeccable accent, begging her forgiveness in far more formal terms than she had used with Lady Jersey, and assuring her that the thought of disregarding her authority had been farthest from her mind. She then, Northover observed with rising admiration, unblushingly enlisted the aid of her brother in softening the hearts of the two offended ladies, and, as Bayard seemed perfectly capable of continuing the conversation his sister had begun with the Countess in the same effortless and idiomatic French, and of addressing Lady Jersey in terms of rather shy but admiring gallantry that could not but please her, coming from a handsome young man of excellent address, Northover judged that the time was ripe to put an end to Lydia's rôle in the proceedings. He therefore bore her off, to Lady Jersey's parting shot, "You had best find her a *respectable* partner instead of dancing with her yourself, Northover! You are an unprincipled wretch, and will only set more tongues to wagging if you stand up with her!"

"What an excellent piece of advice, Sally! I shall!" Northover assured her. He glanced rapidly about the room as he strolled off with Lydia, remarking, "Respectable *and* fashionable he shall certainly be, my dear. And mind that you charm him so thoroughly that he looks to be enjoying himself—Ah! Harlbury! The very man!" he broke off, observing with satisfaction a magnificently tall, classically handsome young giant who was just entering the room. "Come along, my girl!"

"*That* splendid young man? I should rather think so!"

Lydia said, matching her steps to his with alacrity. "Who *is* he?"

"He will be Lady Gilmour's son-in-law one day, if he comes up to scratch," Northover said briefly. "However, that is neither here nor there. I should warn you, though, that for the next half hour you are going to be devotedly interested in scientific farming."

"I *am*? Oh! I see! You mean Harlbury is!"

"I do." The Viscount, purposefully approaching Lord Harlbury, greeted him warmly. "Allow me, sir," he said cordially, "to present this young lady to you as a very desirable partner. Miss Leyland—Lord Harlbury."

Lord Harlbury, appearing considerably startled, looked from the Viscount to Miss Leyland, but good breeding came to his aid and he politely expressed his appreciation of the pleasure of meeting the young lady. She held out her hand; he took it.

"I fancy they are about to begin. You had best take your places," Northover said, shepherding them ruthlessly across the floor to where the set was forming.

Having seen them installed in the ranks of the dancers, he promptly departed, leaving Lord Harlbury to gaze after him with a rather dazed air.

"I daresay it is very remiss of me, but I can't quite place—" he began.

"Lord Northover," Lydia explained helpfully.

"Oh! Northover. Still, I don't quite recall meeting—"

"I have the same difficulty," Lydia said sympathetically. "I practically *never* can recall names, which causes me to make some of the most totally *anachronous* blunders. I daresay it will turn out to be a bond between us."

Lord Harlbury did not appear to find this statement of much consolation at the moment, but he was not so perplexed that he did not presently realise that—however oddly he had come by her—his partner was an excessively pretty girl, and he set himself to the task of making himself agreeable to her. This he did in a manner which struck Lydia

59

as being—in view of his rank and appearance—somewhat overdiffident. His observations to her were all of the most formal nature, and were delivered with a certain air of uneasiness, as if, while enjoying himself, he had a guilty sensation of behaving not quite as he ought.

Since he had not arrived in the ball-room in time to view her error in dancing the waltz, nor could he have had the opportunity of hearing it discussed by others, Lydia was at a loss to account for this attitude on his part, until she observed that it appeared to become more marked whenever he found himself facing a certain middle-aged lady in an impressive purple turban, who had placed herself on a rout-chair drawn up directly in view of the dancers. Her frowning regard, Lydia noted, was fixed unwaveringly upon Lord Harlbury, while he, on the other hand, appeared to make every effort to avoid hers.

"Who *is* that lady?" she enquired at last, with a candid curiosity that would have won her Northover's severest censure.

"That lady?" Lord Harlbury glanced down at her, somewhat startled.

"In the purple turban," Lydia said perseveringly. "She is looking at you very oddly. Do you know her?"

"*Know* her?"

"You really *should* try to lose this habit of repeating everything one says to you," Lydia advised him, somewhat severely. "It does nothing to advance a conversation. I have asked you an extremely simple question, and it *does* seem to me—though perhaps I may be mistaken, for you did appear unable to make up your mind just now whether you knew Lord Northover or not—that you *should* be able to answer it."

"Of course I am able to answer it! She is my mother!" said Harlbury, stung, it seemed, by the extreme frankness of this speech.

"Your mother! Well, she certainly appears to disapprove of your dancing with me!"

"I fancy she expected—that is, she told me Lady Gilmour

60

expected—" his lordship said guiltily. "What I mean to say is, I fancy they *both* expected I should stand up first with Miss Beaudoin."

"With Miss Beaudoin? Oh! You mean Lady Gilmour's daughter. Well, you may stand up with her for the next set," Lydia said magnanimously, "though I *do* wish you will ask me again for the one after *that*, for I can see that it is doing an immense deal to restore my credit to be seen dancing with you, after the horrible crime I have just committed. I expect I had best tell you about that myself, for some utterly corrosive female is sure to do so the very instant you escape from me."

She thereupon confided to her bewildered partner—after first extracting from him a solemn promise to stand up with her for the next set but one—a highly coloured account of the waltzing incident and her subsequent interview with Lady Jersey and the Countess Lieven—"which I *do* think I handled rather beautifully," she said, "for I simply pushed Bayard into the breach, and no woman past thirty can ever *remain* angry with him. He has poise, you see, but at the same time he *looks* shy, which has a totally blighting effect upon them. You might study him; you are somewhat in the same style yourself, you know, though I don't believe you *really* have poise and it's all a bit too stiff, the way *you* do it." She added kindly, seeing the harassed look again appearing in Lord Harlbury's eyes, "Bayard is my brother, and you *haven't* met him."

What response he might have made to this information was never to be known, for Lydia, suddenly recollecting Northover's admonition, immediately turned the conversation into other channels, informing his lordship with some abruptness that she understood him to be an authority on scientific farming, in which, above all other subjects, she was passionately interested. Lord Harlbury, who, in spite of having shown to considerable disadvantage under the series of shocks to which he had just been subjected, was not dull of understanding, looked somewhat skeptical upon hearing this; but, as it was difficult even for the most acute of observers to discover exactly how much of Miss Leyland's conversation was meant to be taken seriously, she eventually succeeded in persuading him that she was in earnest. As a result, she was treated to the spectacle of his lordship in a fluently conversational mood. Such phrases as "crossbreeding" and "rotation of crops" assailed the ears of those standing beside them in the set, and when the conversation was perforce interrupted by the exigencies of the dance, it was once more resumed when his lordship and Miss Leyland came together again.

Northover, watching them from across the room, was discovering that he was finding this ball quite as amusing as any during which he himself had been engaged in the liveliest of flirtations when his appreciative observation of Miss Leyland's skill in drawing her partner out was interrupted by Lady Gilmour's coming up to him and addressing him, not in the kindliest of tones.

"Kit, you wretch! What in the world did you mean by it, flinging that girl at Harlbury's head? It was quite understood that he was to stand up first with Minna this evening."

"Was it? Good God, how maladroit of me!" said the Viscount, with a not very convincing air of compunction.

"And don't try to flummery me! You are not in the least sorry," Lady Gilmour said, laughing in spite of herself. "But I *should* like to know why you felt yourself obliged to help her out of that bumblebath she had fallen into."

"I rather thought you'd be grateful," Northover said virtuously. "After all, she's *your* relation."

"Fiddle! I shan't care in the least if she finds herself in the briars! She appears to me to have the most abominable lack of delicacy—"

She was not permitted to go on, for at this the Viscount broke into a shout of laughter. "From *you*, Trix!" he said, when he was able to speak again.

She tapped her ivory-brisé fan vexedly against the gloved palm of her free hand. "Oh, very well! But I am not a miss in her first Season, you will remember!" She looked at him

with sudden sharpness. "Tell me—are *you épris* there, Kit?"
she asked.

"Of course I am!" retorted the Viscount. "What do you
take me for? I haven't seen anything as amusing in half a
dozen years. I am on tenterhooks to see what next she will
do!"

She shrugged, almost angered, it seemed, by this flippant
reply. "What a cold devil you are!" she said, after a moment.
"Do you know—though I admit I should be abominably
jealous!—I should almost be glad to see you caught at last.
I believe you look upon us as creatures in a raree show,
set up merely for your entertainment."

"Well, you will concede, at any rate, that it was a master-
hand that set this one up tonight," he said, not at all per-
turbed, it seemed, by this thrust. "By the bye, did young
Bayard succeed in propitiating the two offended goddesses?
I saw you talking to Sally Jersey just now."

"Oh, you know very well that Sally is not disposed to ban-
ish anyone from Almack's who promises to be amusing!"
Lady Gilmour said discontentedly. "But I declare I am in
an even worse humour with that troublesome boy than I am
with his sister. Would you believe that this is the third dance
for which Minna has stood up with him? I don't know what
has come over her, for she is usually the most biddable girl
in the world, and she knows she is not to stand up with
anyone—except Harlbury should ask her—more than twice
in an evening."

Northover, raising his quizzing-glass to observe Miss
Beaudoin and Mr. Leyland more closely, let it drop in a
moment and said succinctly, "Romeo and Juliet."

"What!"

"Come, come, Trix, you are not so poorly educated as
that!" he said reprovingly. "They met at a ball, fell in love
at first sight—"

"Don't you *dare* say such a thing! Why, he hasn't a penny
to bless himself with!" Lady Gilmour looked angrily at her
daughter. "She *can't* be such a little fool!"

"Care to lay odds on it?"

"No, I do not! And if she *is* idiotish enough to believe she has conceived a *tendre* for him, that will very soon be put a stop to!"

Northover laughed. "No, no, Trix—don't go to playing Lady Capulet!" he said. "I promise you it won't serve—not if they really *have* fallen top-over-tail in love."

"Love! What do you know of love?" her ladyship said tartly. "I wish you will stop talking such nonsense! People do not fall in love at first sight, and even if they do, it does not signify, for I will *not* have Minna marrying a pauper!"

"He is, you know," Northover remarked conversationally, "a great-nephew of old Rowthorn's, who has, I believe, no closer relations."

"Yes, except for another great-nephew who has been on close terms with him for years!" Lady Gilmour said scathingly. "Thank you, I know all about that situation from Mama. There is not the least hope that young Leyland will come in for so much as a shilling from *that* source."

"Ah, but then Miss Leyland's husband may be expected to do something handsome for him," Northover reminded her gravely, though with a telltale muscle twitching at the corner of his mouth.

Lady Gilmour stared at him in astonishment. "Her husband? But she has not got a husband!"

"She will have, Trix—she will have! What would you say to Harlbury, for example? There is still the Leyland plantation in America, I believe; should not that challenge the imagination of a wealthy young peer with a burning interest in scientific farming?"

"Kit, you are abominable! You *know* I intend Harlbury for Minna. Good God, I am on the very verge of bringing Lady Harlbury round, and if you make mischief now, I'll —I'll—"

"Scratch my eyes out? Oh no, you won't," Northover grinned. "If you must come to cuffs with someone, let me recommend Miss Leyland. But I warn you," he added, as he strolled away, "that I consider you will be engaging a formidable opponent. No holds barred, and the devil take the hindmost! I am not acquainted with the motto upon the Leyland escutcheon, but I should think that would be as suitable as any!"

 LYDIA, SIPPING CHOCOLATE IN HER
bedchamber in Green Street at an
advanced hour the following morning, was indeed inclined to feel a certain satisfaction with the results of
her debut in London Society. She
had stood up twice with Lord Harlbury and twice with Sir Carsbie
Chant, who had paid her several
pretty compliments and engaged him-
self to drive her in the Park in his phaeton the following
afternoon. She had been presented to the Regent's brother,
the Duke of York, who had looked in late in the evening
and bestowed several minutes of jovial conversation upon
her. And even the contretemps with the august Patronesses
of Almack's had had its compensations, for it had ended,
after all, in her being pardoned by both ladies for her lapse,
and it had certainly brought her to the notice of every
gentleman in the room.

When she came downstairs a little later, she found her
grandmother and her brother in equally good spirits. Mrs.
Leyland, who had spent much of the evening in the card-
room, playing whist with some happily encountered acquain-
tances from earlier days, had had an amazing run of luck
which had sent her home with her reticule bulging with her
winnings, and, beyond a brief tiff with Lady Aimer, who had
accused her of being far too casual in her chaperonage of
her granddaughter, she had found nothing in the evening's
events to lessen her enjoyment in her first reappearance in
London Society.

As for Bayard, he was *aux anges* over Miss Beaudoin's
kindness in standing up with him no fewer than three times
in the course of the evening, and was engaged in wearying
his sister and his grandmother for the dozenth time with a
recital of that young lady's manifold perfections when Sidwell, the excellent butler engaged by Mr. Peeke, entered
the room to announce the arrival of Lord Northover.

Lydia, who had been the recipient the evening before of

some chance-given information concerning that gentleman which made her feel strongly that she had a crow to pluck with him, at once desired him to be shown upstairs, and greeted him, as he entered the room, with her customary lack of ceremony.

"Northover, you have deceived me!" she said accusingly. "I have never been so disappointed in anyone in my life!"

Mrs. Leyland looked startled. "Deceived you, my love!" she said. "Lord Northover? Nonsense! I am sure he has never offered you the least—the least discourtesy!"

"Not if you think it courteous to encourage me to believe an outrageous faradiddle, he hasn't!" Lydia said darkly.

Northover grinned. "What 'outrageous faradiddle,' Miss Leyland?" he enquired.

"That you were as poor as a church-mouse! I have it on excellent authority that you are not only very well to pass, but even disgustingly rich!"

"Well, I certainly do not recollect making any statement to you at all about my financial condition," the Viscount said, calmly seating himself. "You ought not to jump to conclusions, Lydia *mia*. It is one of your chief—and, if I may say so—most endearing faults."

"I am *not* your Lydia, *nor* one of your Spanish flirts," Lydia stated categorically. "And if you think *that* is an excuse, it is a very poor sort of one! However," she added handsomely, "I will admit I am in your debt for having extricated me from the scrape I fell into last night, so I have every intention of forgiving you this time."

"Thank you!" said the Viscount, bowing. "Am I to gather that your reason for resenting the delusion into which I permitted you to fall was that you might otherwise have added me to your list of matrimonial prospects?"

"Pray do not flatter yourself, my lord!" Lydia said, with proper primness. "At any rate, you have already told me that you are not a marrying man, so I should merely have been wasting my time if I had spared any of it in attempting to entrap you—which I can assure you I have never had the least intention of doing."

"Lydia! My *dear!*" said Mrs. Leyland, shocked. "One must never make use of such a term in describing one's intentions toward eligible gentlemen, even in jest! Of course you will not attempt to *entrap* anyone!"

"Not even Harlbury?" Northover said wickedly. "My dear ma'am, surely one may make an exception there! I believe Miss Leyland, at least, already agrees with me on that point. What was he saying to you to make you hang so raptly on his words last evening, Lydia? Somehow it puzzles me to picture such a magnificently sober young gentleman paying pretty compliments!"

A gurgle of laughter, immediately repressed, escaped Lydia.

"If you must know," she said loftily, "we were discussing crop rotation and—and crossbreeding." Bayard and Northover burst into simultaneous shouts of laughter. "I daresay it may amuse *you*," she continued, with unimpaired dignity, "but let me tell you that Lord Harlbury considers my understanding quite capable of grasping the intricacies of such subjects."

Bayard gazed at her, awed. "Lyddy, he didn't *say* that to you?"

"Yes, he did," Lydia averred. "What is more, you odious wretches, he meant it! He is a very *worthy* young man—and the most *beautiful* creature I have ever set eyes on—*and* an earl—*and* fabulously rich—"

"Take care, Lydia!" Northover warned. "Harlbury will do very well for you to flirt with, and enhance your consequence in the Marriage Mart, but you had best not allow yourself to be carried away. If his mama and Miss Beaudoin's have anything to say to it, there will be an interesting announcement concerning the pair of them appearing in the *Gazette* before the cat can lick her ear."

Lydia's chin went up. "And what, pray, has Miss Beaudoin to offer that I have not?" she demanded. "*She* has no fortune."

"No," Northover retorted, "but she has something which Lady Harlbury considers more valuable, and which I don't

69

think even *you* have sufficient brass to lay claim to for yourself—a biddable disposition."

Lydia appeared about to utter a spirited rejoinder, but she was interrupted by Bayard, whose face had grown suddenly paler at Northover's pronouncement concerning Miss Beaudoin and Lord Harlbury.

"You must be mistaken, sir!" he jerked out abruptly. "About—about Miss Beaudoin, that is! She—does not love him."

"No?" Northover cynically raised his brows. "And what has that to say to anything?"

"A great deal, I should imagine!" Bayard said doggedly. "Good God, sir, you cannot mean that her relations would force her into a marriage with Lord Harlbury against her inclination!"

"I did not say that," Northover returned, speaking somewhat more gently as he saw the intense earnestness and anxiety with which Bayard was regarding him. "On the other hand, it is quite possible that Miss Beaudoin herself will have no wish to reject such an advantageous offer merely because she has as yet formed no great attachment for Harlbury."

"I don't believe it!" Bayard said. He jumped up and walked to the window, where he stood looking out, evidently unwilling to allow the others to see how strongly disturbed he was. "She has too much delicacy of mind—too great a sensibility—"

Northover shrugged, and Lydia, who had been watching her brother with unusual thoughtfulness, rose and crossed the room swiftly to lay her hand upon his shoulder.

"Never mind, Bayard," she said. "It is nothing but tittle-tattle, at any rate, and I do not believe Harlbury has at all made up his mind to offer for her. He certainly gave no appearance to *me* last night of being a man in love."

"No," the Viscount agreed, amusement lighting his eyes again as he remembered Lord Harlbury's astonishment on being presented with an obviously willing partner by a gentleman quite unknown to him, "I daresay he did not—not with you bursting upon him like a comet! He must be a man of iron nerves even to have been able to carry on a sensible conversation with you under the circumstances. Tell me, Lydia, how did you manage to put together such a bag of tricks as you dazzled the company with last evening? Flawless French, a talent for waltzing that cast every other young lady in the shade—"

"Oh," Lydia said, shrugging, "New Orleans swarms with *émigrés*, you know, and Mademoiselle de Levaillant, who was my governess when I was small, was very willing to continue living with us at Belmaison even after Papa died, until she died herself—poor thing!—last year. And as to the waltzing—pray, what else was there for Bayard and me to do, when we were not riding or reading? We were used to waltz for hours, with Mademoiselle playing *Ach du lieber Augustin* on an impossibly out-of-tune old pianoforte with broken strings."

As she spoke, she still appeared to be giving most of her attention to Bayard, who had not sat down again, but was walking restlessly about the room, paying little heed to the conversation. He was brought back to a consciousness of his surroundings abruptly, however, when Northover signified his intention of taking his leave, announcing that he had stopped in only for the purpose of learning if Bayard wished to accompany him to Gentleman Jackson's famous Boxing Saloon in Bond Street. Bayard's face at once lighted up, and Miss Beaudoin was for the moment forgotten.

"Oh, by Jupiter, that is very kind of you, sir!" he said. "Of course I should like it above anything!"

"For my part," Mrs. Leyland said disapprovingly, "I consider boxing an excessively vulgar form of amusement, and can only regret that gentlemen of the first rank should see fit to indulge in it. What astonishes me even more is that many of them are said to frequent the company of professional pugilists in such places as—Cribb's Parlour, I believe it is called?—where they imbibe a highly intoxicating beverage known as Blue Ruin."

Northover's lips twitched. "Just so, ma'am," he said

gravely, shaking his head. "Now in *your* day, I daresay, such shocking practices were quite unknown."

"Well, no—they were not," Mrs. Leyland confessed unexpectedly. She added composedly, "In point of fact, I daresay your grandfathers were far wilder sparks than you young men are today. But that still does not signify that I approve of your introducing my grandson into low company."

"Low company!" Lydia laughed. "Good God, Grandmama, even I have learned by this time that *Gentleman* Jackson's clientele is as select as his name. Bayard will rub shoulders with quite as many peers in his Saloon, I daresay, as he will at Almack's, if Lady Aimer succeeds in procuring vouchers for us."

She added a few words of obviously sincere gratitude to Northover, which somewhat surprised him, and caused him to realise that Miss Lydia Leyland, in spite of her volatility, was genuinely attached to her brother, and prepared to look kindly upon anyone who exerted himself in his behalf.

However, the brief period of good feeling between them was quickly brought to a close when Miss Leyland, reminded by his doing so again, took exception to the Viscount's making so free with her name as to call her Lydia, and, upon his choosing to laugh at this assumption of propriety, favoured him with such a pungent reproof that all thought that she was about to behave, for once, like any other young lady of quality was removed from his mind.

The Viscount had scarcely taken his leave, bearing Bayard off with him, when the butler announced the arrival of Lady Pentony, Mr. Pentony, and Miss Pentony. Lydia and Mrs. Leyland had time only to exchange glances of surprise before the visitors were ushered in. These were a somewhat faded middle-aged lady, attired in a garnet-coloured walking-dress lavishly trimmed with silk floss, a tall, fair-haired young man who, without being handsome, made an agreeable appearance, and an excessively pretty young girl with melting blue eyes.

Mrs. Leyland had risen to greet the visitors, but her words of welcome were forestalled by Lady Pentony, who in a failing voice begged forgiveness for presuming upon the slight connexion between them—"which I am persuaded you will scarcely consider a connexion at all, based as it is only upon Sir Basil's having married first my dear aunt and then your sister, Mrs. Leyland. But, as I said to Michael only this morning—*do* allow me to present my son Michael—Mrs. Leyland—Miss Leyland, is it not?—and this is my little daughter Eveline—as I was saying, Mrs. Leyland, I should not feel I had done my duty, imperfect as the state of my health is—for dear Dr. Chessick has warned me that any overexertion may cause the most serious damage to my constitution—if I had not made the effort to welcome you to London—"

Lydia, perceiving that Lady Pentony was one of those women whose inability to bring a sentence to a conclusion makes conversation with them a matter of choosing one's opening and dashing in, interposed here to beg the visitors to be seated and, leaving her grandmother to cope with Lady Pentony, herself inaugurated a conversation with the younger members of the party. Miss Pentony seemed very shy, and at first could scarcely be prevailed upon to say a word, but Mr. Michael Pentony, who had very easy manners, followed Lydia's lead in carrying on a civil conversation concerned chiefly with commonplaces until, in answer to an enquiry from him, she remarked that she liked London very much.

"But not more, evidently, than it likes you, Miss Leyland," he said then, with a smile which for some reason made her realise not only how even and white his teeth were, but also how pale were the blue eyes beneath his sandy brows, and how narrow and shrewd the face above his impeccably arranged neckcloth. "Even we—who live rather retired from Society—have already learned of your triumph last night at Lady Gilmour's ball."

"My triumph? Dear me, what an imposing word!" Lydia said coolly, her fine eyes narrowing slightly as she surveyed Mr. Pentony's smiling face. "I should not dream of using it myself! I wonder who can have been so extremely kind as to have exaggerated my small success to you so out of reason, Mr. Pentony?"

"Why, I cannot say that," he replied, with an archness that did nothing to recommend him to her. "It might expose him to your censure, even ridicule, and he has already—poor fellow!—become your slave."

Lydia saw that this speech caused Miss Pentony to colour up and look somewhat self-conscious, and had little difficulty in gathering that the news of what had occurred at Lady Gilmour's ball had actually probably been relayed to Lady Pentony by one of those elderly females whose pedigrees procured them the entrée into fashionable houses, and whose lack of means impelled them to repay invitations from socially aspiring hostesses by relaying to them tit-bits of the gossip they had gleaned in more exalted circles.

"Indeed!" she said, with an assumption of guileless pleasure. "Well, that makes it all quite plain then, for there is only *one* gentleman to whom your description can apply. I shall certainly make a point of it to tax him with running about gossiping to you in the most unwarranted manner of my poor little success!"

Mr. Pentony looked somewhat disconcerted. "No, no!" he said quickly. "I am sure you cannot know—No doubt you are thinking of the wrong person!"

"Oh, I do not think so!" Lydia said, favouring him with a brilliant smile, and then, satisfied that he would think twice before he engaged to impose upon her again with such an obvious fiction, turned her attention to Miss Pentony.

A persevering effort succeeded in drawing a sufficient amount of conversation from that damsel to inform Lydia that she was cast in quite a different mould than her brother. *He* appeared to be keenly determined to put himself forward in the fashionable world, and evidently possessed a degree of intelligence sufficient to guarantee him some success in this, while *her* nature seemed to be one of rather insipid sweetness. Her brother, Lydia saw, held her somewhat in contempt and, when he perceived that Lydia was determined to draw her into the conversation, abandoned his own part in it to devote himself instead to Mrs. Leyland.

His attempts to ingratiate himself with her were far more successful than they had been with Lydia, for on the visitors' departure Mrs. Leyland pronounced him to be a delightful young man, and added that, upon her mentioning that she had a great desire to see Richmond Park again, he had very kindly offered to drive her there—together with Lydia and Bayard, if they cared to join the party—on the Monday of the following week.

"Of course I engaged that you would be very happy to go, my love," Mrs. Leyland said to Lydia, "and I daresay we may count upon Bayard as well. Mr. Pentony will bring his sister with him, he says, but *not* his mother, as her health does not permit her to indulge in excursions of such length. For which, my dear, I cannot but be grateful, for a more disagreeable conversationalist I have never met! Chatter, chatter, chatter—and all in that die-away tone, as if she were preparing to expire before your very eyes! It is no wonder to me that Sir Basil cannot endure her! However, young Mr. Pentony is quite a different matter, and it does not in the least surprise me that Sir Basil intends to make him his heir."

Lydia frowned. "Did *he* tell you that?" she demanded.

"Oh dear, no!" Mrs. Leyland said. "But I gathered, from what Lady Pentony let fall—"

"I am quite sure that what she 'let fall' was perfectly calculated to make you believe a great deal that has not an iota of foundation in fact!" Lydia said. "She is not such a widgeon as she appears, I think—and if she did not decide of her own accord to come here to discourage us from any attempt to make Sir Basil's acquaintance by giving us to understand that he has already decided to make Michael Pentony his heir, I am sure her son took care to put the idea into her head. Scheming is something quite in his line, I should imagine!"

Mrs. Leyland looked startled and not best pleased. "My

dear, you are too severe!" she said. "I will admit that it is the most vexatious thing in the world that Sir Basil's fortune will go to the Pentonys instead of to us, but it is to be expected, after all—"

"Only if we are poor-spirited enough to allow it to happen," Lydia said resolutely, "and that I do *not* intend to be! Only think how Bayard's position would change, Grandmama, if it were known that *he* was to be Sir Basil's heir! He has not the slightest hope of marrying Miss Beaudoin otherwise, I am sure."

"Marry? Miss Beaudoin?" Mrs. Leyland said faintly. "Dear child, what in the world are you talking of? He has only just met the girl!"

"Oh yes, I know that! But I know Bayard as well, and I am certain that this is no ordinary affair with him." She knit her brows thoughtfully. "I shall write to Mr. Peeke today and enquire of him about the state of Sir Basil's health," she declared. "If it is at all improved, I believe we should call upon him at once."

Mrs. Leyland shrugged. "Very well, my dear—but I fear it will be of no manner of use. I have never met the man myself, for Letty did not marry him until after I had left England, but from everything I have heard of him he is excessively set in his ways, and it scarcely seems likely that, after all these years, he will turn against young Mr. Pentony if he has indeed settled it in his mind that he is to inherit his fortune."

"According to Mr. Peeke, he has not at all settled it so," Lydia retorted. "And if he has the least discernment, there will be no question in his mind, once he has seen Bayard, which of the two to favour." She jumped up and implanted a hasty kiss upon the top of her grandmother's head. "At any rate, we must certainly make a push to bring him to realise what a lamb Bayard is," she said. "Dear Grandmama, I shall *just* have time to scribble a note to Mr. Peeke, and then we must positively order out the barouche and go for a shopping excursion in Bond Street. I have exactly the bonnet in mind to wear when we call upon Sir Basil—blue, I think, with just a touch of demureness but decidedly *à la mode*. And one of those dispiriting little shawls with fringe on it, that make one look *quite* fragile and helpless—"

"Baggage!" said Mrs. Leyland.

"Not at all!" said Miss Leyland. "I have the best of intentions: I only wish to help Bayard with my great-uncle. And Mr. Michael Pentony shall most definitely learn that *he* is not the only person who can scheme!"

WHATEVER LYDIA'S IDEAS MIGHT BE concerning the attire suitable to be worn by a young lady paying a first call upon an elderly relation, there was certainly nothing either demure or dispiriting about the costume she donned for her drive in the Park with Sir Carsbie Chant the following afternoon. She wore an extremely dashing promenade dress of coral craped muslin, with gathered sleeves and a high arched collar, which drew an immediate look of approval from her brother when he returned to Green Street shortly before five o'clock to find her just coming down the stairs. When he learned what the engagement was for which she had so adorned herself, however, his air of approbation vanished.

"Good God, you aren't going for a drive with *that* manmilliner!" he exclaimed, with a brotherly lack of tact.

"Oh, but I am!" Lydia retorted. "What is more, I shall enjoy every minute of it, for I have been assured on the highest authority that that absurd creature is one of the chief arbiters of London fashion and fabulously sought after! I shall be the envy of every young lady—*and* her mama—who claps eyes on me in his company."

Bayard shrugged derisively. "Well, I hope you may be, for I can think of nothing else that will make up to you for having to spend an hour with such a dead bore as he is!" he said. "He's a popinjay, you know."

She gave an appreciative gurgle of laughter.

"Oh, the Prince of Popinjays," she agreed cordially. "But beggars can't be choosers, you know, and in spite of Greataunt Letty's bequest I fancy we are very close to fitting that description—even though Grandmama *has* taken it into her head, after her run of luck at Lady Gilmour's party, that she is about to make all our fortunes at the card-table." She added, "If you really *do* wish to do something to make my day a little brighter, you will instantly decide to ride in the Park yourself this afternoon, and manage to bring me someone to talk to who has more to offer in the way of conversation than tales of his own self-consequence. All the world will be there at this hour, you know. Perhaps you may even see Miss Beaudoin."

The arrival of Sir Carsbie put an end to their conversation at that moment, but Lydia was scarcely surprised some half hour later, as she sat bowling sedately along in the Park in Sir Carsbie's yellow-winged phaeton, to find her brother cantering toward them on the raking bay mare he had purchased at Tattersall's a few days before. He was about to spur the mare forward to come up with them, she saw, when his attention was evidently attracted by some object of far greater interest to him. Turning her head, she beheld an elegant barouche a short distance behind her, in which Miss Beaudoin, Lord Harlbury, and the latter's mother were seated.

Lydia at once exclaimed, somewhat startling her escort, "Oh, Sir Carsbie, do pull up your horses for a moment! Here is someone I must speak to!"

She was already signalling for Harlbury's attention, and had the satisfaction of seeing that gentleman give an order to his coachman that brought the two carriages to a halt just abreast of each other. True, the expression upon his face did not indicate any overwhelming delight at this unexpected meeting, but rather the sort of wariness with which a man approaches an object he believes may possibly be capable of some disconcerting action directed against his dignity. Lydia read it very accurately, as the hint of laughter in her eyes betrayed, but she kept her countenance commendably and merely said, with a dazzling smile directed towards her hapless victim, "Oh, my lord, I am so very glad to have had the good fortune to meet you today! You *did* promise—did you not?—that you would bring me the pamphlet on crossbreeding that we were discussing the other evening? I shall be at home all the morning tomorrow expecting you! Have you met my brother Bayard? Lord Harlbury—"

Bayard, who had moved his mare forward at the words,

reached down his hand to take his lordship's civilly extended one; but his eyes, Lydia saw, had gone swiftly to meet Miss Beaudoin's. Nor did it escape her attention that that damsel's lovely little face had coloured up rosily beneath the enchanting Lavinia chip hat that crowned her dark locks, or that the eyes she turned to meet Bayard's wore an expression so worshipful that it must have drawn the notice of anyone not entirely absorbed in his own emotions.

Fortunately, that description exactly suited everyone else in the group. Sir Carsbie, as usual, was wholly occupied with the effect his dress and equipage were making upon the company; Lord Harlbury was mustering up his resolution to present Miss Leyland and her brother to his obviously unreceptive parent; and the parent herself, having received the friendliest of smiles from Lydia, was preparing a frigid rebuff for her.

Unfortunately for her intentions, the guns of her opening attack—the merest inclination of her bonneted head as her son pronounced Miss Leyland's name—were immediately spiked by that young lady's remarking sunnily to Lord Harlbury, "Indeed, I need no introduction to your mother, my lord! Your very striking resemblance to her must inform everyone what the relationship between you is."

As it had long been a sore point with Lady Harlbury that her son—an Adonis by any standard—was universally held to resemble his late father, and to owe nothing of his good looks to her, the delicacy of this compliment was as gratifying to her as it was astonishing. She cast a somewhat suspicious glance at Lydia, but, finding nothing in that accomplished young lady's countenance to suggest that she was *cutting a wheedle*, decided to accept her words at their face value and therefore inclined her head a second time, in a rather more gracious manner.

"As to that, Miss Leyland," she conceded majestically, "I believe he *may* be said to have my nose."

"Not a doubt of it!" said Lydia, regarding without a blink her ladyship's decidedly pug nose, which bore not the slightest resemblance to the classical feature adorning her son's face. "Dear Lady Harlbury, I quite *knew*, the moment I saw how greatly you resembled your son, that I should find in you a sympathetic spirit! *You*, I am persuaded, must share his attachment to country life—which to one like myself, reared in rural surroundings and quite lost in the bustle of a great, noisy town like London, must be of all things most refreshing!"

Lady Harlbury, who, in spite of her pompous manners, was no fool, cast a second rather sharply suspicious glance at Lydia. "You do not care for London, Miss Leyland?" she enquired. "It surprises me to hear that. *I* should have said that you were enjoying yourself excessively at Lady Gilmour's ball the other evening."

"Oh, do you really think so?" Lydia asked cordially. "I am very glad to hear you say so, for it was excessively kind of Lady Gilmour to invite us, and I would not for the world have appeared ungrateful! But I have been used for so long, you see, to living quite retired in the country that I doubt if I shall ever come to care for town life as other young females are said to do."

She flicked a brief glance across the barouche to see that Bayard, who had contrived to bring his mare around into an advantageous position for a conversation with Miss Beaudoin, was in earnest colloquy with her, and hastened to continue the conversation, drawing first Lord Harlbury and then Sir Carsbie into it so that no notice should be taken by the other occupants of the barouche of the fact that Miss Beaudoin and Bayard were pointedly occupied otherwise.

It was Sir Carsbie, in fact, who first discovered that a tête-à-tête was going on under their noses. He gave a waspish titter that drew Lady Harlbury's attention to the situation as well, and her formidable disapproval immediately fell upon the two guilty participants. She sent Bayard an annihilating glance, put an end to Lydia's persevering chatter with the curtest of adieux, and ordered the coachman to drive on by the simple expedient of prodding the tip of her parasol into the small of his back.

Lydia, blinking as the barouche swept past, looked up at Bayard, a gleam of laughter in her eyes.

"*Definitely* unloving," she pronounced. "Do you have the feeling that we were both *de trop*, Bayard my own?"

But Bayard, who seemed in no mood for frivolous conversation, only gave her a brief, rather forced smile and cantered off, leaving her to Sir Carsbie's quizzing.

"You are well acquainted with Lord Harlbury, Miss Leyland?" Sir Carsbie enquired, not, it appeared, best pleased by this supposition.

"Oh dear, no! I met him for the first time only the other night," Lydia replied, composedly unfurling a very fashionable sunshade and raising it above her head.

"Indeed?" said Sir Carsbie, with rather peevish archness. "I gathered, from the freedom of your tone with him—the manner in which you requested him to call—"

"Shall we say '*commanded* him to call'?" Lydia said, on a ripple of laughter. "Dear Sir Carsbie, I believe you are jealous! Shall I command *you* to call upon me—even though I met you, too, for the first time only the other night?"

"I shall be delighted," Sir Carsbie said, unbending a trifle at her flirtatious tone, and glancing about him to make certain that the world was aware he was dallying fashionably with the attractive young lady seated beside him. "Shall I bring you a bouquet as well, Miss Leyland?"

"Oh, by all means! I wish you will do everything in your power to bring me into fashion, Sir Carsbie, and I am sure that if you do so I shall soon achieve my ambition to become the rage of London. *Your* approval, I am told, is all that is necessary for that."

Sir Carsbie, with somewhat half-hearted modesty, attempted to deny this, but, upon Lydia's desiring him not to talk flummery to her, admitted that his taking her up might be the only thing wanted to make her a success in the *haut ton*.

"I may say that even the Prince Regent relies greatly upon my judgement in such matters," he observed, with natural

83

pride. " 'Carsbie,' he has frequently said to me, 'would you call Miss Blank a Beauty or would you not?'—depending upon me, you see, to make those nice distinctions in regard to eyes, nose, teeth, complexion, figure, et cetera, that are so important in such matters."

Lydia, who had rather the feeling of being a prime bit of horseflesh paraded for sale as Sir Carsbie's eyes patently surveyed her own qualifications in each regard while he spoke, bit her lip but, deciding that being brought into fashion demanded its sacrifices, managed to return a light answer. However, her face, as she entered the front door of the house in Green Street a half hour later, bore an expression of such distaste that Bayard, who had apparently come in only a few moments before and was still in the hall, making some enquiry of Sidwell, cocked a questioning eyebrow at her.

"Why, what is it, Lyddy?"

"Oh—nothing at all!" She shrugged, and walked across the hall rapidly to take his arm. "Come with me a moment; I want to talk to you," she said, drawing him toward the small morning-parlour at the back of the house.

He followed her, and she closed the door behind them.

"What is it?" he asked again.

She looked at him, seeing an expression on his face which she—who thought she had been acquainted with all his moods—had never observed there before. He looked resolute, unhappy, and a little desperate, and before she could reply to his question he forestalled her by saying quickly, "No—wait! There is something I must tell you first. I—talked with Miss Beaudoin today—"

"Are you in love with her, Bayard?" Lydia asked directly, as he halted, apparently undecided how to continue.

He threw her a grateful glance. "Yes!" he said. "I thought you must have guessed. How could any man not be—? Is she not an angel? But, Lyddy, it is true, what Northover said! She is being pressed to marry Harlbury; he has not

84

spoken to her yet, but she is sure that everything now hangs only upon her consent."

In spite of herself, Lydia's lips curved in a smile. "You managed to get all that from her this afternoon with the Dowager seated just beside her?" she said. "Good God, I had not realised you could be so adroit!"

Bayard shrugged, but did not respond to the playfulness in her voice.

"Of course it was impossible for her to talk freely," he said, "but a word—a glance—I should have been an idiot if I had not been able to gather the whole situation from what she let fall!" He took a hasty, restless turn about the room. "But it must not be—it *shall* not be, if anything *I* can do can prevent it!" he said, with subdued energy. "If only I were not so new in the country—if I had had time to settle myself in some way, so that I might support a wife!"

Lydia, who had seated herself quietly in a chair beside the table, looked at him keenly and gravely, as serious now as he was himself.

"So it has come to that already!" she said. "I thought as much! But, do you know, it seems quite incredible to me, Bayard—like something one finds in books, but never in real life. Can you really have fallen so much in love with her already—and she with you?"

"Yes!" Bayard said. "That is—of course I can't speak for her, but I believe—I hope—" He sat down suddenly in a chair near hers, sinking his head in his hands. "But, oh God! it is of no use to talk of it!" he said miserably. "I have no fortune, no prospects; Lady Gilmour will never consent to her marrying me! I am a scoundrel even to think of such a thing until I have the means to support her respectably—and how I am to come by them I have not the least idea!"

"Perhaps if you could purchase your commission in a good cavalry regiment—"

He raised his head, giving a shaky little laugh. "Even with

85

that, do you seriously think an offer from me would weigh against one from Harlbury, in Lady Gilmour's eyes? And I have no prospects of being able to do even that."

"Sir Basil—?" Lydia said tentatively. "After all, you do not *know* that he will not make you his heir."

"God, that *is* a forlorn hope!"

"Perhaps." Lydia put up her chin. "We shall see. I did not tell you, I believe, that I sent round a note to Mr. Peeke yesterday, and he says we may call upon Sir Basil on Monday morning." He shook his head unhopefully, and she went on, trying for a lighter note, "At any rate, it may be that we shall do very well without him. Have you forgotten why we came to London? If *I*, instead of Miss Beaudoin, should be fortunate enough to receive an offer from Lord Harlbury—"

Bayard looked up quickly. "You? You do not tell me that *you* have fallen in love with *him*?" he asked incredulously.

"Heavens, no! I seriously doubt that I know what the term means—not as *you* would use it, at any rate. As you well know, I have not had a *tendre* for a man since I was nine years old and tumbled head-over-ears in love with the Esterlys' coachman—and *that* was only his elegant livery, for the moment I saw him out of it, all my affection for him vanished." She had the satisfaction of seeing a faint smile appear on her brother's face and went on, with a gaiety which even she, however, felt was rather forced, "At any rate, Harlbury is certainly all that is amiable—and rich, handsome, and an earl as well—and if I can draw him off from your Minna, why should I not do so, and even marry him if I like? And then he shall do something very handsome for you, and you may marry Minna after all, and we shall all four be as happy as grigs—"

Bayard looked at her searchingly, his face rather pale. "Lyddy, that is horrible!" he said quickly. "Why should I have *my* happiness at the expense of yours?"

"At the expense of mine? Why, what a high flight, my

dear! Why should I *not* be happy, married to a rich, amiable, titled Adonis?"

"If you do not love him—"

"Fiddle! I shall love him well enough for all practical purposes. I am not at all like you, you know, in spite of Grandmama's insisting that the two of us were cut from the same cloth; and if I have reached the age of twenty without once tumbling seriously into love, it does not seem likely that I shall ever do so." She could not prevent a somewhat wistful note from creeping into her voice as she spoke the words, but she threw off the mood in a moment and continued more brightly, "At any rate, don't fall into the mopes, I beg you! I promise you, we shall come about! If Miss Beaudoin has as great a fondness for you as you have for her, Harlbury will never succeed in bringing her to the point of accepting an offer from him, for he is *not* an impetuous lover, I am sure. On the contrary, I daresay he will have to be prodded into matrimony."

Bayard could not help smiling at the mischievous look with which she pronounced these last words, and, as she rose, got up too, slipped his arm about her, and gave her a brotherly hug.

"I expect I should forbid you to meddle in the affair at all, for you are sure to land yourself in the suds, one way or another," he said ruefully. "But, to tell you the truth, I am too much in need of help from any quarter to do that. But you *will* promise me, Lyddy, that you won't do something completely bird-witted only to save my groats?"

"I shall be the soul of discretion," Lydia said virtuously. "Am I not always?"

"No! And, by the bye, what was it *you* wanted to speak to *me* about? I had almost forgotten, in worrying you over *my* affairs."

She laughed. "We had the same thing in mind—as we so often do! My own affairs are prospering splendidly, thank you—Harlbury has promised to call, and the Prince of

Popinjays needed no prodding whatever to invite me to drive out with him to see the flowers in the Botanical Gardens."

"Lyddy! You are *not* to encourage *that* countercoxcomb! I draw the line there!"

She gave his hand a pat, slipping from under his arm and running into the hall before he could restrain her.

"Can you not fancy me as the Popinjay Princess?" she called back provocatively over her shoulder—almost colliding as she did so with Winch, who, halting her, enquired in minatory tones whether or not she intended to come upstairs and sit still long enough to allow her to do her hair before dinner.

 MONDAY MORNING FOUND THE
Leyland barouche arriving in Russell
Square, where Sir Basil Rowthorn had
his town-house, at an hour which Mr.
Peeke had signified would be convenient for a call upon his client. The
Square, which had been built on the
former site of Bedford House since
Mrs. Leyland's departure for America, was unhesitatingly character-
ised by that lady as fit only for the Cits and mushrooms who
dwelt in its massive brick edifices, but Bayard and Lydia,
unacquainted with the nicer points of London geography,
felt that it was all very fine.

Nor were they disappointed with the interior of Sir Basil's
house, when the front door was opened to them by a very
proper butler: everything, from carpets to chandeliers,
seemed in the richest style. They had little time to look
about them, however, for, as it appeared that they were
expected (that would be Mr. Peeke, Lydia thought appreciatively), they were ushered upstairs at once to a large saloon
where, in a corner beside one of the tall windows overlooking the square, an elderly gentleman sat with a gouty leg
propped upon a footstool.

It was a warm, bright June morning, but there was a fire
in the grate and a shawl about Sir Basil's shoulders. At first
glance, Lydia would have taken him for a much younger man
than the eighty years with which Mr. Peeke and her grandmother had endowed him, for the rim of hair encircling his
almost bald head was still black, and there was an expression
of active malevolence on his rather pinched features which
age might have been expected to soften. He looked the three
callers up and down without a word of greeting, and then
motioned them to be seated as cavalierly as if they had been
menials whom he was about to interview for some minor
post in his household.

This was too much for Mrs. Leyland. She threw back her

head, regarding him with a majestic stare, and said bluntly, "My dear sir, if you do not intend to be civil, we are wasting our time. Lydia—Bayard—come, my dears, we shall not stay. I had had the intention," she added acidly, to Sir Basil, "of offering you condolences on the demise of my poor sister, but I see now that it is Letty to whom condolences should have been offered, while she was yet alive—"

"You're Erminia, I suppose," Sir Basil said, opening his lips at last and interrupting her without ceremony. "You don't favour her, but that girl does." He pointed the handsome gold-headed stick that stood beside his chair in Lydia's direction and said to her, "Come over here and let me have a look at you. What's your name?"

"Lydia, sir," said Lydia, casting an irrepressibly mirthful glance at her grandmother, but at once composing her countenance and walking across the room to stand demurely before Sir Basil's chair.

His sharp eyes looked her up and down, the result of his scrutiny being a sardonic, "Humph!" He added, "*You're* a flighty baggage, I make no doubt. Letty to the life! Well, what d'ye want of me—eh?"

"Dear Uncle Basil," Lydia said, looking him straight in the face, "if I told you it was merely to make your acquaintance, you would not believe me—would you? After all, it would be too totally eccentric of us not to be in the least interested in your fortune!"

Sir Basil, taken unawares by this devastating frankness, emitted another—"Humph!"—this one in a somewhat startled tone. He made a quick recover, however, and remarked grudgingly that at least he was glad to see she was not one to use roundaboutation.

"Not," he added, "that that'll do you any good when it's a matter of loosening *my* purse-strings. I'm not such a mawworm as to be taken in by a pretty face and wheedling manners."

"No, I should rather think you are not," Lydia agreed, continuing to survey him with an interested air. "You are not at all as I imagined you—but then I daresay that is for

90

the best, for I do not feel in the least in the mood to play the Dutiful Niece today, in spite of this bonnet, which I purchased *particularly* for the purpose."

"Your bonnet? What's a bonnet to say to anything?" Sir Basil demanded, looking irritated and somewhat bewildered. "You *are* like Letty; there was never any sense to be made of her talk, either."

However, he relented sufficiently to invite the party to sit down, and, ringing a hand-bell that stood on the table beside him, to order the butler who responded to its summons to bring some refreshment for them. He then turned his attention to Bayard, enquiring ungraciously if he was another such skitterbrain as his sister.

Bayard gave him his lazy, good-humoured smile. "As to that, sir," he said, "I should consider it an honour to be bracketed with Lydia, but I fear I am not in her class."

"No, I should think not," Sir Basil said, regarding him keenly. "You don't look to want sense, but *she's* the needle-witted one of the pair of you, if I'm any judge of the matter. Nothing like that simpering, milk-and-water Pentony chit."

"Oh, as to that," Lydia remarked composedly, "I should think Mr. Michael Pentony's wits were quite sharp enough for all *that* family!"

He swung round to her. "You've met 'em, then—have you?" he asked. "How did that come about?"

"Why, they called upon us the other day," Lydia said, "for the purpose, I should imagine, of discovering how much of a threat we should be to their hopes of inheriting your fortune, sir—though, according to Lady Pentony," she added pensively, "you have already quite made up your mind that her son is to be your heir."

"That woman!" said Sir Basil, in tones of strong loathing. "If I thought Michael was fool enough to let *her* get her hands on any of my money, he'd never see a groat of it. But he's a neat article, Michael," he added, with satisfaction—"as shrewd as he can hold together. It's not likely anybody will be able to cozen *him* out of anything, once he has it in his grasp."

91

"Dear me!" Lydia said. "That *does* rather sound as if we were wasting our time here, doesn't it?"

"Nothing of the sort! Don't run to conclusions!" Sir Basil snapped. "I don't say, if I wanted a man to manage my affairs, I might not engage Michael to do it. The point is, that ain't what I want. Damme, I've never been beaten on any suit but one: I've got a knighthood; I've got enough brass to buy and sell half the fine gentlemen in the kingdom; I even married one of their daughters—but I never was taken to their bosom, so to speak." He gave a sudden, quite unexpected crack of laughter. "Well, I ain't done yet, by a long chalk!" he said. "Pentony-Rowthorn or Leyland-Rowthorn —it's all one to me, but I've a fancy to see Rowthorns in the *haut ton*, or whatever they call it these days, and, by Jupiter, I shall do it yet!"

Mrs. Leyland stared at him. "Do you mean to tell me," she demanded, "that you will make the bequest of your fortune contingent upon your heir's adding your name to his own?"

"Yes, I do," he said promptly. "What's amiss with that? Done all the time, ain't it?"

Mrs. Leyland acknowledged that it was, but seemed inclined to make objections. Lydia, however, gave her no opportunity to utter them.

"Why, of course!" she said cordially. "What a splendid idea! But I must say that in that case you have no choice in the matter: you *must* decide upon Bayard, for no one can imagine that Michael Pentony is capable of establishing himself in the first circles."

"And what do *you* know about that, miss," Sir Basil interrupted her sarcastically, "when you've only just arrived from America? *You* hadn't the wit, it seems, not to make yourself the talk of the town at a *ton* party t'other night—"

"That is quite true," Lydia said, with aplomb, "but I doubt that it was a party to which Mr. Pentony could have received an invitation. I know it is excessively vulgar to boast of such things, but did your informant tell you as well, dear sir, that Sir Carsbie Chant has twice driven me out in his phaeton

92

this past week, that we have received invitations to Lady Forward's Venetian breakfast and Lady Micall's cotillion-ball, and that Lord Northover will be kind enough to put Bayard's name up for membership at White's?"

Sir Basil surveyed her with an interested frown, failing to observe that the last portion of her statement had drawn a start of surprise from Bayard.

"No, he didn't," Sir Basil acknowledged.

"What is more," continued Lydia superbly, "Lady Aimer has every expectation of being able to procure vouchers for me for Almack's, where I doubt very much that I shall meet either Mr. or Miss Pentony—"

The arrival of the butler with a tray of refreshments inter-rupted the conversation at this point. Lydia noted that these provisions were laid on with a lavish hand, and that the silver tray upon which they were borne was of a baronial size and opulence: evidently Sir Basil's eccentricities did not prevent him from maintaining a style of living quite in keep-ing with the first circles to which he aspired.

He did not press them to stay, however, once the cakes and sherry had been consumed, nor did he invite them to return for a second visit when they rose to take their depar-ture.

"I shall keep myself informed as to how you go on without the need to hear from any of you," he said bluntly. "And if I want to see you, I'll send for you."

"Thank you!" said Mrs. Leyland, witheringly. "If we should happen to be at leisure, we shall certainly come! Lydia—Bayard—"

She swept them out of the room with her, giving it as her opinion, as soon as the front door had closed behind them, that her brother-in-law was certainly mad, and that, at any rate, there was not the least use in their placing any dependance upon his leaving a penny to them.

But to this Lydia would not agree.

"He was quite taken with us, *I* believe," she said optimis-tically, bringing a smile to Bayard's face as he informed her that it was not generally considered the most suitable way to put yourself into a wealthy relation's good graces to confess candidly that you were interested only in his fortune.

"Well, he must be a perfect cabbagehead if he believes that is not the Pentonys' chief object as well," Lydia said, "and, whatever else he is, he is not *that*. I am rather sorry for him, poor lamb, for I daresay it is horridly uncomfortable to be in the gout, to say nothing of having suffered such a *disgruntling* disappointment as to have been snubbed by the *ton*, when he so much wishes to become one of its ornaments. I wonder if it would satisfy him if I named my first-born for him when I marry? *Rowthorn Chant*—or *Rowthorn* —what is Harlbury's family name? Do you know?"

"I haven't the least idea," Bayard said, "and if you are thinking of having a first-born by Sir Carsbie Chant, I warn you that you will have me to deal with! I refuse to stand uncle to any of *his* brats."

This made Lydia laugh, and Mrs. Leyland frown at such unbecoming language, and the subject of Sir Basil and his foibles was thereupon dropped.

Upon returning to Green Street, they learned that Lady Aimer had called in their absence, and, finding them out, had left a note apprising them that Lady Sefton had agreed to grant the much-desired vouchers for Almack's. Lydia, delighted, at once claimed Bayard's escort to the Assembly Rooms for the very next subscription ball, and was beginning to plan her toilette in detail when Bayard, recalled by the incident to a remembrance of his sister's somewhat vainglorious vaunting of future triumphs to Sir Basil, interrupted to say, "Well, your luck has been in this time, Lyddy; I'll grant you that. But what the deuce were you thinking of when you told Sir Basil that Northover intended to put me up for membership at White's? He has said nothing at all to me of any such intention, and I certainly shan't ask it of him."

"Well, you need not ask him," Lydia said placidly. "I shall do so myself."

Bayard frowned slightly. "I wish you will not," he said. "He has already shown us civility quite beyond anything we deserve from him, and—and it will not do, you know, for you to put yourself under any particular obligation to him."

Lydia turned to stare at him. "And why not, pray?" she enquired. "Surely *you* are not going to warn me, as Lady Aimer did, of his shocking reputation! I assure you, he has no designs upon me."

"Much *you* know about it!" Bayard retorted, galled by her assumption of superior knowledge. "I don't wish to say anything to his discredit, for he's been devilish kind to me, but—but a man of his cut don't put himself out for a chit like you out of the pure goodness of his heart, you know! Oh, I daresay he's not such a rake-shame as to try to give you a slip on the shoulder now, but if you want my opinion, he'll do his possible to see you riveted to some clothhead like Chant, and then hope to enter into a little game *à trois* that will admirably suit his convenience."

"Bayard!" interrupted Mrs. Leyland, who had been a scandalised auditor of this conversation. "You will immediately cease using such improper language to your sister! If you have reason to believe that Lord Northover is guilty of designs upon her virtue, *I* am the person to whom you should confide such thoughts."

Lydia laughed. "Good heavens, I don't know which of you is the more absurd!" she said. "Northover, I daresay, hasn't an idea in the world beyond amusing himself by seeing how far we can rise in the fashionable world with nothing but our wits to aid us—" She broke off, finding that, for some unaccountable reason, this explanation of his lordship's behaviour was no more satisfactory to her than it appeared to be to Bayard, and went on after a moment, rather shortly, "At any hand, I am not in the least afraid of anything he may do. And if he is amusing himself at our expense, that is all the more reason why he should pay for his entertainment. I shall certainly ask him to put your name up at White's when next I see him, and if he will not do so I shall ask Harlbury—"

"Harlbury!" said Bayard, aghast. "Lyddy, you wouldn't! Good God, I have only just met him!"

"I am considering," said Lydia, a somewhat martial light

in her eye, "making him your brother-in-law, so that need not signify. And I am sure *his* principles are far too high to allow *him* to wink at any such arrangement as you have described as being in Lord Northover's mind."

Upon which scathing statement she swept out of the room, leaving Mrs. Leyland and Bayard to gaze at each other in speechless dismay behind her.

The Pentonys arrived in Green Street not long afterward, at the hour appointed for the Richmond Park excursion, in a smart barouche which Lydia—in spite of the derogatory terms in which she had referred to their pretensions of fashion before Sir Basil—privately acknowledged she need feel no qualms about stepping into. Bayard, who had been persuaded to join the party, elected to ride beside the barouche on his bay mare, and, as his good manners led him to direct his conversation chiefly to Miss Pentony, while Mr. Pentony devoted himself to satisfying Mrs. Leyland's curiosity concerning the many alterations that had taken place in the countryside during the years of her absence in America, the drive passed in a generally agreeable manner.

Even Lydia, who was not disposed to be prejudiced in the Pentonys' favour, was obliged to admit that Eveline was a very pretty girl, and that Mr. Michael Pentony's conversation showed that he was deficient neither in understanding nor in address. Her grandmother, she saw, was even quite in the way to making him a favourite, in spite of the peculiar situation in which he and Bayard stood in regard to Sir Basil, for he had exactly that deferential manner and ready consideration for her comfort which an elderly lady must find irresistible in a young man.

It was a fine day, and when they had arrived at Richmond it was discovered that many other parties had been before them in driving out to admire the celebrated view of the Thames from the top of the hill and to enjoy a stroll upon the grass. As the Leylands had so small an acquaintance in London, it was not surprising that they met no one they knew, but Mr. Pentony, in addition to pointing out to them such well-known members of the *ton* as Lord Petersham and Lady Cowper—neither of whom, Lydia noted, did he venture to approach—came across a quietly but fashionably dressed middle-aged lady strolling in company with a younger and more dashing-looking couple, and halted to make her known to the Leylands as a friend of Lady Pentony's, a Mrs. Collingworth. She was persuaded to leave her own party and join theirs for a time, and Mr. Pentony, giving one arm to her and the other to Mrs. Leyland, walked on between the two older ladies, leaving Bayard to squire Miss Pentony and Lydia.

A quarter of an hour later, when the two groups came together again and Mrs. Collingworth made her adieux and returned to her own friends, Lydia learned that her grandmother had been sufficiently taken with her new acquaintance to agree to make one of a card-party she was giving at her house in Curzon Street the following evening. For herself, she would have been little inclined to seek further intimacy with anyone in the Pentonys' circle, but she could not direct her grandmother's conduct, and was obliged to attend with what complaisance she could to Mrs. Leyland's encomiums on the lady. She was, in fact, glad to escape from them when Mr. Pentony, having seen Mrs. Leyland comfortably installed upon a green bench with Miss Pentony, offered her his arm so that they might continue their exploration of the park.

But in five minutes she would, if offered her choice, eagerly have returned to them, for Mr. Pentony, finding himself tête-à-tête with her, at once began attempting to ingratiate himself with her by the most persistent means in his power. She was the target of compliments, flattery, even hints of incipient devotion, delivered to the accompaniment of subtle pressures of the hand which she had unwarily allowed to be drawn beneath his arm—all this with the addition of a series of speaking glances, the meaning of which she could not fail to understand.

His conduct, in short, was such as would have driven most

young females into pleasurable confusion; but Lydia was not an ordinary young female, and she was neither pleased nor confused.

"I don't believe you can have the least notion," she said composedly, after having allowed him to run on in this manner for a few minutes, "how very disagreeable it is, when one wants nothing but the support of a gentleman's arm in walking over uneven ground in absurdly thin sandals, to find oneself involved in an utterly *redundant* flirtation with him. Because if you had, I *do* rather feel that you would give over. You *must* be able to see that I am not at all in the mood."

Mr. Pentony looked considerably taken aback for a moment at this remarkably frank statement. But he made a quick recover and, smiling with a somewhat forced air, murmured something about his feelings no doubt causing him to act in too precipitate a manner.

"Your feelings!" Lydia said reproachfully. "Oh, come now, Mr. Pentony! I am *not* a moonling, you know!"

"No—certainly you are not!" Mr. Pentony said, his eyes narrowing slightly as he turned his head to look into her face. "Though why you should think it beyond the bounds of reason to imagine that a remarkably handsome young woman like yourself should attract admirers—"

"Oh, I do not think *that* is beyond the bounds of reason in the least," Lydia conceded promptly. "But in your case I am *not* a remarkably handsome young woman—or, at least, that is not all I am. I am that *malevolent* Lydia Leyland, who has turned up when she was least wanted to cast a rub in the way of your inheriting a fortune."

Mr. Pentony, though evidently unprepared for this direct attack, demonstrated his native shrewdness by accepting it at its face value and casting aside any further pretence that he was not as cognizant of the situation between them as was Miss Leyland herself. He gave her a slight smile and remarked calmly, "Well, I should not put it in that way, but, if you like, I will admit that the news of your and your brother's arrival in England—before I had become acquainted with you—*did* appear to give me some little cause for apprehension."

"And it does not do so now? Well, I should not be *too* certain of that, if I were you, for it is just possible that Sir Basil may not think quite so poorly of us as you appear to do!"

"I? Not in the least!" Mr. Pentony denied. He seemed quite at his ease, in spite of the rapid reversal of form into which he had been forced, and regarded her with what appeared to her to be the faintly smug air of a man who holds all the trump cards in his own hand. "I am aware, Miss Leyland, that you might be a very formidable opponent. I am also aware—as I believe you are not—that you might be an equally formidable ally."

He paused on the words, observing the suddenly arrested expression upon her face. Of course! she was thinking, castigating herself mentally for not having seen before this moment the glaringly obvious reason for his attentions to her. It would certainly be much to his advantage, in his efforts to bring Sir Basil to make him his heir, if he were to contract an alliance with some highly eligible damsel of the *haut ton*—but, failing that extremely unlikely event, what could do more to forward his claims, and at the same time cut the ground from under Bayard's feet, than marriage with Miss Lydia Leyland? *A neat article*, Sir Basil had called him, and certainly, thought Lydia, the phrase appeared to be justified.

She decided in the same instant, however, not to make things easier for Mr. Pentony by allowing him to see that she understood the meaning of his words, and merely parried them with an innocent—"Well, I do not at all know what that signifies. I only know that if Sir Basil *should* chance to take a liking to Bayard or me, it would go very much against the pluck with you."

"You know very well that he *has* taken a liking to you," Mr. Pentony said, as if he were uttering the merest commonplace—but the words brought her eyes to his face with a jerk.

"He has taken—?" she repeated. "Then you know already that we saw him this morning—?"

"Yes. I do know," Mr. Pentony said baldly. He looked down at her, the slight, self-assured smile again upon his narrow face. "Pray, Miss Leyland," he said softly, "credit me with the ability to be quite as formidable an opponent as you are, if you should choose to cross swords with me. Sir Basil's fortune—as I am certain you know—is not a merely genteel one; it is truly a golden prize. Is it likely then, do you think, that I shall allow anyone to chouse me out of it because of my own negligence in not keeping careful account of everything that concerns it? You saw Sir Basil this morning; you charmed him into complaisance by your audacity, though your brother did little to aid you and your grandmother was a positive hindrance to you—"

Lydia interrupted him indignantly. "You must have bribed the servants, of course, since you know so much so quickly!"

He smiled again. "That will be difficult to prove—will it not?" he said lightly—"since it can hardly be expected that any of them will admit to such a charge, even if it is true. And I should not advise you," he said, as he observed the contempt flashing in her eyes, "to turn your brother and your grandmother against me by repeating such suspicions to them, Miss Leyland. It may make for awkwardness in the future, you see, if you should decide, after all, that you had rather be my ally than my opponent."

It was perhaps unfortunate for Mr. Pentony that he was not better acquainted with Miss Lydia Leyland. If he had been, he would have realised that, in dealing with her, the use of threats—no matter how politely veiled—was even less advisable than the use of cajolery. She made no comment now, but merely advised Mr. Pentony of her wish to return to the others, and when they did so no one would have gathered, from the serene expression upon her face, that she had anything more on her mind than enjoyment of the outing.

Mr. Pentony, driving back to town, might even have congratulated himself upon the success of his little *éclaircissement* with her; but if he did, it was no more than she desired him to do. It was always best, she had decided, to put one's enemy off his guard.

10

ON THE FOLLOWING WEDNESDAY evening the Leyland barouche set Mrs. Leyland, her granddaughter, and her grandson down at Almack's Assembly Rooms well before eleven, after which hour the august Patronesses had decreed that no one should be admitted within its doors. Lydia, when they had been greeted by the Master of Ceremonies and had passed on into the ball-room, was somewhat surprised to find that the rooms, though elegant and spacious, were by no means magnificent, for she had heard so much of the awesome importance to a young female of admission to the club—known as the Matrimonial Mart among the irreverent—that she might have been pardoned for expecting something quite out of the common way.

The toilettes of the ladies, however, and the throng of fashionably tailored gentlemen surveying through supercilious quizzing-glasses the array of hopeful young beauties marshalled for their notice, quite equalled her anticipations; and she was glad that she herself had chosen to appear to her best advantage in a gown of primrose gauze, to which long white gloves, sandals of Denmark satin, and Italian filigree ear-drops added the final modish touches.

The first person to approach them as they entered the ball-room was Sir Carsbie Chant, who at once begged the honour of leading Lydia into the set of country dances that was just forming. She accepted the invitation, casting a droll glance at Bayard as she walked off with her exquisitely attired gallant that prompted the latter to enquire curiously as to its meaning. However, since she had already discovered that he had not the least sense of humour, she carefully refrained from giving him the slightest hint that it was he who had aroused her amusement, and led him instead into a discussion of the merits of a gentleman's coat, selected at random from the array before her. This was a subject that happily engaged his attention during the entire set, as he

103

expatiated upon the rival merits of Nugee, Weston, and Stultz in cutting a coat and pointed out to her various examples of the art of each.

Her attention was thus left free to move about the ballroom, for Sir Carsbie required no more of an auditor than an occasional comment admiring his wide knowledge of his subject. She picked out Lord Harlbury at once, dancing with Miss Beaudoin—much to the satisfaction, it appeared, of Lady Gilmour, who had sacrificed her own enjoyment of the evening so far as to sit chatting with Lady Harlbury instead of standing up with one of her own many admirers. Lady Jersey, stunningly attired in blue silk and diamonds, also took her eye. And there was Northover presently, strolling in to chat with Lord Gilmour and a gentleman attired in the brilliant regimentals of the Dragoon Guards. His gaze raked her appreciatively and, as her eyes met his, he bowed slightly and smiled. She had the feeling that he had looked in at Almack's, which she knew was considered an excessively dull place by men of his stamp, only to appraise her success, or lack of it—a thought which at once put her upon her mettle.

Fortunately, she had no lack of partners. Such a remarkably pretty girl, new upon the London scene and already with the reputation of being very much out of the common way, could not fail to attract admirers, and for a time she was content to flaunt each new conquest under Northover's eyes—until it presently occurred to her, rather uncomfortably, that the quality of these admirers left something to be desired. Middle-aged dandies like Sir Carsbie Chant, who had been on the town for so long that matchmaking mamas had all but given up hope of their being caught in Parson's mousetrap, rackety young men interested only in an *à suivie* flirtation with the latest beauty—these were hardly the stuff of which brilliant marriages were made. She caught Northover's ironical eyes upon her as she went down the set with one of these latter, while he stood idly chatting with Lady Gilmour, and an ireful sparkle, boding no good for the

Viscount when he did deign to approach her, appeared in her eyes.

She had reason to be grateful to him a few minutes later, however, when the musicians struck up a waltz. No gentleman, it appeared, rackety or not, was daring enough to invite her to stand up with him for *that* dance in *this* place, after what had occurred at Lady Gilmour's ball. She was left to sit fanning herself, like the other wallflowers, with what she hoped was an air of indifference, at the side of the room—until suddenly, hopefully, she saw Northover go up to Lady Jersey and say something to her. The next moment the two came across the room toward her.

"You are not dancing, Miss Leyland," Lady Jersey said, a sparkle of mischief in her eyes. "It is a pity to deprive us of so much talent and skill." Lydia had the grace to blush, and Lady Jersey continued, "Northover assures me that he is bold enough to stand up with you; perhaps you will favour him—?"

The Viscount's hand had already taken hers; he was drawing her to her feet, and the next instant his arm was lightly encircling her waist and he was guiding her out into the center of the floor.

"Poor Lydia!" she heard his mocking voice. "What a faint-hearted set of cavaliers you have, to be sure! Believe me, I have no wish to imperil your chances by making you the object of *my* gallantry, but it *did* appear to me that you were in need of someone to break the ice—even someone as ramshackle as myself."

"Don't crow!" she said, regaining her composure beneath this rather blighting speech and regarding him with some asperity. "I should have done very well without you, Northover. I should have contrived *something*."

"Yes, I daresay you would have done," he agreed. "But tell me—how do you go on, Lydia *mia*? It is almost a week now since I have seen you, and I am disappointed to say that no tales of your activities have reached my ears—by which I gather that, for once in your life, you have been

105

behaving with perfect propriety." She cast him a speaking glance and he laughed, continuing, "No new conquests to report? No proposals of marriage from eligible young men?"

"I have," she said with dignity, "received a—a *nibble* in that direction."

He grinned. "Only a nibble? What, is he too timid to speak out?"

"No, he is not in the least timid—only cautious. It is Mr. Michael Pentony, Sir Basil Rowthorn's great-nephew," she confided, "and I rather *think* he believes it would be a brilliant stroke of policy to marry me, as he says Sir Basil has taken a fancy to me, and—well, you can see for yourself how it would favour his chances to inherit if he were to marry into the rival camp."

Northover digested this. "He didn't, I hope," he remarked after a moment, "make you a present of all this information? He must be a skip-brain, if he did!"

"Well, he did," she said. "And he is not a skip-brain in the least; in fact, I think it is far more probable that he is one of the tightish clever sort. But I daresay he saw, after I told him that I was not in the mood for a flirtation with him, that it would be as well for him to put his cards upon the table."

"And did that take the trick for him?"

She glanced up at him, continuing to respond effortlessly to each of his movements as he whirled her expertly around the floor.

"If you mean, will I marry him—of course not!" she said. "I have never met a man I more *totally* disliked!"

"Ah, but if he is to inherit old Rowthorn's fortune—! I thought you had decided that *that* was to be the criterion; and, after all, if it is a fortune you are after, you cannot afford to be too nice in your ideas, you know!"

She gave him a withering glance. "Is it quite natural for you to be such a complete adder, or do you have to try for it?" she enquired. "Besides, I shan't need to marry him to inherit Sir Basil's fortune—I mean, for Bayard to—well, you *know* what I mean! The only thing that seems to be quite devastatingly important to Sir Basil is that we have a great success in Society—which puts me in mind of something I wanted to ask you to do. Will you put Bayard up for membership at White's?"

"At White's? No, I will not," his lordship said promptly.

"You won't!" Lydia's brows drew together in a frown. "*Well*! I had not imagined you would be such a—such a—"

"You may spare the epithets, my dear; they'll gain you nothing," Northover said, with composure. "If you are so remarkably foolish as to wish me to introduce your young cub of a brother into circles that are quite above his touch, and that will be certain to lead him into extravagances that he can ill afford, I am not such a gudgeon as to gratify you."

Lydia did not appear mollified by this explanation. "I think it is *dastardly* of you," she said darkly—"especially since I have already told Sir Basil that you would do so!"

"That was *your* error, my dear. You may plume yourself on your conquests as much as you like, but don't make the mistake of taking them *too* much for granted."

"I don't consider *you* one of my conquests. If you care to know the truth, I practically abominate you—especially when you take that utterly *superior* tone with me!"

"Do I sound superior? That's *my* mistake," he said cheerfully. "What it is meant to be, my love, is merely the tone of one conscienceless adventurer recognising another—or should I say adventuress?"

"I am *not* an adventuress!" she said hotly. "If you had a family quite dependant upon you, you would understand that it is necessary for *me*, at least, to be prudent! There is Grandmama, for instance, who has suddenly taken what *she* thinks is the nacky notion that she is about to make all our fortunes at the card-table, and Bayard, who has fallen in love with the most unsuitable girl—"

"Yes, I want to talk to you about that," Northover said, abruptly becoming more serious as the music wound to a close. "I'll call in Green Street tomorrow—What is it?" he broke off to ask, as her fingers tightened in his and he felt her figure stiffen under his hand.

"Harlbury!" she exclaimed urgently. "Over there! *Could* you contrive it that we shall be just beside him when the music ends?"

"But why—?" he began, amused.

"Never mind! Just *do* it—pray!"

He obligingly turned their circling steps in the desired direction, bringing her up with a swirl of draperies immediately before Lord Harlbury, who had just entered the room from the refreshment saloon. His lordship found himself confronted by a vision in primrose gauze, who smiled at him guilelessly and exclaimed, "Lord Harlbury! Oh, how glad I am to see you again!" A shadow suddenly overspread the radiant face; the vision hesitated and then faltered, looking quite crushed, "Oh! I beg your pardon! I should not have said that! You—you haven't even called in Green Street, as you promised; I daresay I have been *much* too forward—"

"Not at all! Not in the least!" Harlbury denied, casting a harassed glance at Northover, an appreciative auditor of the scene. "I am delighted—that is, I should have been delighted to call—only I was unavoidably—"

"Oh, I *quite* understand!" Lydia said mournfully. "I daresay you had no intention of asking me to stand up with you this evening, either—so if Lord Northover will be good enough to take me back to my grandmother—"

"No, no! Of course I should be honoured!" Harlbury stammered. "Pray allow me, Miss Leyland—"

Northover, with a wickedly quizzing glance at Lydia, made his excuses and strolled off, leaving Lydia to allow herself to be led into the set by Lord Harlbury. Having succeeded admirably in her intention to put him into such a position that he could not fail to dance with her, she was in a mood to be generous, and kindly drew his lordship out of the state of confusion in which she had placed him by leading him on to expatiate upon his favourite subject. Lord Harlbury, already inclined to be bewitched by the bewildering Miss Leyland, was at the end of a quarter hour thoroughly convinced that he had never had a more delightfully attentive auditor, and became so totally engrossed in the pleasure of the dance and of his conversation with his partner that he quite failed to observe that his mama was sitting at the side of the room with an expression as dark as a thundercloud upon her face.

It was Lydia, in fact, who drew his attention to this.

"Your mama," she said pensively, "does not like me a great deal, I fear."

"Does not like—?" His lordship's eyes, following hers, flew across the room to his mother's martially erect figure. "Oh no, you are quite out there, Miss Leyland!" he said, uncomfortably. "Her manner is sometimes not quite—quite *complaisant*, but it means nothing at all, I assure you!"

"Truly? Oh, I am so very glad to have you tell me so," Lydia said, looking up meltingly into his eyes, "for I have a great favour to ask of you, and I was *so* afraid that your mama would say that you must on no account gratify me by doing it!"

"My mother say—?" Harlbury stiffened. "I do not take your meaning, Miss Leyland! Pray, what can my mother have to say to any request that you make of me?"

They were separated at that moment by the movement of the dance, and Lydia found herself sighing almost exasperatedly as she went down the set: really, this handsome young giant was such easy game that it scarcely seemed sporting to lure him into the trap. She much preferred dealing with Northover, who could be counted on to hold his own with her and even to take the trick if it suited him to do so, or with Michael Pentony, who, no matter how greatly she disliked him, was at least an opponent well worthy of her steel.

However, when she came together with Harlbury again there was no hint of these reflections in the appealing smile she gave him, or in the rather hesitant tones of her voice as she said to him, "Yes, but—but it is a very *large* favour, my lord, and I am sure she would think it quite dreadful of me even to broach it to you! Indeed, I should never dare to do so if I were not so certain that I can *utterly* depend upon your understanding and good nature."

The expression upon his lordship's face, as she paused, appeared to indicate that he found this preamble slightly alarming, but he stood his ground and gallantly assured her that she might certainly rely upon him for both.

"Oh!" said Lydia, quite overcome. "I *knew* I could do so! There is something—some sympathy between us—that made me quite sure—You see, I have felt it from the first moment I saw you!"

Lord Harlbury, who was obviously beginning to be aware of the fact that he was getting into very deep waters indeed, replied quite untruthfully, but with an air of conscious bravado implying, *In for a penny, in for a pound*, that he had felt something of the same nature himself.

"Have you, indeed! Oh, my lord!" Miss Leyland, an excellent actress, found that she was being carried quite away by her enthusiasm for her rôle, and managed such a lifelike portrayal of a young lady cast into the most agreeable confusion that Lord Harlbury felt impelled to press her hand reassuringly. This action appeared to give her courage to continue, and she went on bashfully, "But I must not presume, my lord! Your very kindness is reason enough for me not to place you in a situation in which you would feel obliged to—"

"Not at all!" said Harlbury, encouragingly. "Whatever it is, Miss Leyland, I pledge you my word that I shall do my utmost—"

"Oh, in that case—since you are so *very* kind—" Lydia lifted adoring deep-blue eyes to his. "*Would* you put my brother Bayard up for membership at White's?" she breathed.

Harlbury gazed down at her, looking blank. Whatever he had expected, it had certainly not been this, and for a moment he was too taken aback to utter a word. When he did recover his voice, it was to stammer, "Your—brother? Oh, of course! Quite! I met him the other day—didn't I?"

Lydia glanced down, overcome once more. "Oh, I *knew* I ought not to ask it of you! Are you *very* much vexed with me? Indeed you must not do it if it will inconvenience you in the slightest—"

"No, no!" Harlbury interrupted hastily. "You must not blame yourself, Miss Leyland! I am happy to be of service to you—"

"You *are*!" Lydia gave him an ecstatic glance. "Oh, I *do* think you must be the kindest person in the world! Do you know, I asked Lord Northover and he positively *refused* me?"

Harlbury looked grave. "Well, I should not make such a request of a man like Northover if I were in your place, Miss Leyland," he said. "I have nothing to say against him—good God, I hardly know him!—but gossip, you understand—"

"*I* never listen to gossip," Miss Leyland said virtuously, "and I am surprised to learn that *you* do, my lord. Lord Northover," she went on, giving a lofty stare to that gentleman, whom she observed to be propped against the opposite wall, observing her with an appearance of the greatest enjoyment, "is a very good sort of man in his way, I believe—though not in the least obliging when it does not suit him to be."

Having unburdened herself of this remark, which she only regretted had not been able to reach the Viscount's ears, she returned to her former sweetly complaisant tone, thanked her partner effusively for his kindness, and proceeded to enjoy the remainder of the dance—much to the ire of Lady Harlbury, who was obliged to sit for another quarter hour watching her son smiling down in besotted admiration at Miss Leyland, while Miss Beaudoin danced with Bayard.

It may be said that it had not escaped Lydia's observation, either, that, while she had snared Harlbury as a partner, Bayard had succeeded in persuading Minna Beaudoin to stand up with him. Lydia was aware, in fact, that he had led no other young lady on to the floor during the course of the evening, for each time her eyes had sought him out

111

she had found him standing in the same position at the side of the room, his eyes steadily following Miss Beaudoin as she passed from one partner to another. Such behaviour, she knew, could not go unnoticed; she had indeed surprised more than one angry glance cast in his direction by Lady Gilmour, and, as she passed into the refreshment saloon on the arm of a debonair young baronet, Lady Aimer waylaid her for a moment to say to her bluntly, "I wish you will speak to your brother, Lydia. He is making a great cake of himself, standing there all the evening following my granddaughter with his eyes like one of those nonsensical heroes in that fellow Byron's poems. I have spoken to your grandmother, but she is in the card-room, so immersed in her game that I doubt she would attend if the ceiling dropped upon her!"

Lydia smiled, and promised to let fall a word in Bayard's ear if the opportunity should present itself. She spoke carelessly, but she was actually even more anxious than Lady Aimer, and quite vexed with Bayard for having allowed his emotions to betray him into making himself conspicuous. Nothing, she knew, was to be gained by his making it plain to all Miss Beaudoin's connexions that he was in desperate earnest in his attentions towards her; the next thing, she thought, would be that his Minna would be forbidden to have any dealings with him whatever.

She was pondering this thorny matter as she sat in the refreshment saloon, waiting for her young baronet to return with a glass of lemonade for her, when she became aware that someone had slipped into the seat beside her. She turned; it was Miss Beaudoin.

"Oh, Miss Leyland," that young lady said, placing her hand upon her arm and speaking in a rather tremulous voice, "please, may I speak to you for a moment? Bayard—Mr. Leyland—said you would help us if you could—and—and, indeed, I must talk to *someone* who is—who will—"

"Well, of course you may talk to me as much as you like!" Lydia said bracingly, hoping that the obviously almost overwrought girl beside her would not begin to cry under the gaze of the entire assembly. She was reassured, however, on looking into the delicately lovely little face, to see that, although the cheeks were burningly flushed, the dark eyes were quite steady and bright. She continued, "But this is hardly the place, is it? Perhaps we might arrange—"

"Oh, yes!" Minna interrupted gratefully. "That is just what I was about to beg you to do! But I dare not ask you to call upon me, or go to visit you myself, for Mama would be sure to learn of it, and then everything would be in an even worse state than it is in now!"

"Then we must meet elsewhere—by accident, as it were," Lydia said promptly. "Do you often ride or walk in the Park?"

"Oh, yes!" Minna regarded her with respectful admiration. "Bayard said you were very resourceful; that will be the very thing! Mama will not think it at all odd if I go for a walk in the Park with Berky—she is my old governess, and will not breathe a word to anyone about my meeting you if I ask her not to."

Lydia, seeing her swain bearing down on her with cakes and lemonade, quickly concluded the matter by arranging to meet Miss Beaudoin at the Stanhope Gate at eight the following morning, an hour early enough to preclude the likelihood of their meeting's being observed by any of Lady Gilmour's friends, and Minna thereupon slipped away. Lydia saw her a few minutes later being supplied with a glass of orgeat by Lord Harlbury, and toyed for a moment with the idea of removing that earnest young peer from her side by a manoeuvre that would benefit both her own and Minna's cause.

She rejected it, however. An expert angler, she was aware, must allow his fish room to play at the end of his line or risk having his catch escape him, and she quite saw that, if she desired to bring Harlbury into her net at last, she must not be too precipitate in her pursuit.

She therefore allowed the remainder of the evening to pass without doing more than remarking wistfully, during a set of quadrilles in which they both found themselves, that

113

she was still hopeful of receiving from his hands the interesting pamphlet he had described to her on the occasion of their first meeting—an observation which elicited a promise from him to call with it on the very next day, and which sent her home in a mood of modest satisfaction over the results of her evening's work.

LYDIA HAD LEARNED ENOUGH OF London ways not to go unaccompanied to her meeting with Miss Beaudoin on the following morning, and she accordingly enlisted the services of Miss Winch—services which were at first rather grudgingly granted, until that estimable female learned that the excursion was in the interests of Bayard's future happiness. Whatever stringent comments Miss Winch might feel herself called upon occasionally to make on the subject of the shortcomings of the young Leylands, she would have allowed herself to be boiled in oil in order to secure the well-being of either—a sacrifice compared with which that of a June morning walk in good weather, no matter at how unreasonably early an hour, must certainly appear quite insignificant.

She therefore contented herself with the utterance of a severe admonition to Lydia not to allow herself to be up to any of her usual harebrained schemes, since it was Master Bayard's happiness that lay in the balance, and, upon their arriving at the appointed rendezvous, took it upon herself to fall behind her young mistress with the meek elderly lady who had accompanied Miss Beaudoin, leaving the two younger ladies to carry on their conversation in privacy.

Miss Beaudoin's first words, as soon as this had been accomplished, were not calculated to inspire Lydia with the conviction that this meeting was destined to serve any very useful purpose.

"Oh, Miss Leyland, what *am* I to do?" she said, in a distraught voice. "I have been thinking and thinking, and I have not the least idea!"

"Well, I shan't have, either, unless you tell me what this is all about," Lydia said prosaically. "What exactly is it that you feel you ought to do, or want to do?"

"Why, to marry Bayard—Mr. Leyland—of course!" Minna said, her innocent dark eyes opening wide. "Has he not told you?"

"He *has* let fall a few hints in that direction," Lydia acknowledged, "but I hadn't realised there was such pressing haste—"

"Well, there is!" Minna swallowed a sob. "I am sure Lord Harlbury means to offer for me soon—indeed, from something Mama let fall to Grandmama, I believe he may do so in a very few days—and if he does, I shall be in a dreadful case! I have tried to tell Mama that I cannot care for him, but she says that it is only missish scruples on my part, and that I must realise she knows what is b-best for me."

Lydia bit back an impulse to inform her that Lady Gilmour was probably right; certainly, she told herself ruefully, no parent could be expected to believe that her daughter's happiness would be more secure if she were to marry a penniless young man like Bayard Leyland than it would be if she married Harlbury, the personification of any mother's fondest dreams. However, as she was not Miss Beaudoin's mama, but Bayard's sister, it did not suit her to take this view of the situation, and she accordingly said encouragingly to Miss Beaudoin, "Well, that need not signify, if you remain resolute. No one, not even your mama, can force you to marry Harlbury against your wishes—and, at any rate, he may not offer for you, after all."

"But what is to prevent him?" Minna cried. "That is"—she faltered and blushed—"I do not at all mean that he feels an unalterable preference for me, but Mama says *his* mama has quite decided that we shall suit, and—and I believe you cannot know Lady Harlbury well, Miss Leyland, but she is the horridest creature, always ordering poor Shafto about and forever having her own way with him—"

"Shafto!" Lydia interrupted, thunderstruck. "Good God, is *that* his Christian name?"

Miss Beaudoin looked at her wonderingly. "Yes, it is," she said. "Doesn't it please you?"

"No, it does not!" Lydia said, with revulsion. "However, I daresay he has another—perhaps several others—and I shall be able to use one of them." She added kindly, as she

116

saw the wonderment deepen on Miss Beaudoin's face, "I am considering marrying Harlbury myself, you see."

"Marrying—Lord Harlbury—you?" Miss Beaudoin said faintly. "But I don't understand! Has he asked *you*—?"

"Oh, no!" Lydia said sunnily. "I shouldn't think the idea has ever crossed his mind. But it is not at all out of the question, you know. Practically anything can be accomplished if one seriously sets one's mind to it."

Miss Beaudoin gazed at her with an expression of distinctly awed admiration upon her face. "Perhaps it is for *you*," she said. "*I* should never dare—" She broke off, lifting her chin with an air of resolution. "Only I *will* dare anything for Bayard's sake," she corrected herself. "Anything, so that we shall not be parted!"

Lydia accepted this romantic speech without visible gratification; her brow was wrinkled in thought as she began to wrestle with more practical aspects of the situation than those involving valiant self-sacrifice and eternal devotion.

"Do you suppose Lord Gilmour would be prepared to assist you in any way?" she enquired presently. "He seems a very good-humoured sort of man, and I daresay he is fond of you."

"Oh yes, he is," Minna agreed, but not very hopefully. "He is the kindest person imaginable, only—only I fear he will never do anything that Mama dislikes, and she is quite dreadfully set against my having anything at all to do with Bayard, you see. She is *determined* that I shall marry Lord Harlbury!"

"Well, if *you* are determined that you will not, there is really nothing that she can do about that," Lydia reminded her. "But as to gaining her consent to your marrying Bayard —that is another matter altogether, and I confess I do not at this present see exactly how we are to bring it about. He really has not a feather to fly with, you know!"

"He has—he has been telling me about the plantation in America," Minna faltered. "Could not we live there, perhaps?"

"Well, I daresay you *could*, and that you would not starve, for *we* never did; but I should not condemn my worst enemy to be buried there as we were these four years past," Lydia said frankly. "And Bayard is *not* the person to take the place in hand and make a success of it in its present state, though I daresay he might do well enough if there were money to put into it. But if you believe there is no hope of Lord Gilmour's doing something handsome for you—"

Minna shook her head. "Not if I wish to marry Bayard," she said unhappily. "Mama would *never* permit it, I am sure."

Lydia shrugged. "Well, then, we must contrive to do without him," she said. Seeing the downcast expression upon Minna's face, she said more encouragingly, "Never mind! We shall come about, I am sure. *I* shall manage to draw Harlbury off, at any rate—and in the meanwhile, if you are wise, you will say not a word about Bayard to your mama, and will show him in company only the same civility you would show to any other young man—"

She broke off suddenly. They had reached the promenade beside the carriage-way and had been walking slowly along it, paying little heed to the occasional early-morning rider cantering past; but now Lydia abruptly became aware that a good-looking hack had been reined in, snorting, just beside them and that a gentleman was jumping down from it.

"Northover!" she said, in considerable disapproval. "What are *you* doing here?"

"I might ask the same question of *you!*" he retorted, twitching the bridle over his horse's head and fixing a sardonic glance upon the two young pedestrians that sent the guilty colour flooding at once into Minna's cheeks.

Lydia, however, merely said superbly, "As you see, I was having a morning stroll, and was fortunate enough to meet Miss Beaudoin, who had come out for the same purpose." She added darkly, "*If* it is any of your affair—"

They were joined at that moment by Miss Winch and Miss Berker, who, seeing their charges accosted by a gentleman of dubious reputation, instantly came hurrying up to add the

118

respectability of their chaperonage to the gathering. For Miss Beaudoin, at least, their arrival came in the light of rescue; she seized thankfully upon her old governess's arm, stammered a frightened word of leave-taking to Lydia, and scurried off like a frightened mouse.

Lydia gave Northover a severe glance. "I wonder what you can have done to her," she said, "that the mere sight of you casts her into such a taking!"

"Oh, no! Don't try laying that in *my* dish!" Northover said. She turned away, shrugging her shoulders, but he stopped her by the simple expedient of reaching out his free hand and seizing her arm. "No, you are not going yet," he said coolly. "I told you last evening that I wished to talk to you, and this little episode strongly confirms me in that notion. Walk on with me a little way; this will save me a call in Green Street."

Lydia, indignantly detaching her arm from his grasp, appeared for a moment as if she would have denied this very peremptory request, but something in the look on the Viscount's face made her think better of it, and she said grudgingly, "Oh, very well! You may wait for me here, Winch; I shan't be more than a pair of minutes."

Miss Winch, folding her arms tightly across her meagre breast, stood looking the picture of disapproval, but unfortunately neither Northover nor Lydia paid her the least heed. She had her mind set to rest, however, as to the Viscount's having any improper intentions towards her young mistress by his remarking to Lydia, before the pair of them were out of hearing, "I wish you will tell me what sort of mischief you have been up to this morning with that wretched girl. Have you been addlebrained enough to encourage her in that remarkably silly attachment she believes she has formed for your brother?"

"It is *not* silly!" Lydia said. "They are truly in love, and if I can assist them, I shall—whatever *you* may think of it."

"What *I* think of it is of no importance," he said, a trifle grimly. "But what her relations think is another matter, and I can assure you that your young brother has not the least

119

chance of winning their approval of his marrying Miss Beaudoin. If you had the slightest degree of sense you would realise that, and exert any influence you have with him towards warning him away from an attachment that can lead to nothing but distress on both sides."

Lydia paused, looking at him scornfully. "Well, of course, I should expect a man of *your* stamp to take such a view!" she said. "I daresay you have never in your life been in love—I believe that emotion is considered quite unnecessary in the sort of connexions you usually form?"

Northover grinned, showing his teeth, between exasperation and amusement. "You little vixen! What do you know about 'the connexions I usually form'?"

She shrugged. "I know quite as much as I wish to; I am *not* so green as you think me, you know!" She added, goaded by the deepening amusement on his face, "And it is enough to make me feel it necessary to hope, at any rate, that you will not run off at once to your *dear* Lady Gilmour with the tale that you met Miss Beaudoin here in the Park in my company this morning—"

The expression of amusement vanished suddenly from Northover's face; he seized her arm once more, this time so roughly that she gave a gasp of mingled pain and surprise, and swung her around so that she was face to face with him. "Now you *have* gone your length, Lydia!" he said in a harsh voice. "Permit me to tell you, my girl, that your manners are those of a hoyden, and that it would afford me the greatest satisfaction to give you the thorough shaking you richly deserve!"

"Let me go!" said Lydia, in an unsteady voice. Her cheeks were burning, and her heart had begun to beat so hard that she felt he must surely hear it in the sudden silence between them.

Then a stout gentleman trotted by on a rat-tailed grey and Northover released her arm abruptly, quieting his own horse, which had curvetted restively at the approach of the other.

She said then, much annoyed to find that her voice was

still shaking oddly, "I am not going to stay here another instant for you to speak s-so *insultingly* to me! You are a *beast*, Northover, and I am quite sure now that I really do abominate you! And if you do anything to hurt Bayard, I give you fair warning that I shall *strangle* you!"

Her lack of composure seemed to restore his own to the Viscount; he laughed and said, "Well, at any rate, you are welcome to try! But you are mistaken about which one of us is likely to do harm to your brother, my dear! The course *you* are taking is more certain to land him in the basket than anything *I* should be able to contrive—even if I wished to do him an injury, which I don't." He added, in a more serious tone, "Good God, Lydia, you are not such a wet-goose that you cannot realise that you will be doing those two children no favour by encouraging them in an attachment that must come to nothing in the end! It had far better be broken off now, at this early stage, before it is too late—"

"It is too late now," Lydia said. She was still mortified and furious over her momentary loss of command over herself, and spoke curtly, without meeting the Viscount's eyes. "And it is quite false to say that it must come to nothing, for any number of things may occur that will alter the situation."

"Such as your own marriage?" Northover asked, his voice suddenly mocking her unpleasantly. "Which is it to be, Lydia? Chant or Harlbury? I hear they are laying wagers at White's that you will be able to bring Carsbie up to scratch, for he seems uncommonly taken with you, and has reached an age at which he may be thinking seriously of settling down. Yes, on consideration, I believe it would be wiser for you to concentrate on him. Harlbury may be the more attractive game, but then the chances that you will be able to land him are so very much more remote—"

"A beast, and an adder, and completely *loathsome*, besides," Lydia said, regarding him with glowering disfavour. "And if I wish to marry Harlbury, I *will* marry him—in spite of your thinking I could not bring it off!" She added dangerously, "If you say one more uncivil word to

121

me, Northover, I shall hit you—so you had best stand out of my way! I wish you a very good morning, sir!"

She swept him a magnificent curtsey and marched back to Miss Winch, who received her with the air of one snatching a cherished charge from the jaws of perdition. The Viscount, however, merely laughed, gathered his reins, and, swinging himself into the saddle, cantered off.

"Oh!" said Lydia, staring after him with narrowed eyes. "He is the most despicable, odious—! Winch, we must go home at once! Lord Harlbury intends to call this morning, and if I do not utterly *stun* him with the most becoming gown I own and the highest kick of fashion in coiffures, you may call me the greatest mooncalf of your acquaintance! Laying wagers at White's, indeed! And I daresay my Lord Northover foremost among them! Well, I will show him if I must settle for Sir Carsbie Chant! I'll show him, if I must go to perdition to do it!"

LYDIA'S DETERMINATION TO APPEAR
at her most fashionable best that
morning, coupled with the rage into
which her meeting with Northover
had flung her, resulted in her being
in such magnificent looks when Lord
Harlbury dutifully presented himself
in Green Street a little later that day
that he quite forgot the purpose for
which he had come, and it was not
until Lydia had reminded him of it that he collected himself
sufficiently to present to her the pamphlet which he bore
under his arm.

As luck would have it, both Mrs. Leyland and Bayard
were gone out, so that she received his lordship alone. This
quite suited Lydia's purpose, and, after she had exclaimed
in suitable gratitude over his kindness in coming in person
to deliver the pamphlet, and had permitted Sidwell to fetch
some refreshment for her noble guest, she came rapidly to
the point that she had determined to make with his lordship.

"There is a matter," she said to him pensively—"since
your lordship has been so kind as to honour me with
your—may I say friendship?—that I feel I *must* open with
you, difficult as it is for me to speak on such a delicate subject to a gentleman. It concerns," she went on, as she saw
Harlbury looking at her in some astonishment, not unmixed
with alarm, at this portentous preamble, "it concerns Miss
Beaudoin."

"Miss Beaudoin?"

The introduction of the name appeared to do nothing to
enlighten his lordship's mystification. He looked question-
ingly at Lydia, who—having cast herself for the moment in
the role of the devoted confidante—went on with an appearance of self-sacrificial fortitude, "Naturally, *nothing* could
induce me to betray the confidence which she has reposed
in me by speaking of this matter to anyone other than *you*,
my lord. The point is that we are dealing here with a matter

123

of such delicacy—You will not be offended if I speak *quite* openly to you?"

"No, no! Not in the least!" his lordship assured her, looking as if he wished very much that she would do just that and put him out of his suspense.

Lydia nodded. "So kind! So understanding!" she murmured, giving him such a soulfully admiring glance from under dipping lashes that his lordship understandably felt his pulses beating a good deal more rapidly than they normally did. "I must tell you," Lydia continued, "that Miss Beaudoin, in the natural distress she feels in her situation, greatly feared to approach you on the matter, greatly feared that you would not understand—"

Harlbury, who was making a desperate attempt to rally his mental forces sufficiently to comprehend what there was in Miss Beaudoin's situation to cast her into distress of any kind, made an inarticulate sound designed to indicate that he was prepared to be understanding on any suit—an action which encouraged Lydia to continue.

"You see," she said, casting down her eyes and speaking gently but firmly, as if in the performance of a painful duty, "she is under the apprehension—the mistaken apprehension, I must fervently hope—that you are—in short, that you are about to request permission to pay your addresses to her, my lord!"

Lord Harlbury, on receiving thus baldly this totally unexpected piece of information, looked for a moment as if he had suddenly swallowed a red-hot poker, and to compose himself found it necessary to rise precipitately and take a hasty turn about the room. Lydia's eyes flew up to watch him, but when he turned to her again they were once more cast modestly downward to the carpet.

"I am dreadfully afraid that I have wounded you," she said, in obvious self-reproach.

"Not at all! Not in the least!" Harlbury hastily denied. "That is to say—well, I *had* thought—that is to say, my mother thought—"

"Exactly!" Lydia said sadly, raising her eyes to his face.

124

"Your mother is, as I understand, eager for the match; Lady Gilmour is no less anxious to see it concluded—but the feelings of the two unhappy people most closely involved have—alas!—been consulted by neither. But I have told Miss Beaudoin—I have *assured* her that a man as generous as you are, my lord, once he is acquainted with the fact that the young lady concerned in the matter is unalterably opposed to it, will act in such a manner that she no longer need fear being forced into a repugnant marriage—"

She broke off, seeing from the stunned expression upon his lordship's face that he had quite enough to cope with for the moment. He sank, in fact, once more into a chair beside her with the air of a man who has suddenly found the solid ground beneath his feet rocking as precariously as the deck of a ship in a storm.

"But I d-don't understand!" he stammered, brushing his carefully arranged dark locks from his brow into a picturesque disorder that made him look even more romantically handsome than before, the effect being spoiled only by the rather piteously uncomprehending stare in his eyes. "I was given to believe—that is, she never showed the least —the least *reluctance!*"

Lydia shook her head. "Ah," she said feelingly, "you little know the restraints by which a properly brought up young female is bound! *Could* Miss Beaudoin, in the face of her mother's insistence upon her compliance, have behaved towards you publicly in a repulsive manner? You will not yourself say, I believe, that she has *encouraged* you?"

"No," Harlbury admitted. "But she—But I—Good God, this is a dreadful situation!" he exclaimed, jumping up again and striding about the room. It was a rather small room, as the drawing-rooms in the Green Street house did not run to noble dimensions, and Lydia was in some apprehension lest some of the expensively hired bric-a-brac it contained fall victim to the emotions of the very large young man so impetuously traversing it. Much to her relief, he came to a halt presently before her. "I was to have offered for her this very evening!" he said, in an agitated voice. "Everything had been arranged—and now—this! My dear ma'am, what in heaven's name am I to do?"

"Well, in the first place, I should not worry about it, if I was you," Lydia said kindly. "Sit down here"—she patted the sofa beside her—"and we shall put our heads together and think what course you had best follow. I daresay we shall be able to hit upon the very thing—but *do* stop looking so *stricken!*" she added, lapsing into severity as Harlbury sat down obediently beside her. "You *won't* try to tell me that you are in love with the girl?"

"In love? No! But I—" Harlbury appeared to recollect himself suddenly, and said somewhat stiffly, "Naturally, I was prepared to entertain that regard for Miss Beaudoin that is proper to the married state! She is a very amiable young lady, and there is nothing in either her person or her manners to disgust—"

Lydia said irrepressibly, "Oh, if *that* is all you require in a wife, I am sure we shall be able to suit you admirably, half a dozen times over, before the Season is out!" But then, recalling the part she was playing, she once more assumed her pensive air, and said softly, "I am so happy to learn that your feelings are not engaged! Indeed, you do not know what a relief it is to me, for I would not for the world be the unfortunate instrument of causing you pain!"

Lord Harlbury, finding himself confronted, at this staggering crisis in his affairs, by a pair of blue eyes as meltingly sympathetic as any it had ever been his fortune to encounter, discovered with some surprise that his situation was not nearly so black as it had appeared a few moments before, and went so far as to give Lydia a slight, reassuring smile.

"*You* give me pain, Miss Leyland!" he said. "No—I can only honour you for your frankness in laying the matter before me—at a considerable cost, I am persuaded, to your own delicacy of feeling." His brow wrinkled once more. "But I must confess that I am at a loss as to what course I had best pursue now. If Miss Beaudoin's aversion to the match is indeed insuperable—"

Lydia sighed. "Alas, I fear it is!" she said. "Her affections—I should not betray this to you if it were not absolutely necessary, you understand!—her affections are engaged Elsewhere."

"Ah! Indeed!" Harlbury digested this news gloomily.

"It is an attachment," Lydia went on, "which—though the young man is of unexceptionable birth and character—does not, for reasons of fortune, meet with Lady Gilmour's approval. She is quite unwilling to accept it as a reason for breaking off her daughter's projected match with you, my lord—which is why the initiative in doing so *must* come from you."

"Yes, but—dash it, Miss Leyland!" his lordship said, running a harassed hand once more through his dark locks, "I can't just walk smash up to my mother—that is, to Lady Gilmour—and say that I've changed my mind!"

"Certainly not!" Lydia agreed cordially. "They would think that very odd indeed, and I don't doubt that your mother—that is, Lady Gilmour—would be quite unimpressed by such a reason. But if you were to tell them that *you* had formed another attachment—an unalterable one—and had already committed yourself so far as to disclose it to the young lady in question—"

Harlbury stared at her. "Yes, but I *haven't* formed another attachment!" he protested.

Lydia returned his gaze with some impatience. "I know that! It needn't be a *real* attachment," she said. "Merely, if you could persuade some other young lady to allow you to *pretend* an attachment between you until the matter of your marrying Miss Beaudoin has gone off—"

Harlbury shook his head, looking serious. "Oh no, I couldn't do that, Miss Leyland!" he said. "It wouldn't be fair to the young lady."

"Fiddle! If she were your friend, she would think nothing of obliging you in such a matter. I am very sure that *I* should not!"

"You wouldn't?" Harlbury looked at her doubtfully, but with an expression of dawning hope on his face. "You mean *you* wouldn't mind if I were to tell my mother—that is, Lady Gilmour—that an attachment had grown up between us, and that I felt myself bound—because of certain declarations I had made to you—"

"Exactly! Now you are going on beautifully!" Lydia said approvingly. "What could she—they—say, under such circumstances? You have not yet committed yourself as far as Miss Beaudoin is concerned, but in *this* matter, having gone so far, they could not expect you, in honour, to draw back." She went on, warming to her subject, "And then, of course, when the whole matter of your offering for Miss Beaudoin has been laid to rest, you may discover that you have mistaken your feelings, after all, and *I* shall pretend to discover the same, and so you will have escaped from your predicament without the slightest inconvenience to anyone—for we shall have broken off, of course, before any formal announcement is made. Now is not that an excellent scheme?"

Lord Harlbury, who was looking a trifle dazed, said that he supposed it might be, but he added almost immediately, with an air of revulsion, "But it will not do, Miss Leyland! Eternally grateful as I must be to you for so nobly offering to come to my assistance, it will not do! *Your* reputation, *your* peace of mind—"

Lydia curbed an exasperated shrug, and managed a meekly noble expression once more.

"Indeed, my lord, you refine too much upon the matter," she said. "What can such a small sacrifice upon my part signify, if it is to be the means of sparing you and Miss Beaudoin a lifetime of regret? I assure you, I should think the less of you if you declined to make use of my assistance in such a case. Oh, I am well aware that your principles are too high to allow of your accepting it for merely selfish reasons—but there is Miss Beaudoin to be considered. Can you, my lord—because you are too proud to accept my help —condemn *her* to misery?"

"No—no—indeed not!" his lordship said disjointedly. "But have I the right—?"

"The right *and* the duty," Lydia said firmly, and then,

losing patience at last, went on in a far more normal voice, "Good heavens, Harlbury, don't put yourself into such a taking! A pretty hobble you will be in if you don't do it, for you know as well as I do that your mama will never be put off without your giving her some totally *momentous* reason for your crying off at this point in the proceedings!"

His lordship was obliged to agree to this view of the situation, and after a quarter hour more of conversation finally took himself off, his resolution apparently screwed to the point of bearding his mother forthwith and informing her of the alteration in his matrimonial plans. Lydia saw him go and then sat down with a sigh of exhaustion to formulate her own plans for the future—plans which must involve, as she was well aware, the inescapable necessity of a confrontation with Lady Harlbury, who would certainly lose no time in calling upon the young lady who had the effrontery of designing to become her daughter-in-law without her approval and even without her knowledge.

13

LYDIA THOUGHT IT PRUDENT TO acquaint Bayard, when he came in presently, with the turn affairs had taken that day in regard to Harlbury's courtship of Miss Beaudoin; but if she had expected him to be grateful to her for her interference, she soon discovered her mistake.

"*You* marry Harlbury!" he exclaimed, drawing his brows together in a startled frown. "Good God, I thought you were merely jesting when you spoke of that the other day! What can you have been thinking of, to have put the notion into his head? Of all the hey-go-mad tricks—!"

"Handsomely over the bricks, my dear," Lydia said composedly. "There is no need for you to fly into a pelter *yet*, you know! Harlbury has not asked me to marry him, nor have I said that I would. All we have agreed upon is to *pretend* to an understanding, so that he may have a reason to give his mama for not offering for Miss Beaudoin."

"Yes, but I know you, Lyddy!" Bayard said, his face the picture of misgiving. "That may be *his* notion of what he has let himself in for, but if *you* have made up your mind that he is to marry you, he will have no more to say about it than a lamb on its way to the butcher."

A slight flush appeared on Lydia's face. "Now you are talking like Northover," she said. "To hear the pair of you, I am an odious, scheming wretch—"

"Gammon!" Bayard cut her off, throwing an arm about her shoulders and giving her a brotherly hug. "What you are is a heedless madcap, who will fight like a tigress for anyone she takes under her protection. But it isn't your place to protect *me*, love. I shall have to make my own way—though God knows I don't see at present how I am to do it! But I still can't have you entering into an engagement with Harlbury on *my* account!"

"Perhaps it is not all upon *your* account," Lydia said, putting up her chin. "Perhaps I have a fancy to be a countess. And, at any rate, there is nothing that either you or I can do about it now, for Harlbury is already gone to tell his mother. If he has not grown hen-hearted at the awful prospect before him and hedged off," she concluded, with a gurgle of laughter. "He is in the liveliest dread of her, you know—which is absurd, for there is nothing she can do to him if he will only make up his mind to face her down."

She cut the conversation short to run upstairs and communicate the news of her "engagement" to her grandmother, who had also returned to the house after what Lydia assumed to be a round of calls. To her surprise, however, she found Mrs. Leyland stalking about her dressing-room with the air of an offended Juno. At sight of Lydia she said, "Ha!" in a highly dramatic voice, and invited her to guess where she had been.

"I haven't the least notion," Lydia confessed, seating herself in a bergère armchair. "But, wherever it was, something has obviously sent you flying up into the boughs. What on earth has happened?"

"Oh, that wretched little man has nettled me into such a flame that I can scarcely endure to speak of it!" Mrs. Leyland said. "Merely because I told him I had lost a trifling sum at cards and must have the money to pay it!"

Lydia's face altered. "Oh, dear!" she sighed. "I gather you mean Mr. Peeke? But, Grandmama, how could you bear to apply to him when he has been so very generous in advancing you such sums already? Could you not have contrived, if it is indeed a trifling amount—?" She halted, observing the guiltily austere expression with which Mrs. Leyland appeared to be discouraging any further enquiry into the subject. "Grandmama!" she said forebodingly. "How much *did* you lose?"

Mrs. Leyland tossed her head. "Well, well, that is none of your affair, my dear child!" she said airily. "It is merely a temporary embarrassment, for I shall soon be able to recoup my losses."

"How *much*?" Lydia insisted.

Mrs. Leyland gave a pettish shrug. "Well, if you *must* know—two thousand pounds," she said. "But there is no need for you to look so dismayed, for I am quite sure that the next time I sit down to play—"

"Two—thousand—pounds!" Lydia found her voice at last and repeated the figure in appalled tones. "Good God, Grandmama, where could you have lost such a sum? Are Great-aunt Letty's jewels worth so much?"

"I am sure I have not the least idea," Mrs. Leyland said superbly. "At any rate, it does not signify, for, as my dear brother Gerald was used to say, one's luck must always turn if one has but the resolution to continue playing."

"Your dear brother Gerald," Lydia reminded her, a trifle tartly, "lost Great Hayland, I have always understood, by following his own advice in that respect. Oh dear, Grandmama, how *could* you have been so very imprudent? And you have not told me yet where you have lost such a sum. Certainly not at Almack's, for I have heard that the play there is very tame."

"And so it is," Mrs. Leyland said feelingly, "for I was sat down to whist the whole time you and Bayard were enjoying yourselves in the ball-room last evening, and rose from the table not twenty pounds the better for it in the end."

"Then where—?"

"Oh, at Mrs. Collingworth's house," Mrs. Leyland said. "But it was only through the most vexatious run of ill luck that I lost so much—the sort of thing that will not occur twice in a dozen years. I am certain that when I play there again this evening, the cards will fall in quite another fashion for me."

Lydia stared at her. "When you play there again—!" she repeated. "Grandmama, no! Surely you will not be so gooseish as to go there a second time! Besides, how can you?—for you know you have no money."

"My dear child," Mrs. Leyland said impatiently, "what can that signify? Naturally they will accept my vouchers. They must be quite aware, you know, that I shall settle them just as soon as ever my luck turns."

"But if it does *not* turn? Grandmama *dear*, surely you must be able to see what a dreadful situation we shall be in if you cannot pay! We shall be done up—forced to retire from Society—even from England—"

"Nonsense! Now you are running on like that tiresome Peeke, who read me such a scold that I was finally obliged to leave his office without obtaining the least thing I had gone there for! Of course I shall come about; it only needs a little time." She added, casting a somewhat indignant glance at Lydia's stunned face, "I do not at all see why you should get up on your high ropes over the matter. It is entirely for your sake, and Bayard's, that I play at all. Heaven knows I am not desirous of winning a fortune upon my own account!"

Lydia shook her head, a smile irresistibly curving her lips, in spite of herself, at the picture her grandmother had drawn of herself labouring virtuously and unselfishly at the card-table for the sake of her two young relations.

"Yes, but, Grandmama, I assure you that we shall get on a great deal better if you do not go to such lengths to help us," she said perseveringly. "Heavens, are things not in enough of a coil already without our adding debt to the matter! I expect I should tell you, by the bye, that Harlbury has been here today, and has now gone off to inform his mama that, as he has conceived a *tendre* for me and has made certain declarations to me, he is unable to offer for Miss Beaudoin—"

She was interrupted by her grandmother, who exclaimed, in ecstatic astonishment, "Harlbury! Lydia, you have never succeeded in bringing him to the point so quickly! Oh, my dearest girl, why did you not tell me so at once, without talking all this miff-maff about a paltry two thousand pounds?"

"No, no!" Lydia said, laughing. "Pray do not be jumping to conclusions, ma'am! At the present moment Harlbury's interest in me is merely a pretext I have offered him, to

134

allow him to draw back from paying his addresses to Miss Beaudoin. It is to remain the greatest secret; indeed, I should not have mentioned it even to you if I were not persuaded that we must soon receive a visit from Lady Harlbury—in which case it might be awkward if you knew nothing of the matter. But there is *nothing* concluded; you must understand that! Indeed, I have promised Harlbury that he will be perfectly free of any obligation to me as soon as he feels it safe to tell his mama that he does not wish to marry me, after all." She explained patiently, as she saw the stupefaction with which her grandmother was regarding her, "I only made up the scheme in order to help Bayard, love. If I had not stepped into the picture and persuaded Harlbury that he must not offer for a girl who is desperately in love with someone else—and then given him an excuse to present to his mama for not doing so—it would never have entered his mind to tell Lady Harlbury that he was enamoured of me."

"Lydia!" Mrs. Leyland interrupted at this point, apparently unable to contain her feelings any longer. "You *cannot* mean to tell me that, when you have succeeded in bringing him this far, you are going to let him go! That would be *too* much to bear! Even you, I am persuaded, could not be so—so *wasteful* as to do a thing like that! Why, he has forty thousand pounds a year!"

Lydia laughed. "I don't care if he has a hundred thousand," she said. "I have no fancy to trick him into marrying me." She added mischievously, "Oh, I do not say that if, on closer acquaintance, he finds me irresistible, I might not—perhaps!—be brought to find him so as well—"

Mrs. Leyland moaned. "Good heavens, you unnatural girl, what has that to say to anything! Forty thousand a year, and an earldom—and you talk of whistling him down the wind! Why, if you were to marry him, it would be the end of all our difficulties forever! What would a mere two thousand pounds signify in such a case!"

135

The mention of the debt her grandmother had incurred brought Lydia's thoughts back with a disagreeable start to that pressing matter.

"Well, it signifies a great deal now," she said, frowning over a new idea that had suddenly occurred to her. "Grandmama," she asked abruptly, "what sort of house is this Mrs. Collingworth's, that play so deep goes on there? Mr. Pentony said she was a friend of his mother's, but surely Lady Pentony is by no means able to move in circles where such sums can change hands in a single evening."

"Oh, what does *that* matter?" Mrs. Leyland said impatiently, her mind still upon higher things. "I daresay one need not move in quite the same circles as *all* one's friends do. Mrs. Collingworth's house is excessively elegant, I can assure you, and one meets persons of the highest *ton* there."

"Yes, I was afraid of that," Lydia said, with misgiving. "And they have all come with one purpose—have they not? Play!" Mrs. Leyland made a gesture of outraged denial, but Lydia, her eyes narrowing slightly, continued slowly, "And it was Michael Pentony who introduced you to that woman! A polite gaming-house—oh yes, I can see it all now! *That* would take the trick very nicely for him—to see us rolled-up, obliged to leave town—"

"What *are* you talking of, my love?" Mrs. Leyland exclaimed, in the highest dudgeon. "A gaming-house! It is nothing of the sort! Merely a private party where the play ran a trifle deep."

"And you plan to return there tonight? Grandmama, you must not!" Lydia said earnestly. "Believe me, it will not do! Heaven knows how we are to pay the two thousand pounds you have already lost, but if any more is added to it, we shall certainly all go home by way of beggar's bush!"

Nothing she could say, however, had the least effect in altering her grandmother's resolution to endeavour to recoup her losses that evening. Mrs. Leyland would only say bitterly that if Lydia was so unpardonably foolish as not to make a push to bring Harlbury to a public announcement of their betrothal, she herself was not bird-witted enough to cast aside the only means by which they might hope to escape from the predicament in which they found themselves.

Lydia was at last reduced to going downstairs again to seek Bayard's aid in persuading her recalcitrant grandparent; but here too she met with a check, for she was informed by Sidwell that he had already gone out, having an engagement, it appeared, to dine with friends at the Daffy Club.

She was therefore left to her own resources, which turned out to be quite inadequate, for Mrs. Leyland was as convinced of the rightness of her own reasoning as was Lydia of hers, and was even more obstinate in adhering to the course she had chosen to pursue. The matter ended in their dining together very uncomfortably and then parting on somewhat inimical terms, Mrs. Leyland to go on to Mrs. Collingworth's house in Curzon Street and Lydia to sit down alone in the front drawing-room to consider what steps she might take next.

The idea of enlisting Mr. Peeke's aid was the first that came to mind, but it was soon discarded; her grandmother's description of the scene that had already taken place between them gave her little grounds for hoping that any arguments he might make would prevail with her. Lady Aimer? She and Mrs. Leyland—both outspoken and highly opinionated—had all but come to cuffs several times already over much lesser matters, and it was doubtful that interference on her part now would lead to anything more helpful than another quarrel.

All Lydia could hope for—and, suspecting that Michael Pentony was behind the scenes in the matter, she could place little reliance upon her hope's being realised—was that her grandmother might really fall into the luck she was so convinced must come her way, and thus manage to extricate herself from her difficulties. Having come to this conclusion, she then allowed her thoughts to revert to her own affairs, which appeared to her to be also in pressing need of examination, for it was certainly to be expected that she might even that evening receive a call from Lady Harlbury, apprised by this time of her son's change in intentions and hot to do battle with the interfering Miss Leyland.

As it developed, however, Lady Harlbury did not appear in Green Street that evening. Neither did she call there on the following morning, and it was gradually borne in upon Lydia that that lady, far from choosing to cross swords with her, had no intention of dignifying the information her son had presented to her by according Miss Leyland any notice whatever.

To say that Lydia accepted this turn of events with meek complaisance would be to do her a singular injustice. She found her temper rising steadily as the hours progressed, and was almost on the point of taking the bull by the horns and setting out herself to pay a call upon Lady Harlbury when the horrid thought crossed her mind that perhaps that formidable lady knew nothing of the interesting situation in which she and Lydia stood vis-à-vis Lord Harlbury, for the simple reason that Lord Harlbury had not informed her of it.

This was a new and dismaying thought. If his lordship's courage had failed him at the last moment and he had been craven enough, after all, to carry out his intention of offering for Miss Beaudoin, Bayard's hopes must be forever dashed, unless Minna herself had had sufficient resolution to give Harlbury a refusal. Lydia was on tenterhooks to know what had happened, and only the remembrance that she and Bayard and her grandmother were engaged to accompany Lady Aimer to the theatre on the following Monday evening, and that they must surely learn from her if her granddaughter had become betrothed to Harlbury, prevented her from embarking upon some scheme of her own to find out what had occurred in the matter.

Meanwhile, she had other cares, for she found her grandmother, on the morning following her second visit to Curzon Street, in a much subdued humour, scarcely suggesting that she had met with the good fortune there that she had confidently expected. She refused, however, to satisfy Lydia's curiosity on the subject, and only as she came downstairs on the evening they were to accompany Lady Aimer to the theatre, attired in stately purple and ostrich plumes, did she finally confide to her in tragic accents that there seemed nothing for it now but for her to have recourse to Mr. King.

"To *whom?*" Lydia enquired, startled.

"To Mr. King, my dear. I am told that he has an establishment in Clarges Street where one may borrow money—"

"A moneylender? Grandmama, you couldn't—you mustn't!" Lydia felt her heart sink down into the pretty white kid slippers that completed her own diaphanous toilette of sea-green sarsnet. "You *know* how poor Papa was ruined by them! Surely there must be some other way!"

They had no opportunity to discuss the matter, however, for they were interrupted at this point by the arrival of Lady Aimer, who had come to call for them in her barouche. One glance at that redoubtable dame's keen-eyed survey of her as she went to meet her was sufficient to convince Lydia that she had been wronging Harlbury by her doubts, and she was made doubly certain of the matter when Lady Aimer said to her bluntly, "Well, miss, fine doings you have been up to, it seems! So Minna is not to have Harlbury, after all! But I should not be too certain of bringing him up to scratch, my girl, even if you have succeeded in marring that match. Louisa Harlbury is as mad as fire over the affair, and if that boy has the rumgumption to stand out against her, it's more than *I* know of him. Hasn't made you an offer yet—has he?"

"Dear ma'am," Lydia said with a demure look, her spirits rising as she realised the success her strategy had obtained, "it is certainly not to *me* that you should apply for such an announcement. I am sure that Lord Harlbury will say everything that is proper."

Lady Aimer gave her sudden bark of laughter. She was more than ordinarily magnificent that evening in a gown of pomona-green satin, with a turban of green silk shot with orange crowning her square, pugnacious face.

140

"Well," she said philosophically, "you don't lack for wit, at any hand, and if my granddaughter is not to land Harlbury, I had as lief you got him as anyone else, if only to see Louisa made to look nohow for once in her life. But you had best be prepared for battle, my dear. She will be at Drury Lane herself tonight, and, unless I very much miss my guess, you will find yourself in for a thundering set-down from her."

"I daresay I shall," said Lydia, looking not in the least alarmed by the prospect; and, seeing that Bayard had now come downstairs to join them, she drew a delicate Indian shawl about her shoulders and prepared to follow Lady Aimer out to the barouche.

The theatre was full that evening, Mr. Kean being the attraction. Lydia, when the party had settled themselves in their box, allowed her eyes to range casually over the boxes opposite, and was rewarded presently by the sight of Lady Harlbury entering one of them, followed by her son and a group of several other persons. As Lady Aimer's box was almost directly opposite, the members of the two parties could not fail to observe one another, and bows were exchanged—Lady Harlbury's perforce including Miss Leyland. Lydia observed that Harlbury himself, though he appeared embarrassed by the encounter, greeted them with the greatest civility. A few moments later she perceived him in earnest conversation with his mother, and that she herself was the subject of it she could not doubt, from the glances cast in her direction by both.

The rising of the curtain, however, put an end to any further interchange. It cannot be said that Lydia, in spite of the fact that this was her first opportunity of seeing Kean, of whose histrionic powers she had heard so much, attended very carefully to what was going forward on the stage. She was fully occupied in trying to formulate some plan of action for the evening, but could hit upon none that satisfied her. Everything, it seemed, must depend upon Harlbury. She could not very well throw herself at his head in public, and, unless he chose to acknowledge the situation between them, she must accept with what grace she could Lady Harlbury's triumph in publicly displaying the fact that she still had her son in a string.

The curtain came down.

"Well? What d'you think of him?" Lady Aimer's voice demanded beside her.

"Him? Oh—you mean Mr. Kean!" Lydia said. She was observing the opposite box, where Harlbury, after a brief colloquy with his mother, had risen and made his way out. "He is very fine."

"Ay, that is what they all say, but for my part, I had as lief he did not go into such high flights, my dear. It is enough to frighten children, the way he goes on. Lord! you never saw such a to-do as there was in the theatre when he first took the part of Sir Giles Overreach. There were several ladies had to be removed in strong hysterics, and they say Lord Byron had a convulsive fit."

Lydia, quite unable to keep her mind on the overpowering impression Mr. Kean had made in his celebrated revival of Massinger's *A New Way to Pay Old Debts*, gave an absent reply, but then, suddenly recollecting herself, put on for Lady Harlbury's benefit a performance of a young lady enjoying herself to the utmost that rivalled anything the great actor had attempted upon the stage.

She was interrupted by a knock upon the door of the box; the next moment Harlbury himself stood before her. He looked rather red and, after exchanging greetings with the other members of the party, said to her with somewhat uneasy abruptness, "I wonder if you will do my mother the favour of waiting upon her in her box, Miss Leyland. It would be very good of you."

"Yes, of course," said Lydia, rising and accepting sedately the tribute of the surprised and meaningful glances exchanged by her grandmother and Lady Aimer. "I shall be delighted." And she sailed off on Lord Harlbury's arm.

In the corridor her manner changed. "Well?" she said to him conspiratorially. "How did it go? You have told her, of course?—about us, I mean."

Harlbury nodded nervously. "Yes. Oh, yes—I did!" he said, looking pale at the very remembrance of the scene.

Lydia gave his arm an encouraging pat. "Well, it was not so *very* dreadful—was it?" she said. "After all, she could not eat you—and, really, it is quite absurd, you know, that she should have anything to say about whether you choose to offer for a girl or not. It is certainly not *her* affair!"

Lord Harlbury looked as if he were far from being convinced of this, but he had no opportunity to put the thought into words, for Lydia went on at once to enquire whether it had been his notion or his mother's to ask her to visit their box.

He immediately looked, if possible, even graver than before. "Hers," he said. "And I cannot imagine why—for I fear I cannot believe, my dear Miss Leyland, that she wishes to distinguish you publicly by her attention. In point of fact," he said scrupulously, "she has already told me that if I were to marry you she would not receive you."

"Well, as you are not going to marry me, that does not signify—does it?" Lydia said lightly.

He returned no reply. They were by this time approaching the door of the box, and as they entered Lydia composed her features into a smile holding the balance nicely between ease and deference, which she was quite aware would infuriate Lady Harlbury by showing her refusal to be intimidated by the ordeal of meeting her under such circumstances. In tight situations it was Miss Leyland's maxim to attack; nothing, she felt, could be gained by allowing the enemy to take the initiative.

She saw by the tightening of Lady Harlbury's lips as she beheld her presenting herself thus charmingly beside her son that she had succeeded in her purpose. It had been Lady Harlbury's intention, when she had first observed Miss Leyland across the theatre, to ignore her presence there; but this decision had soon given way to a resolution to take advantage of the opportunity afforded by their meeting to put Miss Leyland firmly in her place. She would not deign to call in Green Street, thus acknowledging that she considered her son's infatuation with Miss Leyland a serious threat to her peace. But, since the minx was delivered by fate into her hands this evening, she felt that she might properly make use of the occasion to let her see how little good it would do her to think she might be able to form an alliance with a family so very much above her touch.

The battle lines were thus clearly drawn—a fact of which both ladies were well aware as Lord Harlbury, caught in the unhappy position of being in both lines of fire, placed a chair for Lydia. Fortunately for the combatants, Lady Harlbury had had the forethought to clear the box of its other occupants before her opponent's arrival, and the field was therefore ready for open warfare. This was at once begun by Lady Harlbury, who made a polite enquiry as to when Miss Leyland was returning to America.

"Returning to America?" Lydia opened her eyes with an assumption of naïve surprise. "My dear ma'am, I cannot conceive what you mean! How could I think of being parted by so many thousands of miles from Shafto—*now*!"

She gave Harlbury, who had taken up an uneasy station behind her chair, the flutter of an upward glance, and had the satisfaction of seeing Lady Harlbury's lips thin grimly.

"Indeed!" said Lady Harlbury. "Am I to gather, Miss Leyland, that you consider the remarkably unsuitable influence which you seem suddenly to have acquired over my son to be of a permanent nature? Let me assure you that nothing can be farther from the truth! A gentleman in Harlbury's position may indeed indulge in attachments for persons below his own station in life, but I am persuaded that *my* son has received an education of such a nature that the thought of perpetuating such an attachment in marriage is as abhorrent to him as it is to me."

"Mama—please!" said Lord Harlbury, in an agony of embarrassment. "You do Miss Leyland the greatest injustice!"

Lydia put her hand on his sleeve in a gesture which she was quite aware must cause Lady Harlbury to wish to strangle her out of hand.

"Do not distress yourself, my lord," she said gently, but with her eyes now expressing genuine indignation. "It is not to me that Lady Harlbury does the greatest injustice; it is to you. Permit me to say, ma'am, that your reading of your son's intentions toward me does far more discredit to yourself than any he might bring upon his family by seeking to connect himself with me in marriage. I am persuaded that—"

She was interrupted by the sound of a knock falling upon the door of the box; the next moment it opened, and Lydia was astounded to see Mr. Michael Pentony walk in. She had not been aware that he was in the theatre that evening, and what he was thinking of, to enter the Harlbury box so unceremoniously, she could not imagine, for she did not believe him even to be acquainted with either Lord Harlbury or his mother.

It soon developed that she was correct in this assumption.

"Hullo, coz!" he greeted her, speaking in a broad, rather common tone which she had never heard him use before and at the same time bestowing an offhand nod upon Harlbury. "Saw you from the pit—hobnobbing with all the smarts tonight, ain't you?—and thought I'd come round and do the polite. Well?" He gazed at her expectantly. "Ain't you going to introduce me?"

Lydia, forced into a corner, said from between gritted teeth, "Lady Harlbury—Lord Harlbury—Mr. Pentony." She saw immediately what game Mr. Pentony was up to; he had, no doubt, with his usual enterprise, managed to get hold of the rumours concerning herself and Harlbury that would certainly be flying about London, and, having seen her in the Harlbury box, had taken instant advantage of his opportunity to throw a rub in the way of the match.

He was nodding to Lady Harlbury now with a cheerful air quite at variance with his usual careful manner as he remarked to her familiarly, "Fine gal, my cousin Lydia—don't you agree, ma'am? Not quite up to snuff yet, but give her a little more town-bronze and she'll beat 'em all to sticks, is what *I* say!"

145

"Thank you!" said Lydia, interrupting him scathingly. "I fear you do me too much honour, however, sir, in bestowing the title of 'cousin' upon me."

She cast a swift glance at Lady Harlbury, hoping that her obvious disgust at Mr. Pentony's ill-bred interruption would lead her to take the initiative which belonged to her of obliging him to retire from the box; but she saw at once that that hope was vain. No matter how angry Lady Harlbury might be at the intruder's rudeness, she had immediately realised the advantages it offered her in presenting Miss Leyland to her son in an unfavourable light, and was therefore determined to do nothing to relieve the situation.

Naturally Mr. Pentony was not behindhand in summing up this attitude of her ladyship's, and he accordingly went on in the same manner in which he had begun, now addressing himself to Harlbury.

"If you are Harlbury, I daresay you've been thinking of having a touch at her yourself," he remarked confidentially; "at least, that's what the tattle-boxes are saying. But let me warn you that you've taken the wrong sow by the ear if you think there's a fortune to pick up along with her when old Rowthorn has his notice to quit. *I'm* to be the lucky man there, it seems—I'm his great-nevvy, you understand. Not that it signifies, when a gal is as pretty as Lyddy is. A regular dazzler, *I* call her—"

Lydia rose with decision. There was no hope of stopping his mouth, short of removing him from the box, and she could see that—quite beyond the effect his words might have on Lord Harlbury and his mother—they were already attracting curious attention from the neighbouring boxes. Restraining the impulse to give Mr. Pentony a dagger-glance, she said to him with noncommittal civility, "It is time for me to return to my friends, I fear. If you will excuse me, Lady Harlbury—No, there is no need for you to disturb yourself, my lord; Mr. Pentony will escort me."

She laid her hand upon the latter gentleman's arm, and he gave a broad wink to Lord Harlbury and an exaggerated bow to the rigid Lady Harlbury.

146

"Your servant, sir—ma'am. Well, you see how it is: she can't wait to have me to herself! Always a bit on the impatient side, our Lyddy—"

He had no opportunity to conclude this speech, for Lydia, nipping his arm compellingly, obliged him to retire from the box.

Outside in the corridor she faced him with indignant contempt.

"You really are a despicable person, Mr. Pentony!" she said. "Is there nothing to which you will not stoop to gain your ends?"

"No, I shouldn't think there was," he replied dispassionately, and in his ordinary manner. "I warned you, Miss Leyland, that I was in earnest over this matter. Do you remember? You should have guessed that it would not suit me to read in the *Gazette* of your engagement to Lord Harlbury."

She began to walk on, too angry to remain any longer under his shrewd, considering gaze. He followed her, and after a moment, to her astonishment and distaste, murmured in her ear, "You are magnificent when you are angry! Do not credit me with playing that little scene entirely for monetary reasons, Miss Leyland. Perhaps it does not suit me *personally*, either, to see you married to Harlbury."

She rounded on him scornfully. "Pray spare me your gallantries, Mr. Pentony!" she said. "You have already made it abundantly clear to me—do *you* remember?—what your interest in me is inspired by."

"At one time," he said swiftly. "Believe me, I find my feelings altering more greatly each time I see you! You are—an exceedingly attractive young woman, Miss Leyland!"

She shrugged. "I might be more inclined to believe you," she said, "if you were not doing your best to ruin my family, Mr. Pentony. Oh, yes!" she went on, as she saw him about to utter some remonstrance. "You will not deny, I believe, that it was you who introduced my grandmother to Mrs. Collingworth. Nor need you try to tell me that it was quite by accident that she turned up at Richmond Park on the same

147

day that you were engaged to drive Grandmama there."

She threw him a challenging glance as she concluded, and received in return a slight, composed smile.

"Why, what do you mean?" he enquired smoothly. "What harm can your grandmother have taken from a lady who, to the best of my knowledge, is of the first respectability?"

"Ladies *of the first respectability* do not, I believe, ordinarily keep discreet gaming-houses where unsuspecting people are fleeced of large sums of money!" Lydia retorted. "Don't, I beg you, play the innocent with me! If you are prepared to risk your hopes of attaining a respectable position in Society to gain your purpose—as you plainly showed by your performance in Lady Harlbury's box just now—it can surely be nothing to you merely to play the go-between in a matter of that sort. You ran no risk there!"

They had reached the door of Lady Aimer's box by this time; she was about to enter, without a word of adieu to him, when he put his hand on her arm to forestall her. She cast a glance at the attendant, who stood waiting to open the door for her, and, composing her angry countenance with an effort, said in a low tone, "I have nothing further to say to you, sir."

"But I have something to say to you." He drew her a little away, out of hearing of the attendant. His narrow face, she saw, had a slight, intent smile upon it as he said to her softly, "Come, come, Miss Leyland—would you be making such a bad bargain, after all, if you came to terms with me? Harlbury may be infatuated with you, but it is common knowledge that he will never venture to marry where his mother disapproves. And as for other chances that you may believe will offer—try them and see how many men you find who are willing to take a penniless young woman to wife." She made an indignant movement, as if to turn away from him, but he checked her once more. "One moment!" he said. "You must realise that you have very little time in which to indulge in indecision on this point, Miss Leyland. Of course, if you were to place me in the position of being able to go to Sir Basil and inform him that you have agreed

148

to become my wife, I should be happy to settle the debts that your grandmother appears so imprudently to have incurred. On the other hand, if you do *not* give me the right to make that announcement to Sir Basil, I fear I shall regretfully be obliged to inform him of the insecure foundation on which Mrs. Leyland's hopes of establishing herself and her family in Society presently rest—"

"Yes!" said Lydia, who had listened to quite enough to send her temper soaring once more. "I can well imagine that you will lose no time in running to Sir Basil to tell your tale, Mr. Pentony! But do not underestimate *me*, I beg you! I have not shot my bolt as yet—as certain as you are that you have brought me under your thumb!"

She thereupon moved forward determinedly to the door of the box, which she entered so impetuously that her grandmother looked at her in astonished disapproval. Lady Aimer, noting her flushed, indignant countenance, said shrewdly, "No need to ask you how you and Louisa Harlbury dealt together, my dear! Well, I warned you what you might expect!" She levelled her glass at the opposite box. "Lord! Harlbury looks regularly blue-devilled!" she said. "A pretty scold she is reading him, I'll warrant you!"

Lydia, who for once in her life was too angry and exasperated to return a light answer, made no reply. She was wondering, as the curtain rose, how she could possibly sort out the dreadful tangle into which her own affairs and those of her family seemed to have got themselves. It was a problem, it seemed to her at the present moment, that would require all her best efforts to solve.

IT DID NOT TAKE LYDIA LONG ON the following morning to come to the conclusion that, if she were to succeed in extricating her grandmother from the difficulties that had caused that much-harassed lady to propose again, at the breakfast-table, to seek relief at the hands of a moneylender, she required the counsel of some older and wiser head than her own. It was useless to expect Bayard to take the matter in hand; she had, in fact, advised her grandmother against even acquainting him with the results of her imprudent visits to Curzon Street. Introduced into the exclusive and highly expensive gaming-rooms of White's Club through the promised good offices of Lord Harlbury, he was already elated at having been lucky enough to come off with a modest success in play that was quite above his touch; and Lydia could only shudder at the idea of his taking it into his head that his grandmother's lack of good fortune at the gaming-tables could best be retrieved by his plunging still more heavily there.

Advice, however, she considered, she must have, and, as she sat frowning alone over her second cup of coffee in the breakfast-parlour, it suddenly occurred to her that she might do worse than to enlist Northover's aid.

It was the matter of a few minutes to jump up and run to the escritoire in the back drawing-room to scribble a few lines to him requesting him to call in Green Street as soon as convenient, and to dispatch the note by the hand of the footman, who was rapidly instructed as to those establishments, customarily frequented by gentlemen of the Viscount's sporting proclivities, where he might most probably run his lordship to earth if he did not find him at home. Of course, she told herself severely, as she sat down to await the results of this venture, she had not at all forgotten that she was very much at outs with Northover, and had parted from him in the greatest dudgeon on the occasion of their last meeting in the Park. But that did not mean that it was necessary for her to refuse to enlist his aid when she needed it.

It did occur to her, though, that his lordship might take a less magnanimous view of the situation, and it was therefore with some relief, an hour or so later, that she heard the sound of carriage wheels outside the door and saw—as she peeped through the blinds of the front drawing-room—Northover's athletic form springing down from his curricle.

She hastily sat down and picked up at random a volume of sermons, which he found her interestedly perusing when he was shown into the room a few minutes later. The title immediately took his eye, and he burst out laughing before he was well within the door.

"No, no, Lydia *mia!*" he said, coming across the room and taking the book out of her hands. "If you wish to persuade me that you have not been sitting here waiting on tenterhooks for my arrival, you will have to think of something more plausible than that!" He tossed the book upon the table and drew up a chair so that he could look directly into her darkling face. "You must be in the deuce of a pucker to have to send your fellow out scouring the town for me."

"I suppose he found you in Jackson's Boxing Saloon?" Lydia said loftily, not deigning to dignify the Viscount's undiplomatically direct remark with an equally direct reply.

"As a matter of fact, it was at Manton's Shooting Gallery. I was trying out a new piece there." The Viscount's penetrating dark eyes searched her face. "Cut line, Lydia!" he commanded. "You didn't drag me here only to rake me down. What have you been up to this time?"

"*I?* Nothing at all!" Lydia said, with dignity. "It is Grandmama—"

"Your grandmother?" Northover's black brows went up and he grinned again. "Come now—"

"It's true!" Lydia said, with some asperity. "She has got herself into the most *afflictive* hobble, and it will ruin us

152

all if I cannot manage somehow to bring her about. Are you by any chance acquainted with a Mrs. Collingworth who lives in Curzon Street?"

The brows went up again, and the Viscount gave a long, low whistle. "So that's the game, is it? Yes, I know her. You don't mean to say that your grandmother has let herself be drawn into *that* net?"

"Yes, she has," Lydia replied, her anxiety rising as she saw the suddenly more sober expression upon the Viscount's face. "What is more, she lost two thousand pounds the first night she went there, and heaven knows how much more on the second—and we can't afford to pay such a sum, Northover; truly we can't! I am at my wit's end as to what to do, for she is talking now of borrowing from a moneylender, and I know from what happened to my own father how disastrous such a course can be!"

"Yes, by God!" Northover said, frowning. "If she once gets into the hands of the cents-per-cent, she'll never be clear of them. But how came she to fall into the Collingworth's clutches? Surely you haven't been moving in *that* set?"

"No, of course not; in fact, I don't even know what set you are speaking of. We met her quite by accident in Richmond Park—or at least it seemed so at the time, but Mr. Michael Pentony, who introduced us to her there, has all but admitted that *he* arranged the meeting. Naturally, his purpose is obvious: if Grandmama is involved in a scandal over her gaming debts, it must certainly ruin any chance Bayard may have of inheriting Sir Basil's fortune."

She had been speaking impetuously, too full of her problem to note anything unusual in the Viscount's manner; but it occurred to her suddenly, as she looked into his face, that it wore a rather odd expression. As a matter of fact, she now recollected, it was the same harsh and constrained look she had seen upon it fleetingly as he had walked into the room, before he had burst into laughter at the prim tableau of her sitting there deep in a volume of sermons.

He only said to her, however, in a level, offhand voice,

"That would certainly seem to be a valid assumption. But why come to me with the problem? Why not enlist Harlbury's aid?"

"Harlbury's?" She stared at him.

He gave a short laugh. "I see," he said. "You are not sure that he, too, might not sheer off at the hint of a scandal. Hardly the height of devotion, one would say! However, when one is angling for rank and fortune, perhaps a commodity worth so little in pounds, shillings, and pence as devotion can be dispensed with."

"I don't know what you are talking of!" she said indignantly, and then, in a blank voice, as the meaning of his words broke over her, "Oh! You mean—you think Harlbury and I—?"

He said dryly, "As the news is by this time spread over half the town, you can scarcely believe it has not reached my ears as well. Pray forgive me for being so remiss as not to have offered you my felicitations—or perhaps, in your case, it would be more correct to say 'congratulations.' "

Her cheeks flew scarlet at his tone. "Oh! You are the most *abominable*—! I knew I should never have sent for you!"

"Then why did you? No, no—you needn't answer that. Friendship—it *is* friendship that we are presumed to feel for each other, isn't it, my dear?—can be appealed to so much more safely than—er—love—"

Lydia jumped up. "If this is your idea of *friendship*," she said fulminatingly, "to come here and insult me, when I am in the briars and merely want your advice, it is not mine! And if you don't care to give it to me, you can go away! I—I shall manage somehow!"

He gave a rather jeering little laugh. "What, and jeopardise such a promising arrangement as you have come to with Harlbury? No, no—I am not so hard-hearted as *that*! What is it that you really want me to do, Lydia? Lend you the money? Very well; you have only to find out from your grandmother the sum you require and I'll write you a

154

cheque on Drummond's. No doubt, once you are married to Harlbury, you will find the means to repay me."

"When I am—? I am not going to marry Harlbury! How can you be such a—such a *gudgeon!*" Lydia, incensed, took a rapid turn about the room and came up to stand before him with flashing eyes. "If I were, I should not need *your* help!"

Northover looked at her, the rather ugly, jeering look still there on his face. "Come, my girl, that cock won't fight," he said shortly. "I have it from Lady Gilmour herself that Harlbury's match with her daughter is off, and that his intentions toward you are known at least within his family."

"Yes, they are known there, but that is all—or, at any rate, it *should* be all!" Lydia said. "I am not betrothed to Harlbury; I only offered to allow him to tell his mama that he had an attachment for me so that he might have an excuse for not offering for Miss Beaudoin."

"And why didn't he wish to offer for Miss Beaudoin?" Northover enquired skeptically. "It appears to me that he was quite willing to do so before you thrust *your* finger into that pie. But I will give you credit for being up to every move on the board, my love. If *this* was the ruse you used to bring him into your net—"

"Oh!" Lydia choked. "How *can* you be so hateful! I did it to help Bayard!"

"Very pretty! So, out of the purest altruism, you have scotched Harlbury's match with Minna Beaudoin. It will never have occurred to you, of course, that, having brought him so far, it will no doubt be a simple matter for you to bring him a little farther, into the bonds of matrimony. A fitting end for him, I should think; after all, his mother has kept him in leading-strings all his life, and he will merely see them transferred now from her hands to his wife's." He grinned suddenly, not very pleasantly. "No, don't look at me as if you'd like to murder me, Lydia *mia*," he said. "Have you forgotten? There is still a favour you want me to do for

155

you. It would be too bad if all these beautiful plans of yours were to go astray merely for the lack of a few thousand pounds at the crucial moment."

Lydia said, from between gritted teeth, "I would not take a penny from you, Northover, if it was to save myself from—from the gallows! I wish you will go away! I have nothing more to say to you!"

"Gammon!" he said coolly. "You are angry now, but when you have had time to think it over you will realise that the use of four or five thousand pounds at a critical moment is well worth having a few disagreeable home truths put to you."

It was this inauspicious moment that Sidwell chose for his entrance with the news that Lord Harlbury had called to see Miss Leyland.

For a moment neither of the participants in the rather spirited scene that had just been taking place appeared to comprehend this statement: then Northover gave a crack of laughter and Lydia, flushing and biting her lip, ordered Sidwell curtly to show his lordship upstairs. Sidwell departed, and Northover, turning to follow him, said mockingly, "Send me word of the sum you must have, Lydia. No, there is no cause for you to get up upon your high ropes; I have been a needy rascal myself in my day, and am quite aware of the shifts one may be forced to in such a situation." He had moved to stand beside her, and now, reaching out a hand, flicked her cheek with a careless forefinger. "Don't despair, my sweet love," he said. "You will come about. I am not in the position to go into detail on the matter as yet, but I am strongly of the opinion that there is no need for you to worry as far as old Rowthorn's intentions toward your family are concerned. And if you succeed in inducing Harlbury to leg-shackle himself to you, that should certainly clinch the matter."

He did not stay to give her the opportunity to utter the startled questions that rose to her lips, but walked out of the room, encountering—as she was able to hear—Harlbury on the stairs. A brief greeting passed between them, and then, as Harlbury entered the room, she was forced to compose herself sufficiently to smile and extend her hand to him.

She saw at once that he was looking very serious, and as soon as he had seated himself he said to her, with an air of resolution, "Miss Leyland, I am come to ask if you and your brother and Mrs. Leyland will do me the honour to make a party for Vauxhall tomorrow evening. It will be a gala night, and I believe I may promise that you will enjoy it."

The manner in which he brought the words out suggested that they held a great deal more significance than a mere party of pleasure would imply. Lydia, who had sat down opposite him, wrenched her mind with difficulty from its wrathful contemplation of the scene with Northover and replied with somewhat absent civility, "I should be delighted, of course—and so, I believe, will Grandmama and Bayard." She then added, not entirely tactfully, "Does your mother know you have come here?"

A dark-red flush overspread his lordship's handsome face. "I cannot think," he said rather stiffly, "what my mother should have to say to it!"

"Can't you?" Lydia said. "Then you must be a greater moonling than I would have believed possible!" She saw him staring at her, and realised the rather startling change in manner from the sweetly sympathetic tone she had used during their last conversation in this room that he was being required to digest; but she was too hot still from her encounter with Northover to alter her course. "You know very well," she went on frankly, "that she was as mad as Bedlam over the whole affair last night—and that outrageous scene Mr. Pentony put on for her benefit must have capped the climax. So if she knew you were coming here—"

"She didn't," Harlbury said, the flush still high upon his face. "But I fail to see what concern it is of hers if I escort you to Vauxhall tomorrow evening, Miss Leyland!"

Lydia, who was still wondering what Northover had meant by his cryptic parting remarks concerning Sir Basil, was roused sufficiently by this declaration to say with some

157

appearance of approval, "Do you know, I believe you are coming on, Harlbury! That was very nicely said. Of course it is none of her affair, and the sooner you realise that, the better it will be for you." She conceded after a moment, "I daresay, though, that she read you a horrid scold last night, and that cannot have been very agreeable."

His lordship gloomily agreed that it had not been. He appeared to be in a far from happy mood, and showed distinct traces of the nervousness engendered within him by the knowledge that this visit to Green Street, if it were to come to Lady Harlbury's ears, would no doubt cause her to put him through exactly another such scene as he had been forced to participate in the night before. Lydia, who was scarcely in frame, considering her own difficulties, to humour him out of his depression, was relieved when another pair of morning callers arrived to interrupt their tête-à-tête, even though these callers turned out to be Lady Pentony and Miss Pentony.

Neither of these ladies betrayed the slightest knowledge of what had taken place at the theatre the evening before, but Lydia was very certain, after five minutes' conversation, that Lady Pentony, at least, knew all about it, and that the purpose of her call in Green Street was to discover what effect it had had upon Lydia's matrimonial prospects. The presence of Harlbury himself in the Leyland drawing-room could give her little comfort, Lydia considered with some gratification, and she was ungenerous enough to twist the knife further in Lady Pentony's bosom by behaving towards his lordship in the offhand manner of a young lady so certain of her conquest that she need make no attempt to call attention to it.

So she devoted her conversation amiably to Lady Pentony, leaving Harlbury to entertain Eveline—a task in which he appeared to succeed a good deal better than Lydia had hoped. This, however, was not entirely surprising, for Miss Pentony, in addition to being an exceptionally pretty girl, was obviously so much in awe of his lordship's rank and magnificent good looks that she attended to every word that fell from his lips with the worshipful interest she might have accorded the utterances of a god. Lydia observed in some amusement the manner in which Harlbury gradually blossomed under this unfeigned admiration; the poor fellow, she thought, must rarely have had such an experience. Courted and sought after as he was by the young ladies of his own circle, his grave, stiff manners could never have made him a favourite with them, and he was not so deficient in understanding that he could have failed to realise that no warmer sentiment than ambition lay behind the many lures cast out to him.

Miss Pentony, on the other hand, was casting out no lures at all. She was too dazzled by her good fortune at being allowed to sit beside the handsome young Earl of Harlbury, and even to converse with him, to think of doing more than drinking in the words he uttered and, when necessary, replying to them with a blushing phrase of respectful assent. When his lordship rose to make his adieux, saying politely that he hoped they should meet again, she said, "Oh, so do I!" in accents so nicely divided between a mournful realisation of the unlikelihood of this event and a shy, desperate hope that it might indeed come to pass that his lordship could not but have felt complimented. He said reassuringly that he was certain they would, and then, having reaffirmed his engagement to escort Lydia to Vauxhall on the following evening, took his departure, in a much more cheerful frame of mind, it seemed to her, than that in which he had arrived.

His exit was the signal for Lady Pentony to set to work, with half-hints and smiling innuendoes, to discover how matters really stood between Lydia and his lordship. It was perhaps fortunate for her that the entrance of Mrs. Leyland within a very few minutes put an end to Lydia's being required to cope with her manoeuvres singlehanded, as that young lady was on the point of giving vent to one of her singularly frank expressions of opinion when her grandmother providentially arrived on the scene.

Mrs. Leyland, who detested Lady Pentony, soon put her to rout; but the martial spirit evoked in her by this encounter faded into gloom at once on the visitors' departure, and only the news that Harlbury had called to invite them to Vauxhall stirred her into some slight cheerfulness again.

"But, there!" she said pessimistically, upon Lydia's immediately turning the subject and putting a question to her as to whether she had had any fresh ideas on how to deal with her financial difficulties, "I know how it will be! You will do nothing to fix his interest, and it will end with his mama's prevailing upon him to offer for the Beaudoin girl, after all. I vow, my love, it is *too* provoking of you, for it is not as if you had an inclination for any other gentleman! Do but think of the pin-money you might have, and the gowns, and the carriages, to say nothing of the position you would occupy in Society as the Countess of Harlbury! And then poor Bayard might be comfortable, too, for I daresay Lord Harlbury would be happy to purchase a commission for him in an excellent regiment."

"Nothing," said Lydia shortly, "will make Bayard comfortable except being able to marry Minna Beaudoin. Have you *looked* at him lately, Grandmama? He is quite miserable, I know, though he does his best to conceal it from us."

"Nonsense!" said Mrs. Leyland. "He will probably tumble in and out of love with half a dozen girls before he is ready to settle himself. And I have it from Lucinda Aimer herself that Miss Beaudoin's fortune is nothing at all, which makes it highly unsuitable that Bayard should fix his choice on her." She shook her head with a desponding air. "I do not know how it is," she said, "that you both *refuse* to take advantage of the opportunities I have provided you with by bringing you to London, at the greatest sacrifice of my own health and convenience! And the result—if I am able to escape a debtors' prison—will be that we shall be obliged to retire again to that *odious* plantation, where *you* will dwindle into an old maid and *I* into my grave!"

Lydia could not help being diverted by this highly coloured statement of the situation, and a gurgle of laughter

160

escaped her. She was at once reproved for her levity and required with some severity to inform her afflicted grandparent what she found to amuse her in the bleak picture of their joint future that had just been drawn for her—a task which she declined to undertake, on the grounds that Mrs. Leyland's mood was such that she would be quite unable to find amusement in anything at the present moment.

"But we shall come about somehow, Grandmama, I promise you," Lydia said. "If the worst comes, I can always borrow the money from Northover to preserve you from the dire fate you are imagining for yourself—though I confess I had rather go to prison myself than be obliged to do so."

Mrs. Leyland stared at her. "From Northover! But—will he lend it to you? Why should he do such a thing?" A gleam of hope suddenly appeared upon her face. "Lydia! Tell me the truth!" she exclaimed. "Has *he* made you an offer? Oh, my love, that would be beyond anything great, for, though he has *not* the kind of reputation I should choose to see in your husband, he is splendidly rich, and I daresay quite amiable if one can bring oneself to overlook a certain sarcastic levity—"

Lydia, upon whose face a sudden flush had risen, got up quickly.

"Oh, Grandmama, do give over!" she said rather sharply. "Of course he has not made me an offer—nor has he the slightest intention of doing so! Indeed, I shall be surprised if he ever marries. Why should he, when he is so well entertained by his *chères-amies*?"

"*That* statement," said Mrs. Leyland, disapprovingly, "is not what I like to hear from your lips, Lydia! Not that I see what his having mistresses has to say to anything, for I am sure that *that* does not prevent a gentleman from wishing to set up his nursery when he reaches a certain age—particularly one in Northover's position—"

"Grandmama, if you do not stop, I shall scream!" Lydia threatened, her face still suffused with angry colour. "You may put Northover quite out of your mind as a matrimonial

161

prospect for me, I assure you! Nothing is more unlikely than that he will make me an offer. He is so odiously rich that he can afford to tow us out of the River Tick for his own amusement and never count the cost—that is all!"

Mrs. Leyland, on whose face an expression of increasing foreboding had appeared during this speech, at this point could contain herself no longer.

"Good God, Lydia," she said, in a failing voice, "do not tell me that you have conceived a *tendre* for Northover, and *that* is why you are being so gooseish about Harlbury!"

"For Northover!" Lydia, who had been about to leave the room, swung around, stung on the raw, it seemed, by this accusation. "For—*Northover!*"

"Really, my dear, there is no need to fly into such a taking if it is not so," Mrs. Leyland said. "I am sure nobody could be happier than I should be to hear I am mistaken, but it *does* appear to me—"

"I," said Lydia, controlling herself with a great effort and speaking in a quite calm voice, "am going to leave this room. Carrying on a conversation with one's grandmother when she has obviously taken leave of her senses—"

"But it will be *you* who have taken leave of *your* senses if you have been foolish enough to fall in love with a man who has no intention of marrying you!" Mrs. Leyland pointed out, piteously. "Oh, my love, surely you would never be so lost to all propriety as to let him make *you* his mistress—for if he has indeed offered you the money to bring us out of our present difficulties, without having the intention of marrying you, you may depend upon it that that is what he has in mind! And *that* would quite ruin everything! It is not as if you were married and settled, you know; I should *never* be able to find a husband for you!"

She got no further, for at this point Lydia made good her threat and swept from the room.

It was quite beneath Miss Leyland's code of behaviour to give way to tears, as other young ladies might have done under the agitating influence of the facts that had suddenly been brought into the open by the frank speaking of the scene she had just taken part in; but it must be reported that she stood for a full quarter hour, with her eyes unnaturally bright and her lips ominously quivering, at the window of her bedchamber before she was calm enough to go on about the ordinary business of her day. To which it may be added that when she did emerge from her room she appeared unwontedly subdued, and even endured a scold from Winch on the subject of a rent in the sea-green sarsnet gown she had worn the evening before without attempting so much as a single saucy word in her own defence.

16 LYDIA, WHO HAD NOT HAD THE least intention, even before her disastrous conversation with her grandmother, of obeying Northover's injunction to let him know the extent of Mrs. Leyland's debts, sent no message to the Viscount on either that day or the next, and was therefore more than a little surprised, on the afternoon following his visit, to receive from him a brief missive, brought by hand, and containing a cheque in the amount of five thousand pounds made out to her grandmother.

It is not like you to be missish, Lydia, my love, with so much at stake, the accompanying careless scrawl ran. *If this doesn't cover the lot, let me know. Yours, etc. Northover.*

"What is it, my dear?" Mrs. Leyland, who was sitting with Lydia, forebodingly enquired, seeing her granddaughter's face alter and the colour rush up into her cheeks as she perused the note. "I hope it is not from Harlbury, saying that he must relinquish the Vauxhall scheme."

"From Harlbury? No! It is from Northover!" Lydia tossed the cheque across the table to her contemptuously. "You see at how high a rate he sets me!" she said. "I should be flattered, I daresay. And more if I desire it! There are no limits to his generosity, it seems!"

Mrs. Leyland, who had picked up the cheque, eyed it incredulously. "Five thousand pounds!" she gasped. "Oh, my love, it is a great deal more even than we require! Was there ever anything so providential!—for now I shall be able to settle that odious Celeste's bill as well, and you may have the jaconet muslin with the Russian bodice that so becomes you, after all—"

"Grandmama!" Lydia's startled voice cut into these delighted reflections. "What can you be thinking of? Of course we cannot accept it! I shall send it back to him at once!"

"Send it back—" Mrs. Leyland's voice faltered, and then

strengthened into tones of outraged incredulity. "Send
—it—back! My dear child, you must be all about in your
head! Do you realise that I have been driven quite to des-
peration by our situation over these past days? First you say
I am to have no dealings with Mr. King—and now you wish
me to return this—this *honeyfall* to Northover!"

"But, Grandmama," Lydia protested, "*you* were the one
who said that Northover could have only one idea in mind
in offering me such a sum! Surely you cannot wish me to
keep it!"

Mrs. Leyland looked at her with some hauteur. "Naturally
we shall not *keep* it," she said. "We shall merely accept it
as a loan. No doubt I shall be able to repay the entire sum
within a very short time, for I am quite convinced that my
luck must turn—"

"*No!*" Lydia said, snatching the cheque from her grandmother's fingers. "Grandmama, you *would* not be so imprudent as to sit down to play again, after what has happened—and with Northover's money! It would be infamous!"

"Infamous! To attempt to establish my granddaughter and
grandson respectably in life?—for that is the *only* reason,
you must know, that I indulge in cards at all—"

"Well, I will not have it!" Lydia said implacably, carrying
the cheque over to the escritoire and sitting down there.
"I shall send this back to him at once."

"Lydia!" intoned Mrs. Leyland dramatically. "Unnatural
girl! You cannot do it! I implore you—to save us all from
the Fleet—!"

"No!" said Lydia ruthlessly, already scribbling furiously
upon a sheet of hot-pressed notepaper. "Don't put yourself
into a taking, Grandmama! I shall marry Harlbury if it is
necessary—or Sir Carsbie Chant—or even that odious
Michael Pentony—*anything* rather than give Northover the
right to think he has been able to—"

She broke off to reread with satisfaction what she had written. *My lord, I herewith return the cheque you have sent,
and must beg that you will not call in Green Street again.*

166

It will be quite useless, as I do not aspire to the honour of the position you have designed for me. L.L. She then folded the paper, enclosed the cheque within it, and, having sealed it with a wafer, rang the bell for the footman and directed him to carry it immediately to Lord Northover.

Having accomplished this, she fell into a very cheerful and light-hearted mood, if one were to judge by her conversation, and embarked upon a highly interested discussion as to whether she should wear green ribbons or white with the gown of jonquil sarsnet she had chosen for the Vauxhall party that evening. Only the arrival of a bouquet of yellow roses in an elegant holder, with the compliments of Lord Harlbury, prevented her grandmother from characterising her as the most unfeeling girl it had ever been her misfortune to become acquainted with, the posy having the effect of diverting her mind once more to the happy prospect that Lydia might yet exert herself to bring that unexceptionable young man to the point.

It was therefore a moderately cheerful party that set out for Vauxhall Gardens that evening. Harlbury, who was apparently intent on doing everything in his power to make the project a success, had hired sculls to carry them from Westminster to the water-gate of the famous gardens, and Lydia, who had never visited Vauxhall before, was in transports—slightly overdone, her somewhat amused brother considered, but obviously quite satisfactory to Lord Harlbury—over the sight that greeted her eyes as she was handed ashore. The gardens, which were lit by thousands of lanterns, glittering in brilliant colour about the giant kiosk where the orchestra played and hanging in graceful festoons to illuminate the long pillared colonnades, had all the appearance, she assured Harlbury, with some lack of originality, of a fairyland, and as they trod the leafy walks towards the Rotunda where they were to attend a concert before partaking of supper, she indulged in a constant flow of exclamations of wonderment that could not but have been gratifying to his lordship.

He seemed, however, to be in a somewhat distrait mood

that evening—a circumstance that was presently explained by his confiding to Lydia, as they were taking their places in the concert-hall, that his mother had also decided to visit the gardens that evening in company with Lord and Lady Gilmour.

"I told her, of course," he said, "that I should have invited her to join *our* party if I had had the least notion she would have cared to do so. It will look very odd, you know, for her to come with Lord and Lady Gilmour instead."

"Which is exactly what she desired, of course," Lydia said, quite unperturbed. "Well, if she wishes to parade her differences with you before the world, that is *her* affair, and certainly need not concern you in the least." She added, looking up and bestowing a brilliant smile upon a party making their way to seats in the row just before them, "But here they are now. Dear Lady Gilmour, how do you do? And Lady Harlbury—what an agreeable surprise!"

Both ladies returned exceedingly cool bows to this cordial greeting, but Miss Beaudoin, following in her mother's wake, cast a glance upon the group behind her—including, as it did, both young Mr. Leyland and Lord Harlbury—which immediately sent a suffocating flush up to mantle her clear olive skin. She stammered a word of greeting, her eyes seeking Bayard's with such beseeching intensity that it must have required a man far less in love than he was not to understand that she urgently wished for an opportunity to speak to him alone that evening.

But it was impossible for him, with the concert about to begin, to do more than acknowledge this mute message with a fervent glance. Both parties then settled back in their chairs to find what enjoyment they could in the music, Lady Harlbury's rigidly erect pose suggesting, however, that she, at least, found it impossible to do anything of the sort in such close proximity to Miss Lydia Leyland.

If the truth were told, it is probable that few of the members of either party—with the exception of the pair of very fashionable young gentlemen who had come in Lady Gilmour's train—were able to concentrate sufficiently upon the music to know whether they were listening to a much-admired oratorio by Handel or to a street-singer's ballad bawled in their ears. Lydia spent the greater part of her time in endeavouring to contrive a scheme by which it might be possible to detach Miss Beaudoin from her mama and Lady Harlbury, so that she might have the interview with Bayard she evidently so much desired; but even her ingenuity boggled at the task, and she was obliged at last to give it up and to hope that chance might later be kind enough to present the lovers with the opportunity they craved.

When the first act ended, the Gilmour party, disdaining to view the spectacle of the Grand Cascade, in which a waterfall, with a mill, a bridge, and a succession of vehicles crossing the latter, was represented upon the stage with a lifelike similitude extending even to the sound of rushing waters and rumbling wheels, passed out of the Rotunda. With the exception of Lord Gilmour, who paused for a friendly word with Mrs. Leyland and Harlbury, no communication took place between the opposing parties, unless the term might be applied to the dagger-look Lydia received from Lady Harlbury as she passed by.

"I *do* think," Lydia said to Harlbury, looking thoughtfully at the pretty painted fan she carried, "that if I were you I should make arrangements to live apart from your mama, Harlbury. She could not drive you into such a panic if she were not able to see you whenever she wishes—"

"I am *not* in a panic!" his lordship said, in a low, indignant voice.

"Yes, you are, Harlbury," Lydia contradicted him, incurably frank. "I can scarcely blame you, for there is nothing horrider than being raked down by someone for every least thing one does; but if you saw her less frequently it would not signify so much. And it would be excellent practice for you to begin living without her, you know, for when you are married you must expect to do so."

"When I am married—!" His lordship cast a somewhat startled glance at her. "But I am not—"

"Of course you are not—just now," Lydia said, giving his

169

arm a reassuring pat. "But you will wish to marry some day, and once we have quite put the idea to rest that you are to offer for Miss Beaudoin, we shall set about it to find a more suitable young lady for you."

Lord Harlbury appeared to be about to enter some protest to this scheme, but was silenced by the resumption of the entertainment. His handsome countenance, however, had taken on an even more harried look than that which it had worn at the start of the evening, and it was apparent that he looked forward with no great anticipation to the hours that must still elapse before he could decently bring his party away from the gardens.

But if one of the apprehensions he harboured was that Lydia meant to set about it immediately to implement her matrimonial plans for him, he need not have concerned himself. Miss Leyland, with Bayard and Minna on her mind, had other things to think of. And, as if that were not enough, she was greeted, when they left the Rotunda and repaired for supper to one of the boxes overlooking the principal grove, by the sight of Northover lounging in the box just opposite, chatting easily with Lady Gilmour.

A slight flush appeared upon Lydia's face; she shut her fan with a snap, and Bayard and Minna and all their tribulations, together with Harlbury and all of his, instantly flew out of her head.

Of course it was not lost upon Harlbury that, by the most vexatious of coincidences, he was for the second time that evening obliged to attempt to enjoy himself under the basilisk stare of his offended mama. But he pulled himself together with commendable fortitude and ordered an excellent supper for the party, which included the ham-shavings and rack punch for which Vauxhall was famous.

He had scarcely completed this task when Northover, having left the Gilmour box by the simple method of vaulting over the low barrier in front, instead of using the more conventional form of egress by the door at the back, strolled across and, after exchanging casual greetings with the company, enquired pointblank of Miss Leyland, "Just what the deuce did you think you were about, Lydia, to send that remarkably henwitted message to me?"

Lydia, in the act of swallowing a morsel of chicken, choked, and gave him a glance that fully expressed her indignation at the unfair advantage he was taking in bringing the matter up in a situation in which she could not speak openly. She controlled herself, however, and merely said loftily, "I do not care to discuss the matter, Lord Northover."

"You don't, don't you? Well, I do—and, what is more, I shall call in Green Street tomorrow to do exactly that."

"I have asked you *not* to—" Lydia began, fulminatingly.

"I am aware, my dear." His mocking dark eyes appreciatively surveyed her flushed face. "It was abominably ill-bred of you, but I shall overlook it. No," he added to Bayard, who had started up with an irate exclamation at this uncomplimentary speech, "never mind looking like bull-beef, halfling. Your sister is quite capable of fighting her own battles; in fact, I should think it hardly sporting of you to deprive her of the privilege when it affords her so much harmless amusement."

With a nod to his stunned auditors, he walked off, leaving Mrs. Leyland, who recovered herself first, to say in a rather anguished voice to Lydia, "Indeed, he is the oddest man! But need you have been so very abrupt with him, my love? After all, he—"

"Abrupt!" exclaimed Bayard wrathfully. "I should rather hope she was! What the deuce does he mean by it, to speak to her so?"

"I do *not* wish to hear another word on the subject!" Lydia said ominously. She saw Lady Gilmour, who had been looking very ill-pleased at Northover's departure from her box, laughing now as he re-entered it, and tapping his arm with her fan while glancing in Lydia's direction. Her bosom swelled. "He is rude and—and unprincipled—and if he thinks I am another Lady Gilmour, I promise you that he shall very soon learn his mistake. Harlbury, where in the world are you going?" she broke off to enquire in surprise, as his lordship arose and evinced a sudden intention of leaving the box.

He turned a slightly flushed face upon her. "You are my guest, Miss Leyland," he said, "and if Lord Northover has insulted you—"

"For heaven's sake, Harlbury," she said severely, "do not be so absurd! Of course he has insulted me; he has been doing it since the first day I met him—but that does not mean that either you *or* Bayard need feel called upon to interfere! *I* shall deal with Lord Northover, and I promise you that he will be very sorry indeed before I have done that he has dared to cross swords with me."

Harlbury and Bayard exchanged glances, the former looking uncertain and rather puzzled; but a rueful grin gradually replaced the lowering expression upon Bayard's face.

"She's right, you know, Harlbury!" he said cheerfully. "We had as well both sit down. We should only make cakes of ourselves, trying to force a quarrel upon Northover because he and Lyddy have come to cuffs again."

"I should rather think so!" Lydia said, and added darkly, "Never believe I shall not get my own back with him! I have my methods!"

Lord Harlbury, resuming his chair, looked as if he could well believe this latter statement. But his rather bemused mental contemplation of the unorthodox Miss Leyland was interrupted almost at once by the appearance of a newly familiar face among the strollers passing by: Miss Eveline Pentony, wearing a pale-blue gown with a bodice cut in the Austrian style, which made her look rather more sweetly angelic than usual. She was on her brother's arm, and it was probable that Harlbury, seeing them together, for the first time made the startled connexion in his mind between the vulgar young gentleman who had invaded his mother's box at Drury Lane and the worshipping young lady he had met in Green Street the day before.

As for Lydia, one glance at the pair was sufficient to bring to *her* the exasperated remembrance that both Lady Pentony

172

and Miss Pentony had heard Harlbury refer to his Vauxhall scheme the day before—a fact which was undoubtedly responsible for Mr. Michael Pentony's having determined to visit the gardens that evening himself.

It was impossible for her to pretend that she had not seen them, however, for Harlbury, starting up at once, had already greeted Miss Pentony. Mrs. Leyland was not behindhand in doing likewise, and Lydia was resigning herself to the prospect of a repetition upon Mr. Pentony's part of the scene he had played in Lady Harlbury's box when she saw his eyes fix themselves suddenly upon Harlbury's face. She turned her head, and observed in an instant what it was that had no doubt caught Mr. Pentony's attention.

Lord Harlbury was gazing upon Miss Pentony with the intent, earnest, self-revelatory expression which only a very sober and literal-minded young man could have been betrayed into allowing upon his countenance in a public place. What was more, he was inviting her—stammering a little over the words—to join his party, an invitation which naturally had to include Mr. Pentony as well. Miss Pentony, looking much as if the heavens had suddenly opened and deposited before her a magnificently handsome angel in a well-fitting blue coat and starched neckcloth, gave an immediate and dazzled assent, which she then recollected herself sufficiently to qualify by a shyly enquiring glance cast at her brother.

But even she, Lydia reflected resignedly, could not have been gooseish enough to anticipate opposition from *that* quarter; and the upshot of the matter was that in the space of a pair of minutes both Mr. and Miss Pentony had entered the booth and joined the party there.

If Lydia had expected Mr. Pentony to resume the boorish manner he had displayed in Lady Harlbury's box at Drury Lane, she was doing an injustice to that gentleman's powers of observation. It had taken him no more than thirty seconds to note that Lord Harlbury, far from being absorbed in Miss Leyland's charms, was showing a lively interest in his sister's; and it required very little longer for him to come to

173

the surprising conclusion that Miss Pentony's milk-and-water disposition and total lack of pretension to anything in the nature of liveliness or wit were exactly what Lord Harlbury liked.

The idea that anything might come of this very odd—to her brother, at least—predilection was not one on which he laid much weight, particularly in view of his lordship's notorious lack of independence from the wishes of his mama. But Mr. Pentony was not the man to neglect a possible *coup* because it seemed a long chance, and he determined on the instant to do nothing that might jeopardise it in any way.

He therefore remained discreetly in the background, devoting his conversation chiefly to Mrs. Leyland, and sustaining with an appearance of perfect equanimity the cold shoulder that Lydia turned to him.

As for Lydia, the chief amusement she was able to obtain from the trying hour that followed was the sight of Lady Harlbury's burning curiosity as to the identity of the ethereally blonde young lady to whom her son was paying such marked attentions. As Miss Pentony was entirely unknown in the exalted circles in which Lady Harlbury herself, and the other members of Lady Gilmour's party, moved, this curiosity perforce remained unsatisfied until, the supper being concluded, the members of Lord Harlbury's party chose to leave their box to stroll through the grounds and watch the exhibition of fireworks that was about to take place.

This instantly decided Lady Harlbury that she, too, wished to watch the fireworks. The rest of the company rose to accompany her for civility's sake, with the result that the two parties came face to face with each other in the neutral territory between their boxes.

"Shafto," Lady Harlbury said, coming up immediately to the attack as she confronted her son, "I do not believe that I am acquainted with this young lady." And she favoured Miss Pentony with a comprehensive stare, from the crown of her fair head to the tips of her little kid slippers, that had that modest young lady instantly in a blush.

174

Lord Harlbury, looking startled but resolute, presented Miss Pentony to his mother.

"Pentony?" Lady Harlbury repeated, her brows on the rise. "Pentony? I seem to have heard the name—"

"I had the honour, my lady," Mr. Pentony, stepping forward, suavely remarked, "of making your acquaintance the other evening at Drury Lane. Miss Pentony is my sister."

A look of horror overspread Lady Harlbury's face. "*Your* sister!" she ejaculated. "*Your* sister! Good heavens!"

"I am afraid," Mr. Pentony said, himself having the grace to colour slightly, "that I must apologise for my behaviour upon that occasion, my lady. The truth is that I was labouring at the time under the double difficulty of a strong misapprehension and considerable emotional stress, which may have caused me to appear in a somewhat invidious light to you. I must beg, however, that—even if you feel it impossible to pardon *me*—you will not extend your disapprobation to my sister."

But Lady Harlbury, far from being mollified by this speech, appeared on the verge of suffering one of the spasms which—as her son had bitter reason to know—invariably attacked her iron constitution on the occasion of any shock caused to it by her offspring's behaving in a manner not entirely in accord with her own ideas. On the present occasion the attack was sufficiently violent for her to demand his arm upon the instant, and, though Lord Gilmour and the other gentlemen in the party immediately offered her any assistance that lay in their power, it was Harlbury alone whom she would allow to lead her to a seat and extract, under her directions, the hartshorn that she carried in her reticule.

Her indisposition naturally threw both parties into confusion. Lady Gilmour, hovering over her afflicted guest, forgot entirely for the moment the danger that lay in permitting Minna to remain unguarded in Bayard Leyland's company; Lydia, who, in spite of her dislike of Mr. Pentony, was kindhearted enough to pity his sister's embarrassment, was occupied in preventing that damsel from bursting into tears

175

by addressing some bracing small talk to her; and Mrs. Leyland, who cared nothing for Lady Harlbury's dramatic indisposition, but who had not yet given up hope that Northover might be induced to return, on the strictly businesslike terms of a loan, the cheque that Lydia had so cavalierly flung back at him, was endeavouring to take advantage of the brouhaha around her to drop a word to this effect in his lordship's ear.

It was the opportunity for which the two lovers had been waiting. Miss Beaudoin saw her mama's preoccupation; Bayard was not behindhand in noting that his inamorata was, for the moment, unguarded. An exchange of glances, a murmured word—and two figures detached themselves quietly from the now twinned parties and melted into the darkness of a leafy walk.

"I HAD TO TALK TO YOU!"
Minna said. They had reached the
darkness of one of the secluded
paths leading to the little tem-
ple at the end of the Long Walk
and had halted there, feeling themselves at last safe from pursuit or
observation. Huge trees rose above
them, their branches motionless in
the summer night air; the strains
of distant music came softly to their ears. "The most dreadful thing has happened!" she said, swallowing the sob that
threatened to choke her voice. "Mama has decided that we
are not to go to Brighton at the end of the month, after all;
she is taking me to Scarborough instead. I shall be miles
and miles away from you—and, oh, Bayard! I fear that is
not the worst! If you should find the means to come to Scarborough, too, I am quite certain that she will take me even
farther away, perhaps to Paris, for she is determined that,
even if I am not to marry Lord Harlbury, I shall never marry
you!"

All this grievous news came tumbling from Miss
Beaudoin's lips in a mournful torrent, and the effect upon
Bayard was to impel him irresistibly to take her in his arms
and assure her, with the fervour of young lovers from time
immemorial, that, come what might, they should not be
parted; somehow they would find a way.

"Yes—but how?" said Minna despairingly, her head resting against his well-tailored blue coat. "We cannot marry
—you have no money, and I am not of age—and, oh, I cannot bear it, to lose you forever!"

"Nor I to lose you," he said. "And we shan't, my darling!
I shall contrive something—"

She raised her head, looking at him trustfully. "Oh, I
knew you would do so!" she said. "I am too stupid to think
of the least shift myself that will serve us, but *you* will do
so—will you not, Bayard? Only we must act quickly or it
will be too late. We are to leave on Friday, you see."

177

"On Friday!" Bayard looked appalled. "But—good God!—that is only two days from now! How can we possibly—?"

"Perhaps we could go to America," Minna suggested timidly. "I have—I have a little money put by from my quarter's allowance, and there are my pearls—"

Her hand rose to touch the single valuable strand that encircled her slender neck.

Bayard shook his head emphatically. "No, my God! I couldn't let you do that! Besides, it's not necessary; I'm not so purse-pinched as *that*, though I'm in no position to set up as a married man—you know that!"

Minna's dark eyes looked up at him tragically. "Not even in America?" she asked. "You have Belmaison still, and Lydia says we shouldn't starve there."

"No, no, we'd not starve, sweetheart—but how could I take you there, thousands of miles from your home, miles even from any other society than my own and that of a few ignorant servants?"

"I should not mind it, if *you* are there," Minna said forlornly. "But I—I daresay it would be different for you."

This assumption was sufficient to cause Bayard to fold her tightly in his arms again, and to declare fervently that *she* was the only thing necessary to *his* happiness—after which it somehow seemed to be settled between them that they were to spend the rest of their days in idyllic bliss at Belmaison, the only matter remaining to be settled being by what means they were to succeed in reaching this secluded Paradise, and to manage to be married on the way.

Meanwhile, Lydia had been the first of the party gathered around Lady Harlbury to realise that Bayard and Minna had disappeared. She herself would have been quite content to have them spend the remainder of the evening in each other's company, but only a few moments after she had made her own discovery of their absence she saw Lady Gilmour begin to look about her as well, and then speak a few hurried words to her husband. Lord Gilmour laughed, and returned a reply that caused Lady Gilmour to say in a voice of sufficient asperity to reach Lydia's ears, "I don't consider that amusing, Ned! Do you wish the child to ruin herself? Do go off and find her, for I cannot leave Lady Harlbury as yet!"

Lord Gilmour shrugged good-humouredly and moved off down the path. It occurred to Lydia that Lady Gilmour herself would doubtless join in the search before many minutes had passed, and that the guilty couple would be in for an uncomfortable scene if they were discovered by her ladyship alone in each other's company; and with her usual resolution she made up her mind to join the two culprits herself, if possible, before Lady Gilmour succeeded in coming up with them.

She had, of course, no idea in which direction they had gone, and, as she was entirely unfamiliar with Vauxhall, she could do no more than wander at random along the paths, hoping that chance would sooner or later bring her to the pair she sought. She soon discovered, however, that Vauxhall on a gala night was scarcely the most comfortable place in the world for a young lady unencumbered by an escort, for a number of town bucks, attracted by the sight of a remarkably pretty young woman straying alone down dimly lit paths, had approached her with overtures of gallantry before she had been five minutes absent from her party. The most importunate of these, a young blade whose gigantically high neckcloth and striped green-and-gold waistcoat proclaimed his aspirations to dandyism, had, after following her the length of the path she trod, actually had the audacity to come up beside her and seize her arm when, to her relief, she suddenly caught sight of Sir Carsbie Chant standing in a group at the end of the path.

He saw her at the same moment and, grasping her predicament, came at once to her rescue. True, the impressiveness of his action was somewhat impaired by the slurring remarks cast upon his appearance by the encroaching buck, who addressed him as "old spindle-shanks," and enquired derisively how many pounds of buckram wadding were required in his coat to give him more of a figure than a starving clerk. But some indignant flourishing of the gold-headed cane Sir Carsbie carried, together with the interloper's knowledge that his opponent's friends stood nearby, ready to aid him if it should come to blows between them, eventually decided the matter in Sir Carsbie's favour.

"Puppy! City mushroom!" Sir Carsbie ejaculated as he watched the intruder make off, and he dusted his coat-sleeve with an exquisite cambric handkerchief, as if he felt himself contaminated by having merely stood in near proximity to such a person. "My dear Miss Leyland, how very fortunate that I chanced to be by! You have become separated from your party, I apprehend? Allow me the honour, pray, of escorting you back to them."

"Oh yes, that would be very kind of you!" Lydia said immediately, suppressing a tiny gurgle of laughter at her rescuer's air of self-congratulatory heroics. "Indeed, I did not think I should encounter such difficulties merely by walking alone for a few minutes in a place as fashionable as this!"

Sir Carsbie, who was feeling quite puffed up with his own bravery in putting the annoying buck to rout, assured her that a young lady of such ravishing appearance must always be prepared, in any surroundings, to find admiration overleaping the bounds of civility. He then enquired, a trifle jealously, in whose party she had come to Vauxhall that evening.

"In Lord Harlbury's," she replied. "But I do not wish to return to it quite yet, if you please. I left it, you see, on purpose to try to find Miss Beaudoin, who has become separated from *her* party, so if you would be so very kind as to help me to look for her—"

Sir Carsbie obviously considered it a trifle odd that the search for one unchaperoned young lady should have been placed in the hands of a second; but he was more than willing to stroll with Lydia through Vauxhall Gardens, and therefore made no demur to this plan. In point of fact, as he stole surreptitious glances at her exquisite profile and perfectly proportioned figure, it occurred to him forcefully that he might do worse than to benefit from his present opportunity by pressing upon her the suit which he was just

180

about determining to make for her hand. The news concerning an imminent engagement between her and Lord Harlbury had recently reached his ears, and, though he had pooh-poohed the idea of such a match at his clubs, it had been more than a little disagreeable to him to feel that he was generally considered to have been cut out by his lordship.

It was unlike Sir Carsbie, who had reached his middle years, when it was possible for him to contemplate such a step as marriage with entirely dispassionate consideration, to permit himself to be rushed into precipitate action; but he could not but feel that, to a young lady, this was the very kind of romantic setting and occasion that must appeal, and he therefore somewhat unwisely allowed himself to be hurried into taking advantage of it.

Thus it came about that Lydia, walking along rather absently beside him, her mind occupied with quite other matters than her companion's intentions towards her, was suddenly startled to find herself seized about the waist and Sir Carsbie's voice murmuring fervidly into her ear, "I can no longer contain my ardor! Miss Leyland—Lydia—you must allow me to express my feelings toward you!"

With this, he attempted to implant a kiss upon her lips, but Lydia, wresting herself free of his grasp, succeeded in receiving it only as a glancing salute upon her cheek. She gave a gasp, half of indignation, half of amusement, and said in a reproving tone, "*Dear* Sir Carsbie—not in this place, I beg you! Someone may come upon us at any moment!"

"Do you think I care for that?" Sir Carsbie, who had dined at White's with a party of friends, by whom he had been encouraged to imbibe rather freely of the excellent wine procurable there, was a trifle pot-valiant as well, and, once excited to action, was not to be so easily fobbed off. "My dear—*dearest* girl, you must know that you have bowled me out at last—yes, damme, though I am sure the town has said these fifteen years that Carsbie Chant was far too downy ever to become a tenant-for-life!"

This was accompanied by another attempt to implant a kiss

upon Lydia's lips—again, owing to that young lady's artful manoeuvring, an unsuccessful one.

"For heaven's sake, Sir Carsbie," she said, with slight severity, "do give over behaving in this totally *unnecessary* manner!"

"But I am proposing marriage to you, Miss Leyland!"

"Marriage!" Lydia for the first time looked a trifle startled.

"Yes! Marriage, Miss Leyland!" Sir Carsbie reiterated magniloquently, himself as impressed, apparently, by the immense condescension of this statement as he obviously expected her to be. "The fact that you have no fortune," he continued, "that your position in life is such that you could not anticipate that a gentleman holding my position in Society would consider an alliance with you, weighs nothing with me, I assure you! I consider that you will admirably fill that position in the *haut ton* to which marriage with me will raise you."

"But I do not *wish* to marry you, Sir Carsbie!" Lydia said, with more truth than civility—and, having said it, found herself genuinely surprised at the sound of such an immediate negative issuing from her lips, since it had been only that day that she had declared her complete willingness to wed Sir Carsbie or any other gentleman who would relieve her of the necessity of accepting Northover's largesse.

But if her utterance of this statement was surprising to her, to Sir Carsbie it was perfectly staggering.

"Not wish to marry me!" he ejaculated incredulously. "Not wish—! Nonsense, my dear Miss Leyland! You are distraught—you do not know what you say—and this is not, after all, surprising, since you can have had no notion of such an offer's being about to be made to you."

"No, no, of course I had not," Lydia said soothingly, recovering her own poise as Sir Carsbie appeared on the verge of losing his. "But, dear Sir Carsbie, honoured as I must be by your offer, it is definitely my opinion that we should not suit. Besides," she added, candour getting the better of good intentions once more, "I do not think you would *really* care for being married, after all—having chil-

182

dren, I mean, and giving up all your flirts to become a settled sort of man—"

The reference to his amorous conquests somewhat mollified Sir Carsbie; the mention of the production of children offended his sense of the delicacy suitable in a young female upon such an occasion; but by far the chief emotion engendered in his breast by Lydia's speech was a dark suspicion that, in rejecting such an advantageous offer, she must have another even more advantageous in mind.

He tittered suddenly, and said, "Oh, if you are thinking of Harlbury, my dear, you had best put the thought quite out of your head. He will never marry without his mother's approval, and I assure you she has been running about the town these three days telling everyone who will listen to her the most dreadful stories about you—that you have low connexions, and that you positively *entrapped* poor Harlbury by the most shameless manoeuvres. To be sure, she does not go *quite* so far as Lady Gilmour, who has termed you, it has been reported to me, a scheming wench—"

Lydia unexpectedly bestowed a dazzling smile upon him. "How very kind of you to tell me this, Sir Carsbie!" she said cordially. "And how much kinder, even, of you to make an offer for a young lady of such a shocking reputation! I wonder that you could bring yourself to do it!"

"Ah—well—er—" Sir Carsbie looked somewhat taken aback. "Of course *I* didn't believe a word of it," he hastily disclaimed. "Very respectable families, the Leylands—the Tresselts—though they have fallen on bad times—"

"Thank you!" Lydia said. "But *not* on such bad times, I assure you, as to oblige me to marry where I feel no inclination." She added briskly, "And now *do* let us get on with our search for Miss Beaudoin, for I fear we have wasted our time far too long already."

"Wasted—our—time!" This description of the tendering of an offer of marriage from himself to Miss Leyland was too much for Sir Carsbie. He stiffened visibly, drew himself up, and uttered a—"Well!"—of such explosive hauteur that it brought Lydia, who had already taken a step or two along the path, around to gaze at him enquiringly. "Perhaps you do not realise, Miss Leyland," he continued waspishly, "that it is not likely you will soon again find a gentleman of fortune and high position who is willing to overlook certain deplorable facts concerning your situation in life and—if I may say so—a somewhat unseemly levity in your conduct as well—"

"But you are *not* overlooking them, Sir Carsbie," Lydia said reasonably. "Indeed, I cannot conceive why you should wish to marry me at all, since they appear so offensive to you, and I am quite sure that when you have had time to think the whole matter over, you will be very glad indeed that I did not accept you. You *are* a trifle foxed, you know," she added, looking at him critically. "Perhaps, after all, you had better remain here and I shall go on looking for Miss Beaudoin alone, for I certainly cannot be stopping every half minute to engage in an argument with you."

The expression on Sir Carsbie's face had by this time become indicative of such outraged indignation that even Lydia realised that she had said quite enough, and deemed it prudent to slip away without any further discussion. She was obliged to stifle a ripple of laughter as she did so, for the picture of Sir Carsbie standing in all his offended dignity in the middle of the path, with the first of the evening's rockets rising in a great burst of whizzing light behind him, as if in apt symbolism of his mental state, appealed irresistibly to her risibilities.

Not, she told herself ruefully, that she was likely to find it so amusing, when she returned to Green Street and all her problems there, to think that she had whistled Sir Carsbie and the undeniable advantages of an alliance with him down the wind.

But she had no time in which to consider her lack of prudent conduct further, for around the next turn in the path she came upon a pair of familiar figures—Northover and Lady Gilmour, standing together in conversation beside one of the fountains that dotted the gardens. Its graceful cascades, with the falling drops glittering in the light of the coloured lamps above it, made a charming background for

184

Lady Gilmour's diaphanous, spangled gown, but Lydia did not find the tableau before her at all charming. Her eyes narrowed slightly, and she would undoubtedly have gone on, with only the briefest of acknowledgements of the couple's presence, if Lady Gilmour had not halted her by enquiring if she had seen Minna.

"No," said Lydia shortly, looking at Northover so disapprovingly that his lordship grinned and said virtuously, "Don't pull that Friday-face at me, Lydia! *I* didn't slip off to a rendezvous, as you did; *I* came merely to find Miss Beaudoin."

"A rendezvous!" Lydia repeated indignantly. "It was no such thing!"

"It's no use your trying to bamboozle *me*," Northover said cheerfully. "I saw you."

"You *saw* me? *You*? And you—you merely stood there and allowed that abominable little creature to maul me about!"

"I most certainly did," the Viscount admitted shamelessly, his black eyes wickedly alight, "and then retreated in good order. Somehow I scarcely thought you would thank me for interrupting what was obviously a proposal of marriage."

Lady Gilmour, who had been attending with some impatience to this interchange, at this point interrupted sharply. "A proposal of marriage!" she exclaimed. "What—was it Harlbury?"

Lydia, framing a spirited rejoinder to Northover's last speech, checked as she found herself confronted by a pair of icy blue eyes in Lady Gilmour's delicately flushed and very handsome face. Turning her attention to that lady instead, she remarked, with very little attempt to moderate the baldness of the statement by a civil tone, that she did not believe *that* to be an affair that concerned her ladyship.

Lady Gilmour's fan closed with a snap. "My dear Miss Leyland," she said, with a somewhat excessive sweetness, "you will permit me to differ with you. It may do very well in the wilds of America for a female to pursue a *parti* who is all but affianced to another young lady with the same ardour that gentlemen use on the hunting-field; perhaps that is the way in which such matters are arranged there. I am thankful to say I know nothing of that. But—"

She got no further, for Lydia, with a ruthless sweetness that rivalled her own, broke in to remark, "Is that indeed so, ma'am? Then it only goes to show one how mistaken gossip may be, for I am sure if I have heard once since I came to London I have heard a dozen times that my Lord Gilmour was quite on the verge of offering for Lord Aubry's youngest daughter when she was *cut out* by your ladyship."

Northover's shoulders shook slightly—a sight which did nothing to cause the flush on Lady Gilmour's face to abate. Her fan was flirted open again; she said rapidly, "Your manners, Miss Leyland, are deplorable. Let me warn you that your position in Society is not such as to allow you to indulge in such insolence without losing the precarious foothold which you now hold there—and which, I might remind you, you owe entirely to my mother's condescension in taking you up!"

"Oh, yes!" Lydia agreed cordially. "Lady Aimer has been everything that is kind! But do you not think that such a *scheming wench* as I am—I believe that that was the term your ladyship has applied to me?—is sufficiently clever to make her way even without Lady Aimer's kind offices? I have, you see, the advantage of having a respectable reputation, in spite of my *deplorable manners*, so that at least *one* handicap your ladyship was obliged to surmount in your own rise to affluence is quite lacking in my case!"

What response Lady Gilmour might have made to this last truly outrageous speech was not to be known, for Lydia, with a slight curtsey directed impartially at her and Northover, was gone the next moment along the path.

Lady Gilmour, stiff with rage, rounded on the Viscount. "*Oh!*" she exclaimed. "Was there ever a more impertinent, odious—!" Her blue eyes shot fire that rivalled the showering sparks of a rocket descending the summer night skies above them. "And you—!" she ejaculated. "You can *laugh*—!"

"No, no, Trix!" Northover bit his lip, attempting to speak

soothingly, but the situation was too much for his gravity; he gave one gasp and broke into a shout of laughter. "Oh, lord, Trix, I warned you not to cross swords with her!" he said, when he could speak again. "Don't come to dagger-drawing with *me*! Didn't I tell you how it would be?"

**BUT LYDIA, RETURNING HOME TO** Green Street later that evening, was little in the mood to congratulate herself on the successful outcome of her encounter with Lady Gilmour. Harlbury's obvious interest in Miss Pentony, her own refusal of Sir Carsbie, and above everything, the strained, desperate look in Bayard's eyes that she had noted when he had at last returned to the company with Miss Beaudoin to face the icy censure of that young lady's mama—all these combined to cause her to feel that events were fast hastening to a climax, and that something must be done at once to avoid catastrophe.

As if this were not enough, Mrs. Leyland, to whose dressing-room she repaired before retiring to her own chamber that night, was found to be equally on the fidget over her own affairs, and capped the sum of her granddaughter's woes by announcing her intention of going early on the morrow to see Mr. King, it being her firm conviction that, since Lydia had refused Northover's assistance, her only hope now lay in borrowing from a moneylender.

Lydia was notoriously an excellent sleeper, even when her own affairs were not in good train; but it could not be said that she enjoyed peaceful slumbers that night. She tossed and turned, while Northover's sardonic smile, Bayard's haggard face, and Sir Carsbie's eyes starting, affronted, at her, chased one another through her mind; and when she fell asleep at last it was to dream of being cast out from Polite Society, like Eve from the Garden of Eden, by Lady Gilmour in the guise of an avenging angel.

She awoke with only one clear idea in her head—that she must do something, and do it at once. Winch, whom she encountered in the upstairs hall as she was going down to breakfast, informed her that her grandmother was already gone out, and she thought, with a sinking of the heart, that this early excursion could have only one meaning—that Mrs.

Leyland was in truth making good her threat to visit Clarges Street and Mr. King.

She went into the breakfast-parlour, sipped a cup of coffee, and nibbled half-heartedly on a piece of toast. It was while she was engaged in this occupation that she suddenly started up, exclaiming—"Sir Basil!"—in a tone that considerably startled Sidwell, who was just entering the room to enquire if there was anything more she desired.

"'I beg your pardon, miss?" he said, in some disapproval.

"Never mind!" Lydia turned a slightly absent but highly determined face upon him. "Tell me, Sidwell—did my grandmother take the barouche when she went out this morning?"

"No, miss, she did not." Sidwell, who was far from considering the erratic Leylands among the more desirable parties by whom he had been employed, put on his primmest face. "She desired me to fetch a hackney-carriage for her, instead."

Lydia had become acquainted, during her sojourn in London, with the convention which wisely decreed that a lady visiting a gentleman's lodgings should engage one of these anonymous vehicles rather than risk her own carriage's being seen and recognised on such an adventure, and she had a moment's diverting curiosity as to whether Sidwell suspected her grandmother of slipping away to an assignation. But her own affairs were too pressing to allow her to pursue it.

"Good!" she said. "Then will you have the barouche brought round as soon as possible, Sidwell? You may tell my grandmother, if she returns before I do, that I have gone to call upon Sir Basil Rowthorn in Russell Square."

She ran upstairs immediately to change the simple morning-dress she was wearing for a modish promenade gown of primrose craped muslin with sleeves *à la mamelouk*, and to tie a very fetching Italian straw bonnet over her dark curls. Thus attired, she ran down the stairs again to find the barouche waiting at the front door, and, mounting into it at once, ordered the coachman to drive to Russell Square.

It was a sultry morning, threatening rain, but Lydia had no thoughts to spare for the weather; she was fully occupied in considering what she would say to Sir Basil. It had seemed an inspiration of a high order, in the breakfast-parlour in Green Street, to approach her great-uncle frankly with her difficulties and to request his aid before Mr. Michael Pentony should have presented the matter to him in the worst possible light; but by the time she descended from the barouche in Russell Square it had somehow become much less clear to her that she had done the right thing, and she was almost hoping that Sir Basil's butler, when he opened the door to her, would inform her that his master could not, or would not, receive her.

The butler, however—a different man, she noted, from the one who had admitted her on her previous visit—though he looked at her a trifle doubtfully, did nothing of the sort, but invited her instead to wait in a small saloon opening off the hall while he acquainted Sir Basil with her arrival. Lydia, too preoccupied with the importance of her errand to wait quietly, walked up and down the room, inspecting its elegant appointments without the slightest notion of what she was doing, until the butler returned to tell her that Sir Basil would see her. She then followed him up the stairs to the apartment in which she had been received on her first visit to Russell Square, where she found Sir Basil, as on that occasion, seated in a chair beside the long windows with a rug drawn over his knees. He was not alone this time, however, for a very small, red-faced man with a very large head, wearing a shabby, old-fashioned, full-skirted coat and the knee-breeches that had been popular in the last century, was in the act of bowing himself out of the room. He gave Lydia a frank, scrutinising glance, which appeared satisfactory to him, for on concluding it he laid his finger alongside his nose, winked broadly at Sir Basil, and said in a hoarse aside to him, "Ay, guv'nor, she'll do! Knocks 'em all into horse-nails! Lay your blunt on *her*, and you'll have backed the right filly this time!"

He then favoured Lydia with a bobbing bow, advised her

not to try to cut any wheedles with the guv'nor, since he still knew one point more than the devil, and departed, leaving Lydia staring at Sir Basil in considerable astonishment.

"Well, well—sit down, sit down!" Sir Basil said testily. "Have you never seen a dwarf before?"

"Not in a drawing-room," Lydia replied truthfully, recalling Mr. Peeke's ambiguous reference to the odd circle of friends Sir Basil enjoyed.

"Well, you've seen one now," Sir Basil said, summarily dismissing the subject and going on at once to more important matters. "Now then, what do you want—eh? I thought I'd told you and that brother of yours I'd let you know if I cared to see either one of you in this house."

Lydia, who had seated herself in the chair drawn up before him in the window, perversely found her spirits reviving under this Turkish treatment.

"You have a very good memory, sir," she said composedly, "for that is exactly what you did say. However, as it happens—"

"Of course I have a good memory! Why shouldn't I have a good memory? I ain't in my dotage yet!" Sir Basil interrupted, wrathfully. "Don't put on airs to be interesting with *me*, miss! I asked you what you wanted, and you can give me a plain answer, without any skimble-skamble roundaboutation, or you can take yourself off, and that's all there is about it!"

"Oh, very well," said Lydia, unperturbed. "I *had* thought we might have enjoyed an agreeable quarter hour of conversation first, but if that seems *totally* redundant to you, I shall come to the point at once." She drew a breath. "I want four thousand pounds—that is, not *personally*, but for Grandmama—and I want you to decide at once that you will make your will to divide your fortune between Bayard and Mr. Pentony. Well, you *must* do so one day," she went on hastily, seeing the choleric colour rising in Sir Basil's face—"that is, decide to make your will, I mean—and it had as well be now, for I daresay it would make all the difference to that *odious* Lady Gilmour if she knew Bayard was to inherit at least half your fortune, and then he may marry Miss Beaudoin, after all—"

She halted, observing that Sir Basil was by this time looking quite alarmingly red.

"Are you well, sir?" she enquired solicitously, after a moment.

"Well! How should I be well," Sir Basil demanded, in almost apoplectic ire, "when a slip of a minx sits there telling me what I must and must not do? Have you run mad, girl?"

"No, I do not *think* so," Lydia said cautiously. "But I am so put about that I daresay I am behaving a little strangely. It *did* seem to me, though, that it would be much the better plan to come directly to you with the matter, rather than allowing you to learn of it from Mr. Pentony."

Sir Basil's brows shot up. "Pentony?" he barked. "What's Michael to do with it?"

"Well, nothing at all, actually—though he *did* introduce Grandmama to Mrs. Collingworth, and it was at her house that Grandmama lost four thousand pounds at play. But you *must* know that he is very desirous of inheriting your fortune, and will do everything in his power to accomplish that—"

"Including," Sir Basil interpolated grimly, "bribing my servants!"

Lydia halted, looking at him in surprise. "Oh! Do you know about *that*?" she enquired.

A tiny, almost inward smile appeared upon Sir Basil's face, erasing not a jot of its grimness.

"Ay, I know it!" he said. "I told you, I ain't in my dotage yet! Damned rascally set of fellows, the servants you come by these days, ready to sell you to the devil if he'll but take the trouble to grease their fists—but they don't pull the wool over *my* eyes!" He nodded with an appearance of some satisfaction, and after a moment went on, in the same vindictive tone, "And so Michael was behind that, too—your grandmother getting into the hands of those sharps! Well, that's one more point against him, but it don't make a ha'porth of odds now, for he queered his game with me the day I

193

found him going behind my back with my own servants. Damme, that brother of yours may be a soft 'un, but he's a gentleman, at any rate—not a curst sneaksby!"

Lydia stared at him, her brain reeling a little under the import of the words he had just uttered.

"But—but—do you mean," she managed to say at last, "that you have decided *not* to make Mr. Pentony your heir?"

"Why should I make him my heir?" Sir Basil demanded irascibly. "He's a—a twiddle-poop! Coming around here all these years, turning me up sweet like a damned simpering macaroni-merchant! *He* knew I knew what he was about, for he ain't bacon-brained, but what he didn't know was that he might have carried the business off if he hadn't tried to run sly with me as well. Well, he caught cold at that! Coggins is right—I still know a point or two more than the devil!"

Lydia, who could scarcely believe the good fortune that seemed to be tumbling into her—or, at least, Bayard's—lap, said in a rather stunned voice, "But, dear Uncle Basil, do you mean, then, that you will leave your fortune to *Bayard*?"

"Yes, I do," snapped Sir Basil. "Or, at any rate, I shall if he don't put me off it by giving me reason to think as ill of him as I do of Michael, for you'd have to say I had windmills in my head if I was fool enough to cut Michael out for another good-for-nothing Jack Straw as bad as he is. But if your young brother don't queer himself by running off to Gretna with some silly chit, or getting caught fuzzing the cards, or doing any of the other ramshackle things a man can ruin his chances by in the *ton*, I'll have him in here next week and make things all right and tight, as soon as I've settled with Northover about Great Hayland."

"Great Hayland!" Lydia exclaimed, neglecting, in her astonishment at this new matter introduced at the conclusion of her great-uncle's speech, to assure him that it was totally unlikely that Bayard would commit any of the social solecisms against which he had so strongly inveighed. "Good gracious, do you mean—?"

"Well, naturally!" Sir Basil said, with some acerbity. "It's the family seat—ain't it? Letty was forever after me to buy it back for her, but while old Northover was alive I wouldn't touch it, for the old snudge held out for twice what it was worth. This present man, though, wants nothing better than to be rid of it, and he's agreed to a fair price—"

"So *that* was what he meant!" Lydia exclaimed, recalling Northover's cryptic words to her implying that there was no need for her to despair over Sir Basil's intentions towards her family. Her indignation kindled suddenly. "Well, he *might* have told me," she said, "instead of allowing me to believe—"

She halted abruptly, seeing that Sir Basil was looking at her keenly.

"What's this?" he demanded. "Did Northover tell you of the business, then?"

"No, he did not," Lydia said resentfully, "though he *knew* what straits I was in."

"Humph! Didn't think he would," Sir Basil said, with satisfaction. "Asked him to keep it close till it was settled. Not that I had any reason to expect he'd let it out to you. Didn't know he was that particular a friend of yours."

"He isn't," Lydia said, with dignity. "In fact, I *practically* loathe him."

"Not much use in that," said Sir Basil unfeelingly. "*He* won't care what a chit like you thinks of him. You ain't in his line, by all *I've* heard of him." He added abruptly, "You've caught Harlbury on your hook, though, I hear. Has he made you an offer?"

"No!" said Lydia unequivocally.

"Well, you'll have better luck, I don't doubt, when it comes out what I mean to do for you," said Sir Basil, with his usual lack of civility. "Yes, yes, throw a good dowry into the balance and you'll go off like a shot, for you're a fetching piece, for all your damned queer manners. But what about that brother of yours—eh?" he went on. "You were saying *he* had it in mind to get himself riveted. Who is the gal?

195

Is she a lady? Or is she the sort of high-flyer a young ram-stam's as like as not to dangle after, and come to perdition on the head of it?"

Lydia said, rallying to do her best for Bayard, "By no means, sir! Miss Beaudoin moves in the first circles of Society. She is the daughter, by her first marriage, of the Viscountess Gilmour, and is making her come-out this Season. She and Bayard are very much in love indeed, but I must tell you that Lady Gilmour has set herself strongly against the match. It is not, I believe, that she has objections to Bayard personally, but his lack of fortune—"

"Well, she sounds like a sensible woman," Sir Basil said coolly, "so it's Lombard Street to a China orange she'll change her tune in a hurry when she learns what I have in mind to do for young Leyland. *Leyland-Rowthorn*, I should say, for the name goes with the bargain, you know!" He rubbed his hands together gleefully. "Ay, we'll have the notice in the *Gazette* and the *Morning Post*," he said, "and the wedding at St. George's in Hanover Square—everything in the first style! And I mean to bring Great Hayland up to what it was in your great-aunt's day—"

Lydia could only sit nodding in stunned assent as Sir Basil unfolded his plans for Bayard's future, her one wish being that Bayard himself were with her to hear them as well. She was on tenterhooks to return to Green Street so that she might acquaint him with his good fortune, and made not the slightest objection when Sir Basil, abruptly winding his peroration to a close, informed her baldly that he had had quite enough of her company and that she might go.

"You'll be hearing from Peeke," he said as she rose, trying to gather the proper words in which to thank him. "No need for you to come around here again, interfering in matters that are none of your concern! Told you more than I intended already, and I daresay it's too much to expect you to keep it to yourself!"

"Well, sir," Lydia said, with proper meekness, "you can scarcely expect me not to tell Bayard—though I shall *endeavour* not to, if you really wish it."

196

"You had better tell him, instead, to take care to conduct himself like a gentleman, or he'll find he's whistled *his* chances for a fortune down the wind," Sir Basil said testily. "As for that grandmother of yours—I expect I shall have to tow her off Point Non-Plus, since it was Michael who lured her into the business. But she needn't think I'll do it without ringing a peal over her! I cured Letty of gaming, and I daresay I shall be able to do the same for her, for I won't have her playing wily beguiled with *my* brass after I've gone to roost! And now go away, go away!" he concluded, violently ringing the hand-bell that stood on the table beside him. "I've no more time to spare for you this morning! Beal! Beal! Where is the fellow?"

The butler arrived almost immediately, and in another moment Lydia found herself being ushered out of the room and down the stairs to the door.

The return journey to Green Street was accomplished perfectly prosaically in the Leyland barouche, but if Lydia had found this vehicle suddenly transformed into a golden coach, and herself set down in it in company with a beaming fairy godmother, the circumstance would scarcely have appeared strange to her. Her brief interview with Sir Basil had indeed wrought such a total change in her family's prospects that she believed no further transformations, however magical, would have had the power to astonish her. All her anxieties had been laid to rest: she need no longer fear Mr. Pentony's disclosure of her grandmother's debts to Sir Basil, or the dire consequences of those debts' remaining unpaid, and that Lady Gilmour would soon be brought to abandon her opposition to her daughter's marriage to Bayard, if he were to become heir to one of the largest fortunes in the kingdom, she had not the slightest doubt.

When the barouche arrived in Green Street she descended from it quickly and entered the house, enquiring of Sidwell, the moment she was inside the door, where her brother might be found.

"Mr. Leyland is not in the house, miss," the butler informed her.

"Not—?" Something in Sidwell's face, which bore an expression nicely balanced between the desire to impart some portentous piece of news and the feeling that it was beneath his dignity to concern himself with the eccentric starts of his employers, caught Lydia's attention. "Has he gone out, then?"

"Yes, miss."

"Did he say where?"

"No, miss." The desire to communicate conquered Sidwell's severe reserve; he went on, with a carefully wooden countenance, "He *was*, however, carrying a cloak-bag, so that I can only assume he was contemplating an overnight stay."

He paused, observing with some satisfaction the effect that his words had had upon Miss Leyland. She was gazing at him with obvious astonishment, not unmixed with apprehension. But, seeing his eyes fixed upon her, she managed to control her countenance and said, with a fair attempt at sang-froid, "Oh, yes—I believe he did mention something about going out of town. Has my grandmother returned yet, Sidwell?"

"No, miss, she has not," said Sidwell, looking disappointed at Lydia's quick recover, which promised nothing to gratify his curiosity.

She nodded dismissal to him and mounted the stairs with the calm air of a young lady who had no other thought in mind but to retire to her own chamber to remove her hat and gloves. But once upstairs she called immediately for Winch and, when that austere handmaiden appeared, enquired of her in considerable agitation if she knew when Bayard had left the house and where he had gone.

"*That* I don't know, miss," Winch replied, folding her arms with the resigned air of one whose patience was about to be tried yet again by the vagaries of the young master's behaviour, "for I have been out of the house myself, on an errand for Madam. But he was here when I left an hour ago, if that's of any help to you." She looked forebodingly

198

into Lydia's flushed countenance and enquired, "What is it now?"

"I don't *know*," Lydia said, "but Sidwell told me he went out carrying a cloak-bag."

Her troubled blue eyes met Winch's grey ones, and a mutual suspicion, communicating itself between them, was given voice by Winch.

"Merciful heavens, Miss Lydia," she said hollowly, "he's gone and run off with that Miss Beaudoin!"

Lydia winced. From the moment she had first heard from Sidwell of Bayard's having gone out carrying a cloak-bag, that horrid idea had been haunting her own mind, but, with her conviction of what such a scandalous action on his part would do to jeopardise what only half an hour before had appeared the certainty of his becoming Sir Basil's heir, she had not dared to acknowledge it.

She said hastily to Winch, "No, no, you must be mistaken! There is some other explanation, I am sure! He has received an invitation from one of his friends to go into the country, and has merely forgotten to mention it."

Winch shook her head, unconvinced. "I knew how it would be!" she said, with the gloomy satisfaction of a prophetess whose dire foretellings have at last been proved correct. "Ever since Madam took this notion into her head to come to London, I knew no good would come of it! He's gone off to Gretna Green with Miss Beaudoin, as sure as check, Miss Lydia, for when a young man's as deep in love as he is he'll never give a thought to consequences."

"Nonsense!" said Lydia, with a certainty she was far from feeling. "I am sure he would never do anything so improper, nor would Miss Beaudoin. She has been *very* carefully brought up, you know!"

"So was Madam, but that didn't stop *her* from running off with the Major," Winch said incontrovertibly. "You wait till *your* time comes, Miss Lydia, and you'll know how it is when you're to be parted forever from the creetur you adore."

"Oh, *do* give over talking such fustian, Winch!" Lydia said crossly. She pressed one hand to her forehead, as if she could somehow succeed in this way in quieting the turmoil of anxiety behind it. "He must have left *some* word if he has indeed gone off on such a journey, for he would know he could never be absent for so many days without our scouring the country to find him!"

She broke off abruptly, remembering the habit she and Bayard had long had of scribbling notes and leaving them in the other's room when obliged to go off somewhere in the other's absence. Parting from Winch without ceremony, she went swiftly down the hall and entered her own bedchamber. A quick glance around it showed her the object she was seeking—a sealed and folded sheet of notepaper laid upon her dressing-table. She pounced upon it and tore it open.

Lyddy, love, the firm black letters covering the page read, *this is a despicable thing to do to you and Grandmama, but you must see, when I tell you all, that there is no other way. Lady G.'s intention was to take Minna to Scarborough tomorrow, and, if I succeeded in following her there, to Paris. So my dear, brave girl has consented to go with me to America, where we shall contrive to be married and then go to live at Belmaison. I never thought, Lyddy, that we two should part in such a way, without so much as a word of farewell between us, but there is no help for it, my dear, for I know you too well to think you would not try to stop me if you knew what I was about.*

But when you read this I shall be on my way to Bristol with Minna, and it will be too late for you to throw a rub in our way. This news, of course, is strictly for your eyes alone. Lady G., I apprehend, will believe us gone to Gretna when Minna is missed, and I do not think you will be so unkind either to me or to Minna as to disabuse her mind of this idea until it may reasonably be expected that we have taken ship for America.

One last word, Lyddy, my own. Don't marry Harlbury. You do not love him, and I should not like to think of your missing forever what Minna and I have. Believe me, it is well worth waiting for. B.

By the time she had come to the conclusion of this letter, Lydia's face was as white as the paper on which it was written. She found herself, for the moment, quite unable to put together two coherent thoughts: the one dire realisation drumming desperately through her head was that, by this single rash act, Bayard was irrevocably throwing away all hope of inheriting Sir Basil's fortune. The scandal that such an elopement must give rise to would prevent his ever being able to take that place in Society to which Sir Basil vicariously aspired, and it was not to be expected that that irascible gentleman, once it reached his ears, would adhere to his plan of making him his heir.

And the most damnable part of the whole affair was that it was only by an hour, or even less, that Bayard had missed his good fortune. No doubt, Lydia thought, he and Minna were even now seated in a post-chaise rattling along a road not a dozen miles from London, and she was ready to scream with frustration at the realisation that, were she able now to converse with him only for five minutes, he would certainly agree to abandon the projected elopement and allow his and Minna's affairs to follow the socially accepted course of a conventional marriage, with parental approval, in the full light of public knowledge.

Standing with the note crumpled in her hand, her mind grappling hopelessly with the problem of how she might succeed in recalling Bayard from his mad venture, she did not hear Winch approach the door behind her, and it was only when that long-suffering handmaiden spoke her name that she whirled about.

"Yes? What is it, Winch?"

"Lord Harlbury," Winch said succinctly, her eyes upon the paper in Lydia's hand. "He's below, and wishful to see you, Sidwell says. Is that from Mr. Bayard, Miss Lydia?"

"Yes—no!" Lydia placed the note hastily in a drawer of her dressing-table and looked distractedly at Winch. "I cannot see Lord Harlbury now!" she said. "Tell him—"

201

She halted, struck by a sudden thought. Harlbury, she knew—though he had no desire to ape either the fashions or the morals of the Corinthian set—had one thing in common with those dashing blades: he was a first-rate whip, who took justifiable pride in the beautiful team of matched chestnuts he was accustomed to drive. Lydia, still under the influence of that sudden inspiration, flew to the window, which overlooked the street, and peered down. As she had hoped, she was rewarded by the sight of his lordship's lightly sprung curricle standing before the house, with a groom at the heads of his team of glossy chestnuts.

"Oh, famous!" she exclaimed.

She turned back impetuously into the room, snatched up the gloves she had thrown upon her dressing-table, hastily retied her bonnet-strings before the mirror, and moved quickly towards the door, only to find that aperture blocked by Winch's angular figure.

"And what," enquired Miss Winch, ominously folding her arms, "do you think you are up to *now*, Miss Lydia?"

"Oh, Winch, *do* stand aside!" Lydia said, almost dancing with impatience. "I am going after Bayard, of course!"

"After Mr. Bayard! And how do you know where he may be? And you'll *not* be starting a journey in *that* dress, with never so much as a nightgown put up in a portmanteau, and with no one to escort you—*Miss Lydia!*"

Winch's voice rose as Lydia determinedly thrust her aside and emerged into the hall, but Lydia was already flying down the stairs.

"Never mind, Winch! I shall have Lord Harlbury to escort me!" she called back; and thereupon vanished from sight into the drawing-room below.

**LORD HARLBURY, FINDING HIMSELF** confronted by a very flushed and eager young lady, already attired for the outdoors and demanding to know if he would instantly drive her out of town in pursuit of her brother, had for a moment the startled conviction that Miss Lydia Leyland had finally taken leave of her senses. No less distressing reason, he felt, could account for such very odd behavior, and he was wondering in some alarm how he might get Sidwell into the room and, through him, acquaint Mrs. Leyland or some female servant with the necessity of her coming immediately to assist the young lady, when Lydia observed the distraught expression upon his face and gave vent to a rueful chuckle.

"Oh, dear! I daresay you think I have run quite mad!" she said. "But indeed I have not; it is only that there is such desperate need for haste that I cannot spare the time to tell you properly what I am about! But will you not at least humour me sufficiently to take me for a drive in your curricle in the direction I wish to go, while I tell you exactly what I have in mind? And then, if you do not wish to oblige me by going further, you may bring me back here—only I do not think that you will. *Nobody* could be so hardhearted as *that!*"

His lordship looked down indecisively into Lydia's pleading face. He was a chivalrous young man, and it would go sorely against the pluck with him, he felt, to deny such an urgent request from so charming a young lady—but at the same time he was a sensible man as well, and he was damned, he told himself firmly, if he was going to embroil himself in such a harebrained business as this promised to be.

He was about to open his mouth to utter a kind but decisive negative when Lydia, on whom the growing look of resolution upon his face had not been lost, abruptly abandoned her cajoling air and took command.

"Harlbury," she said with perfect civility, but with an ominous ring of determination in her voice, "I warn you that you had best not say *No* to me! If you do, I shall drive those chestnuts of yours myself—oh, yes! I am quite capable of handling a team!—for I *must* come up with Bayard before he has utterly ruined his entire future. Now—you may come with me or not, as you choose, but *I* am going after Bayard!"

With these words she turned and walked towards the door. Harlbury, who by this time knew enough of Miss Leyland to realise that she was perfectly capable of carrying out her threat, had no choice but to follow her, and emerged, remonstrating, into the street behind her, greatly to the interest of Sidwell and his own groom.

"For heaven's sake, Miss Leyland," he urged her in a low voice, desperately trying to keep up the appearance that he was conducting a perfectly normal conversation with her, "do let us return to the house and discuss the matter there! We cannot do so in the street!"

"No!" said Lydia obdurately. She stood beside the curricle, her eyes running rapidly and approvingly over the chestnuts. "There is no time, my lord. Every minute we waste here lessens our chances of overtaking him in time. Now—do you intend to drive, or shall I take the ribbons myself?"

Harlbury cast an anguished glance at his gaping groom and closed his eyes for a moment, as if in prayer.

"Very well," he capitulated, handing her up into the curricle and mounting beside her. He took the reins from his groom and said to him, with a praiseworthy attempt at achieving a casual tone, "I shan't need you, Hemlow. You may walk back to Harlbury House."

"Very good, sir."

The man touched his hat and stepped back from the curricle as his master gave the horses the office to start. As the curricle rolled off down the street, Lydia said, "Bayard has set out for Bristol, so that is the road that we must take. I daresay you will know the way?" She added approvingly, "That was very clever of you to dismiss your groom. The fewer people who are aware of the matter the better it will be, for you know how easily gossip spreads."

"My dear Miss Leyland," Harlbury said, in a voice that, for him, was unwontedly stern, "the reason I have dismissed my groom is so that we may discuss this matter in privacy before I set you down again at your own door. Surely you cannot believe that I am going to drive with you to Bristol in an open carriage, without a chaperon, and without our having informed anyone of our intention! I have not been able to gather exactly why your brother has gone off to Bristol, but certainly, if it is essential that someone pursue him, *you* are not the proper person to whom the matter should be entrusted!"

Lydia sighed. "Oh, dear!" she said. "I daresay I shall have to tell you the whole story. But you must solemnly swear, Harlbury, before I do, that you will not divulge it to *anyone!*"

"I see no reason," his lordship said austerely, "why you should believe I would violate any confidence you may choose to entrust to me, Miss Leyland."

"*That*," Lydia pointed out to him, "is *not* solemnly swearing, Harlbury."

"Yes, but, my dear Miss—"

"Oh, *do* stop saying, 'My dear Miss Leyland!' " Lydia said. "You *know* you are as cross as crabs with me, and would like nothing better than to tell me to go to the devil!"

"No, indeed!" Harlbury said, shocked.

"Then why won't you swear?"

His lordship gave up. "Very well, I swear it," he said resignedly. "But we shall *not* go to Bristol!"

"Well, not the *whole* way, certainly," Lydia agreed, mollified, "for I should not think that will be at all necessary. I am quite sure, you see, that Bayard has no money to spare, and so has hired only a pair of horses. And he cannot have had more than an hour's start of us, and perhaps not nearly so much as that, so that it is entirely likely, if you spring your horses, that we shall be able to come up with him before he has got anywhere near to Bristol."

"And why," enquired his lordship, "is it so imperative for you to bring him back, Miss Leyland?"

"Because he is eloping with Miss Beaudoin—Oh! *Do* look what you are about!" she broke off to say severely, as Harlbury started so violently at this announcement that he jobbed at his leaders' sensitive mouths. "What a cow-handed thing to do!"

"I beg your pardon!" his lordship said stiffly. "But to hear such a shocking piece of news—! How is it possible! Miss Beaudoin! I should not have thought it of her!"

"Well, she is in love with him, you see," Lydia explained, "and Lady Gilmour is planning to take her to Scarborough tomorrow, and then to Paris, if necessary, to separate her from Bayard. So of course they were driven to do something desperate—only I have been to call upon Sir Basil Rowthorn this morning, and have discovered that it is his intention to make Bayard his heir, so that there is no need for them to elope, after all. In fact, if they succeed in doing so it will spoil everything, for all depends upon Bayard's being accepted in the first circles of Society—which he *never* will be, of course, if he does anything so ramshackle as running off to America with Miss Beaudoin."

She paused for breath, and Harlbury, who was looking rather dazed, said, "Good God, if this is true—"

"Of course it is true!" Lydia said indignantly. "Why should I lie to you about it? And that is why I *must* stop Bayard before he has got clean away—and if you can think of any other way to do so than what I am doing at this moment, I shall be very much obliged to you if you will tell me of it!"

But to this request his lordship had no answer. It was perfectly clear, as Lydia had said, that if the runaways were to be overtaken before they had irretrievably committed themselves to their reckless scheme, the utmost haste was necessary. Even if they were not able to engage passage immediately on a vessel leaving for America—and Harlbury had no way of knowing that a stroke of good fortune might not allow them to do just that—it was obvious that, once they had reached Bristol, they might easily manage to evade pursuit in that populous port until their joint disappearance had become one of the scandalous *on-dits* of the town and it was too late to salvage the reputation of either.

The situation therefore presented his lordship with a truly dreadful dilemma. The reputations of two young ladies, it seemed, lay in his hands, and it appeared impossible that, whatever decision he now made, both could emerge scatheless. If he acceded to Lydia's request that he pursue the fleeing couple, he was exposing her to the censure of her acquaintance, should any of them come to learn of this most unorthodox journey. On the other hand, if he refused it, Miss Beaudoin would most certainly be ruined.

A very short period of earnest cogitation was sufficient to convince his lordship that the latter alternative presented by far the darker consequence. If he were able to come up quickly with the young couple, he told himself, they might all return to London together that same day with reasonable propriety, whereas, if he turned back now, there could be no hope of rescuing Miss Beaudoin from the consequences of her romantic folly.

With great misgiving, therefore, he informed Lydia that he would do his best to overtake the fleeing pair—a statement which caused her to remark handsomely that she had never really doubted that he would stand buff.

Now that agreement had been reached on the course to be followed, Harlbury lost no time in directing his curricle out of town by way of Knightsbridge and Hammersmith, and was soon able to let his team out on the open road. Lydia, whose spirits had risen quite to their accustomed buoyancy as soon as she was assured that there was now a reasonable hope that they might overtake Bayard and Miss Beaudoin within the next several hours, at first occupied herself with questioning Harlbury as to the roads and towns that lay before them, with which she was but imperfectly acquainted, having passed this way only once, on her journey from Bristol to London on first arriving in England. But she soon realised that if she conversed with her companion

207

it must be to the detriment of his handling of his team, and accordingly fell accommodatingly silent. She was able to see, at any rate, that his lordship was now quite as anxious as she was to come up quickly with the eloping pair, and she determined to leave in his hands the necessary enquiries at turnpikes and posting-houses along the way.

Harlbury did not halt to change horses at Hounslow, declaring that his chestnuts were good for two stages, but at the Crown Inn at Slough, where he turned in to have a fresh team put-to, they came upon definite news of the runaways. An ostler, his memory jogged by a handsome *douceur* slipped into his hand, clearly recollected that a chaise-and-pair containing a young gentleman and a young lady had come through not half an hour before, and the description he gave of the pair left no doubt in Lydia's mind that they had indeed been Bayard and Miss Beaudoin. Moreover, the ostler informed them, the young gentleman had been in something of a fret, one of his horses having pulled up dead lame a few miles before Slough, and the chaise consequently having been obliged to come halting into the Crown at a snail's pace.

Lydia could scarcely wait until they were back on the road again to express her jubilation.

"Could anything be more fortunate!" she exclaimed. "We are certain now to come up with them at least not long after they pass through Reading. And then we may all return quite comfortably to London, with no one the wiser for what has occurred except Lady Gilmour. And perhaps even she need not know, if Minna was prudent enough to make some excuse to her that would account for her being gone from home the whole day, so that she and Bayard might be farther on their road before any alarm was raised."

Harlbury, whose wishes in this regard most emphatically coincided with Lydia's, said that he earnestly hoped she might prove to be correct in this assumption. He was beginning, however, to be concerned on another account. The sultriness of the weather was increasing as the afternoon

208

advanced, and ahead of them the western sky was darkening ominously. It was probable, he thought, that they might be driving into a storm, and, though this was a matter of little concern to him personally, the thought of driving a young lady, attired in a thin dress and a modish straw bonnet, through a pelting rain in an open carriage was not one which he could face with equanimity.

He held his peace, however, hoping that his forecast of the weather might prove incorrect, until, as they were approaching the outskirts of Reading, a rumble of thunder and the pattering down upon their heads of a few widely spaced drops of rain alarmed him in earnest. He turned to Lydia.

"I fear," he observed, "that we are in for a storm, Miss Leyland."

Lydia cocked an eye aloft at the sky. "I daresay you are right," she agreed, with composure. "Must we change horses here? I do not like to take the time, now that we must be so close upon them, but it appears to me that this team is flagging, and it may save time in the long run if we have a fresh one put-to here."

Harlbury glanced over at her, a trifle nonplussed. "Yes, but—my dear Miss Leyland," he said, "you will not like to be driven through a storm in an open carriage!"

"Pooh!" said Lydia. "As if I should care for that when Bayard's whole future is at stake!"

Harlbury shook his head disapprovingly. "I have been thinking," he said, "that it would be best for me to leave you at the George here in Reading while I go on alone. If it should come on to rain hard—"

Lydia gave him an astonished glance. "Leave me behind!" she said. "You must be all about in your head, Harlbury! What does a wetting signify in such a case? I daresay you have a rug that I can throw over me—"

She was interrupted by a crash of thunder and a sudden quickening of the rain, which began to pelt down now in good earnest. They were by this time just entering Reading

209

on the London Road, and as they progressed farther, along New Street, the traffic thickened, obliging Harlbury to give all his attention to his team. He was still determined, in spite of Lydia's objections, not to continue on in the storm, which gave every promise of becoming a severe one; but, as events transpired, the decision was very shortly taken out of both his and Lydia's hands.

For as he was threading his way skilfully between an over-burdened wagon and a gig being driven by a dashing-looking young man in a sporting neckcloth, a sudden brilliant display of lightning, followed by a terrific thunderclap, caused the bay mare drawing the gig to rear up between the shafts in terror, overturning the gig directly in the path of the curricle. There was a moment of complete pandemonium, full of plunging horses, startled curses, and colliding vehicles; then, as Lydia clung to the madly rocking curricle, it went over abruptly with a splintering shock and she was flung out into the road.

When she came to herself she was lying on a sofa in what appeared to be an inn parlour, inhaling the pungent odour of the burnt feathers that were being waved under her nose by a very stout female in a mobcap. Dazedly, as her eyes blinked open, she saw Harlbury distractedly pacing the room, his coat darkened with damp and his wet hair clinging in disordered dark locks to his brow. He was insisting that a surgeon be fetched at once, to which the stout female responded soothingly that he need not put himself into a fret, for his lady wife was coming round very nicely now.

"She is not my—" Harlbury began, still in that half-distracted voice; and then, suddenly observing Lydia's now sapient and rather quelling gaze fixed upon him, he swallowed visibly, stopped short, and said hastily, "Yes, yes, I see that she is recovering. My dear Mi—" Lydia's minatory eye again halted him, and he continued awkwardly, "My dear *Lydia*, how do you feel? Are you in pain? Only lie still, pray; I shall have a surgeon called to you at once."

"Nonsense!" said Lydia, endeavouring to raise herself

from the cushions against which she was reclining, but sinking back upon them immediately, overcome by a wave of giddiness. "I shall be all right in a *very* few minutes," she said firmly, but with tightly shut eyes, as she strove to steady her swimming senses.

"You may have broken something!" Harlbury said anxiously. "And you have certainly sustained a dreadful shock! Good God, when I saw you lying there on the paving-stones, I made certain that you were dead!"

Lydia opened her eyes cautiously, found that the walls of the room had become reassuringly steady after the disconcerting waltz they had been performing a few moments before, and said, "Pray do not go off into any high flights! Do you think I have never been overturned before?" She managed a little laugh. "Don't look so frightened! I am quite sure that nothing is broken. What is more to the point—is your curricle damaged?"

"Yes," said Harlbury. "But *that* is quite unimportant—"

"Unimportant!" Lydia shot up again from her recumbent position, but was once more obliged to own herself vanquished and lie back against the cushions. She went on, again with tightly shut eyes, "It is *not* unimportant; it is the most important thing of all! You must hire some other vehicle at once. I am sure to be better in a few minutes, and then we can be on our way again."

But to this scheme Mrs. Yarden, the landlady—for such, it appeared, the stout female was—added a negative as shocked and decided as his lordship's. It would be madness, she averred, for Madam to think of resuming her journey that day. Betty would have the best bedchamber ready for her in a trice, and when she had taken off her wet clothes and laid herself down on the bed there with a handkerchief soaked with lavender water on her forehead, and had swallowed a few drops of laudanum to compose her nerves, she might later on fancy a little Cressy soup and a bit of the chicken that was roasting in the kitchen at that very moment.

"And then in the morning, *after* you've had a good night's

211

sleep, you may be fit to go on again," she said severely. "But jauntering about the country after a nasty accident like that is something *I* wouldn't wish to have it on *my* conscience to let you do, and I'll be bound your husband feels the same!"

Harlbury, meeting her expectant gaze, said hastily that he quite agreed with her, and, waiting for no further authorisation, she thereupon bustled out of the room to hasten the preparation of the best bedchamber, leaving Harlbury to confront Lydia with a harassed frown upon his face.

"Good God, what a dreadful situation, Miss Leyland!" he said, running a hand distractedly through his already dishevelled locks. "I cannot think what had best be done! You *must* remain here—but since that woman obviously believes that you are—that is, that I am—in short, that we are married—"

An irrepressible gurgle of laughter escaped Lydia. "Oh dear, Harlbury, *don't* look so dismal!" she begged. "It does not matter what she believes, for I have no intention of remaining here."

"That," said his lordship, with unwonted asperity, "is nonsense! You are scarcely able to lift your head from the pillow; you are undoubtedly suffering from severe bruises, if no worse injury has occurred; and it is raining torrents outside! If you believe that, under such circumstances, I shall *allow* you to go on, you are quite beside the bridge, I assure you! I should be worthy of being clapped into Bedlam if I permitted such a thing!"

Lydia lay blinking at him in some surprise. "Well, you *are* coming along, Harlbury!" she said approvingly. "I have never heard you speak in *this* vein before! If you will only use that tone to your mama, I should not at all wonder if your difficulties with her would come to an end." She raised herself as she spoke to a sitting position and cautiously lowered her feet to the floor. "But I *must* go on, nonetheless," she said. "You must see that, Harlbury! Under ordinary circumstances it might be different—but these are not ordinary circumstances."

212

She passed her hand in a rather dazed fashion over her forehead, looking so pale as she did so that Harlbury was constrained to move forward quickly and support her in his arms, lowering her gently to the cushions once more.

"There! You see!" he exclaimed anxiously. "You are not fit to go on!"

It was at that precise instant that the parlour door opened and Mrs. Leyland, her dress soaked with rain and her fashionably plumed bonnet drooping horribly over one eye, surged into the room, closely followed by Lord Northover.

IN ORDER TO ACCOUNT FOR THE
sudden appearance of the Viscount
and Mrs. Leyland in Reading at
this point, it is necessary to turn
to Green Street in the period immediately following Lydia's departure
from it in Harlbury's curricle.

Scarcely half an hour had passed after the curricle had disappeared
from before the front door when Mrs. Leyland, in a hackney-carriage, arrived there and, entering the house, was
met by Winch, who confronted her with a face of doom and
urgently requested the favour of a few minutes' conversation
with her.

"Why, whatever is the matter?" Mrs. Leyland demanded,
drawing off her gloves as she stepped into the small saloon
just off the hall. "You look as if you had seen a ghost!"

"Oh, it's far worse than that, Madam!" Winch said, tearfully. "Oh, Madam, that we should live to see this day!
There's Mr. Bayard run off with Miss Beaudoin, and Miss
Lydia gone after him in Lord Harlbury's curricle, for all the
world like she was a brass-faced lightskirt instead of a young
lady of quality!"

Mrs. Leyland gazed at her elderly handmaiden with an
expression of amazement, not unmixed with strong disapproval, upon her face.

"Winch," she pronounced awfully, after a moment's consideration, "you are drunk!"

Winch gasped. "Drunk! No, you daren't say such a thing
of me, Madam—not for your life! As if you ever knew me
to do such a thing, in all the years I've been in your service!"
Her indignation at this unfounded accusation was so strong
that for a moment she appeared likely to be drawn off from
her original topic, but she mastered herself with an effort
and, taking a folded sheet of paper from her pocket, thrust
it upon her mistress. "If you don't choose to believe my
word, Madam," she said, with dignity, "perhaps *this* will

give you reason to think otherwise. I have not read it myself, being as I extracted it unbeknownst to her from a drawer of Miss Lydia's dressing-table, but if I'm not sadly out it's from Mr. Bayard, telling her all he intends to do."

Mrs. Leyland, her brows still drawn together in a frown, received the letter and, unfolding it, rapidly perused its single page. As she did so, Winch saw a look of horror appear upon her face, and nodded her own head in a Cassandra-like gesture of grim satisfaction.

"Ay, now you've seen for yourself how it is, Madam!" she said. "And Miss Lydia no sooner reads that letter, and hears me say Lord Harlbury is waiting to see her downstairs, than she flies out of the room with no more of a word to me than that she's going after Mr. Bayard, and the next I know she's mounting up into his lordship's curricle, and him looking as queer as Dick's hat-band, Sidwell says, and trying his best to get her to change her mind. *Which*, you know, Madam, he might have saved his breath doing, when Miss Lydia once takes a notion into her head! And then in the twinkling of a bed-post the two of them were driving off together down the street, *without* his groom, too, for at the last minute his lordship gave orders he was to stay behind."

"But she *cannot* have set off for Bristol with Lord Harlbury in such a fashion!" Mrs. Leyland, finding her voice, said faintly. "Bayard and Miss Beaudoin—and now Lydia—No, no I cannot believe it! She would not do such a dreadful thing!"

She was about to collapse into a chair when a sardonic voice behind her interrupted her grimly.

"Oh yes, she would, ma'am!" said the voice.

Mrs. Leyland, uttering a suppressed shriek, turned around to see Northover regarding her from the doorway. As she stared at him, she was alarmed to observe such an oddly baleful gleam in his dark eyes that her hand flew instinctively to her breast.

"My lord!" she exclaimed, summoning all her dignity to her aid. "What, may I ask, are *you* doing here?"

"I beg your pardon for the interruption, ma'am,"

216

Northover said, coolly advancing upon her and taking from her nerveless hand Bayard's letter, which he rapidly proceeded to peruse, "but I only this moment arrived to pay a call upon Lydia, and, as this door was open when I entered the house, I could not avoid overhearing something of what was being said inside. Young fool!"

These latter words, apparently, were his comment upon Bayard's letter, which he proceeded to drop upon a table. Mrs. Leyland again rallied her forces.

"Sir," she said in a quelling voice, "if it is your intention to reveal to anyone outside this room what you have learned in this clandestine way, give me leave to tell you that you are no gentleman!"

This was sufficient to bring a smile to Northover's face, but the grim look remained in his eyes.

"You may make yourself easy, ma'am," he said. "Not only will I not reveal what I have heard here, but I will make it my business to see that no one else learns of this double folly. I gather that Lydia has set out with Harlbury in his curricle in pursuit of the love-birds? How long ago was this?"

"I have no idea," Mrs. Leyland said distractedly; but here Winch came to her aid with the information that little more than half an hour had passed since the curricle had driven away from the house.

"Good!" said Northover. "Was Harlbury driving those chestnuts of his?"

Winch nodded.

"Well, he has a bang-up set-out of blood and bone there," Northover said, "but I expect I can contrive to come up with him! The point is, though, ma'am," he went on, to Mrs. Leyland, "that I shall want your company. *My* presence can do little to add propriety to this harebrained escapade, but *yours* will make all right, so I fear I must ask you to accompany me."

"To—accompany you!" Mrs. Leyland stared at him. "To—to what place, my lord?"

"To Bristol, if it is necessary!" Northover replied impatiently. "But I scarcely think we shall need to go so

217

far if you will come with me immediately."

"But—but—" Mrs. Leyland appeared to be having difficulty in collecting her thoughts. She looked at the Viscount in some bewilderment, enquiring, "But have you a post-chaise outside, my lord?"

"A post-chaise!" Northover gave a bark of laughter. "No! We should not have the least chance of overtaking them in a chaise. We shall go in my curricle, ma'am."

"In your curricle! To Bristol! Why, it will be a matter of a hundred miles or more! And without luggage!" Mrs. Leyland looked despairingly at Winch. "He is *quite* mad! Do show him out, Winch, and let me sit down quietly and think what I must do—"

"If you sit down here quietly, ma'am," Northover said bluntly, "you will see your grandson an outcast from Society and your granddaughter ruined—or, what is as bad, a partner in a contrived marriage that will be regretted by both. *You* are the only one who can prevent that from happening—so, damn it, you are coming with me, and there's an end to it!"

Mrs. Leyland, who had experienced long years of matrimony with a military gentleman who, in moments of stress, had been wont to use the same kind of unequivocal language to enforce his commands, recognised the voice of authority. She had just time to snatch up her gloves from the table where she had laid them before she found herself being ushered firmly and inexorably from the room. A moan escaped her as she emerged from the house and saw the exceedingly sporting vehicle in which she was to be transported upon her journey, but she uttered no further protest, and allowed herself to be handed up into it by his lordship with nothing more than an anguished backward glance at Winch and Sidwell, standing goggling on the doorstep.

The next moment the Viscount had mounted beside her and, gathering his whip and reins, given his team the office to start. His diminutive Tiger swung himself up behind, and off went the trio in a clatter of hooves and a rattle of wheels on the paving-stones.

Not for many, many years had it been Mrs. Leyland's fortune to be driven at such breakneck speed as she was called upon to endure for the ensuing hours. Of conversation between her and his lordship there was very little, for Northover's attention was fully concentrated upon his team, but she did startle him once, when they had progressed some dozen miles beyond the town, by enquiring abruptly, and with some asperity, "A *contrived* marriage! Pray, what did you mean by such a remark, my lord? How could Lord Harlbury possibly have *contrived* this most unseemly journey, since he had no means of knowing that the opportunity for it would arise?"

"Not Harlbury. Lydia," Northover said succinctly. He cast a brief glance at his companion, who he saw was ruffling up at this imputation. "Oh, very well," he conceded. "Perhaps I am mistaken. But you can scarcely blame me, ma'am, for believing that not even your remarkably impetuous granddaughter could go haring off into an adventure of this sort without realising that she was very likely to come out of it with a husband! Harlbury may be hag-ridden by that mother of his, but he is a man of honour, and Lydia must know very well that he will marry her, in spite of Lady Harlbury, if he feels that he has compromised her."

"Oh! Do you think so?" Mrs. Leyland asked, brightening momentarily; but dejection quickly overcame her once more. "Well, well, but I doubt that it will come about," she said. "She is the most vexatious girl, and it is very likely that, even if Harlbury *does* offer for her, she will be selfish enough to refuse him, without a *thought* for the hardships she will be inflicting upon Bayard and me by such an action."

She broke off, conscious of Northover's keen eyes upon her.

"Is that your opinion, ma'am?" he asked abruptly.

"Well—no," she conceded, giving the matter some thought. "That is—if we do not overtake Bayard and he really *does* succeed in carrying Miss Beaudoin off to America, I daresay even Lydia cannot be so utterly without

219

feeling as not to do her possible for her family by accepting Harlbury, if he should offer for her."

"I daresay not," Northover agreed dryly, the grim look again settling about his mouth.

No more was said upon the subject, and their journey progressed thenceforth with very little more in the way of conversation between the travellers than Mrs. Leyland's lamentations over the discomforts of being driven at such high speed in an open carriage.

When they arrived at Reading, however, not a quarter hour after Harlbury's curricle had reached the same point, they were greeted by the new discomfort of the thunder-shower that had caused the accident to his lordship's vehicle. Here the complaints of Northover's unwilling companion rose to such a pitch that even the Viscount could no longer remain proof against them. She would not, Mrs. Leyland declared, in accents of doom that might have done credit to a Siddons, wish him to be obliged to carry through the remainder of his days the remorse occasioned by having obliged an elderly lady of weak constitution to drive unprotected through a rainstorm, thereby bringing down upon her the inflammation of the lungs that was sure to carry her off before her time.

Whether the Viscount would actually have given way before these tragical representations was never to be known, however, for at this point they came upon Harlbury's curricle lying overturned in the road, while various zealous persons still attempted to clear the way of the entangled horses, the gig, and the wagon that had all been involved in the accident.

The Viscount, having brought his own horses to a halt, entrusted them to the care of his Tiger and, jumping down, made a few rapid enquiries of the assembled throng. These immediately elicited the information that a young lady who had been a passenger in the curricle had suffered some serious (perhaps even fatal, one onlooker helpfully added) injury in the accident, and had forthwith been carried by her male companion into an inn nearby. The inn having been pointed

220

out to him, the Viscount quickly returned to his curricle, his face now so set and drawn that Mrs. Leyland felt the shock of the news he had to communicate to her before he had so much as uttered a word; he then proceeded to escort that lamenting lady with all possible speed to the inn to which it was said the injured young lady had been borne.

Thus it came about that Mrs. Leyland and the Viscount, after a few hasty enquiries of the chambermaid who was the first person they encountered upon entering the front door of the inn, were directed by this damsel to the private parlour where Lydia was at that precise moment being assisted to lie back upon the cushions of her sofa by a solicitous Harlbury.

The tableau presented by the handsome and interestingly dishevelled peer and the afflicted young lady was doubtless an exceedingly romantic one; but, in spite of the relief both Mrs. Leyland and the Viscount felt on finding that Lydia was neither lifeless nor severely injured, it appeared to awaken no correspondingly soft emotions in the breasts of either. Mrs. Leyland's first words, in fact, were, "Unfeeling girl! You will yet bring my grey hairs down to the grave!" (This was a slight hyperbole, her locks being, either by art or by nature, of the same raven hue they had possessed in her youth.)

She thereupon tottered to the nearest chair, while Northover, with a very unfriendly glint in his eyes, which were fixed upon Lydia, said to her in sardonic tones, "I should have guessed, I daresay, that any accident you were involved in would only serve to further your ends. I gather that we may felicitate you and Harlbury, then?"

Lydia had fallen back against the cushions in the liveliest surprise at sight of her grandmother and Northover entering the room—an action somewhat facilitated by Harlbury's relinquishing his hold upon her as rapidly as if she had suddenly turned into something in the nature of red-hot metal. At the Viscount's words, however, she started up again, exclaiming with considerable vehemence, "No, you may not! I don't know what you may be doing here, Northover, or

221

how you got here, but if you intend to behave in this tiresome way I wish you will go away again! You have no more sympathy than a—a goat!"

"I have a great deal of sympathy—but it is for Harlbury, not for you, my girl!" Northover said unfeelingly.

He turned his eyes upon that harassed young man, whose fingers were tugging at his once beautifully arranged neckcloth as if that much-abused article of clothing were still in a state to interfere with his breathing.

"Sir—ma'am!" he stammered, turning from Northover to Mrs. Leyland. "I assure you that it is my intention—I am aware that my presence in this place with Miss Leyland may be construed as highly compromising to the young lady—"

"Oh, for heaven's sake!" interrupted Mrs. Leyland piteously. "Do not stand there talking to no purpose, Harlbury, but ring the bell for some refreshment for me! Lydia, you are a wicked, wicked girl, and your brother, as I have always said, is twice as bad, but if he chooses to run off with a penniless bride to Belmaison I wash my hands of him, for not another step will I take after him!"

"Not another step! Oh, but you must, Grandmama!" Lydia exclaimed, raising herself again from the cushions in a new access of energy that set her senses swimming once more. She shut her eyes, endeavouring to command herself, and said, urgently passing her hand over her forehead, "You don't understand, love! If you let Bayard go off with Miss Beaudoin now, the consequences will be far worse than you imagine! I called upon Sir Basil this morning, and he told me positively that he means to make Bayard his heir, but that his intention depends entirely upon Bayard's conducting himself in such a way that he will be able to hold a respectable position in Society. You *must* know, then, what will happen if he creates a scandal by this elopement! It will ruin all his chances forever!"

She let her hand fall as Harlbury, looking half-distracted with worry and embarrassment, again obliged her to lie back on the sofa, while her grandmother stared at her with an almost ludicrously stricken expression upon her face.

"Merciful—heavens!" that good lady ejaculated at last, with every evidence of being about to be overcome by a fit of strong hysterics. "Do you mean—*can* you mean that Sir Basil—?"

"Yes, yes!" Lydia assured her. "It was that that made me so desperate to overtake Bayard. But then we had that horrid accident, and now I cannot prevail upon Harlbury to let me go on! But all that is of no consequence, since you are here. Dear ma'am, you *must* go on at once, and not waste any more time in talking to me. How did you get here? Surely you did not overtake us in a chaise?"

"No, no," Mrs. Leyland said feebly. "Lord Northover drove me—in his curricle."

Lydia looked at Northover. "Well, then, you must go on with her," she said to him decisively. She saw the ambiguous, somewhat sarcastic expression upon his face and added, in imploring vexation, "Northover, even *you* cannot be so totally malignant as to refuse now! You *must* see how much depends upon it!"

Northover looked unimpressed. "And leave you here alone with Harlbury?" he said. "I think not!"

"Oh, what does that signify!" Lydia said impatiently, and was about to go on when Harlbury himself interrupted seriously, "As to that, my lord, I can only say that you may consider Miss Leyland and myself from this moment as a betrothed couple, for I have every intention, after this unfortunate episode, of making her my wife—"

"Of making me *what!*" Lydia gasped, bouncing off the cushions again, her pale cheeks suddenly flying scarlet.

Northover spoke briefly. "Never mind!" he said. "I'll deal with this." His dark eyes raked Harlbury; there was a slight and not entirely pleasant smile on his lips. "So, my lad," he said, "you intend to offer Miss Leyland the *amende honorable*, do you? Very *galant* of you, to be sure, but has it never occurred to you that you have been led down the garden path—?"

He got no farther, for Lydia at once repeated, her eyes blazing, "Led down the garden path! Northover, what do you mean? Do you believe that I—?"

"I don't believe it. I know it!" Northover retorted, giving her no more opportunity to finish her speech than she had given him to finish his. "Why else should you have sought out Harlbury, of all men, to escort you upon this charming little excursion à deux?"

"I didn't seek him out! He h-happened to come to the house just as I—" It might have been fury that caused Lydia's voice to stammer and break; certainly the Viscount believed this to be true, and he was cutting into her angry words in a tone quite as intemperate as her own when, to his blank astonishment and that of everyone else in the room, his antagonist suddenly burst into tears. "You are a b-beast!" she sobbed. "If you th-think I would do such an utterly l-loathsome thing as that—"

"My love!" Mrs. Leyland, startled at the rare sight of her granddaughter in tears, rose to comfort her, as Harlbury stepped nobly into the breach.

"My lord," he said, looking rather pale, but speaking determinedly, "I must tell you that I find your insinuations offensive in the extreme! I consider that Miss Leyland's conduct in this affair has been unexceptionable throughout, and if you persist in speaking of her in such—I can only say, such insulting terms, I shall feel myself obliged, as Miss Leyland's affianced husband, to call you to account."

Northover, who sustained this warning with complete equanimity and even with an appearance of some amusement, merely said softly, "You are a gudgeon, Harlbury!"—a remark which caused Lydia, who was being offered succour by her grandmother in the shape of the vinaigrette she had extracted from her reticule, to say to him in tones of strong loathing, her eyes flashing through her tears, "He is not a gudgeon! And I wish he will shoot you! I would do it myself if I were a man! Grandmama, I don't want that! I am perfectly all right!"

This last statement she proceeded to demonstrate by crying even harder than before—a mode of behaviour which caused Mrs. Leyland to declare in helpless tones that she feared she must really be suffering from some more severe injury than they had at first believed, and that a surgeon had best be called to her.

"Exactly my own feeling, ma'am," Harlbury said earnestly, and was starting towards the door when he was interrupted by the reappearance of the landlady, who stood gazing in some astonishment at the scene before her.

"Well, I'm sure I never—!" she exclaimed, looking to Harlbury for some explanation. "Who had the impudence to show *these* people into your private parlour, sir? No wonder your lady wife—"

"I am *not* his lady wife!" Lydia said through her teeth, thrusting the vinaigrette aside and regarding the startled landlady with an expression so stormy that that worthy dame instinctively retreated towards the door. "I shall never marry *anyone*—and—and"—she bit her lip, struggling with the sobs that threatened to overcome her again—"and what is more, I wish to be left *alone*! Totally *alone*!"

"My dear—" Harlbury began anxiously.

"I am *not* your dear! And there is *nothing* the matter with me—except people with m-minds like vipers' and no feelings whatever, who won't lift a f-finger to stop other people from ruining their whole lives—"

Northover flung up a hand. "Very well!" he said. "That will do, Lydia! The picture is clear." There was an odd gleam in his eyes and a suppressed, taut excitement in his manner that might have given Lydia to think if she had been in a calmer state of mind. He went on, "As the one sensible thing you have said since I entered this room is that your brother had best be brought back to London before he has completely ruined his chances of inheriting old Rowthorn's fortune, I propose to do just that. On that head, at least, you may make yourself easy, for, if I know Minna, she won't be in the least agreeable to travelling in a storm. With luck, we shall find the two of them at an inn not far along the road, waiting for the weather to clear." He crossed the room

225

in three long strides and, with one hand on her arm, assisted—or, rather, compelled—Mrs. Leyland to arise from her seat on the sofa beside Lydia. "With your permission, ma'am," he said, "we'll be on our way."

"On our way!" Mrs. Leyland stared at him, dumbfounded. "Sir, you cannot be serious! Leave my granddaughter in such a situation—!"

"You have already heard her say that it is her wish to be left alone," Northover said coolly, "and, as a matter of fact, I think that is an excellent idea. A period of calm reflection should do her a great deal of good."

"But it is still raining!" Mrs. Leyland said piteously. "And in an open carriage—!"

"No doubt the landlady will be happy to accommodate you with a cloak and an umbrella," Northover said ruthlessly. "Come, ma'am, you will not deny your grandson a fortune merely because of a wetting! Harlbury"—he turned to his lordship, who was looking on rather dazedly at what was occurring—"I should advise you—strongly advise you!—to await our return in the coffee-room. In Miss Leyland's present agitated state, I fear that any further discussion of her affairs cannot be beneficial to her. I trust I make myself clear?"

Harlbury, who had been about to protest this rather high-handed arrangement, read at that moment an expression in the Viscount's glinting dark eyes which caused him to suffer an emotion that could readily have been identified by a number of Northover's former subalterns who had suddenly been confronted by the iron behind their superior's ordinarily easy-going manner. He said rather hastily, to salvage his dignity, "Perhaps you are right. Miss Leyland will wish to rest—"

"Oh, go away—do!" Miss Leyland said cordially. "Go away! Go away, all of you!"

She had stopped crying, and, after looking vainly for a handkerchief with which to dry her wet cheeks, was reduced

226

to accepting—with a dagger-glance—the one thrust upon her by Northover.

"There, Lydia *mia!*" he said soothingly. "Dry your eyes and compose your temper, and when I return we'll sort this all out."

"There is nothing to sort out! And I *never* wish to see you again!" Miss Leyland flung at him; but her words fell disregarded.

Northover, shepherding Mrs. Leyland and Harlbury before him, was already out of the room, leaving the landlady, with the bobbing of a quick, scared curtsey, to whisk herself out behind him.

IT WAS GROWING DUSK, AND candlelight was glowing warmly from the windows of the inn, when a post-chaise-and-four turned into the yard and a gentleman, quickly alighting from it, strode—after bestowing a word upon his postboys—hastily across the courtyard and in at the front door. Encountering the landlady in the hall, he accosted her without ceremony.

"I understand," he said, "that a young lady who was injured this afternoon when her carriage overturned was brought here by her companion. Can you inform me, ma'am, whether she is still in this house?"

Mrs. Yarden, somewhat startled at having this question flung at her at the very moment when she had been endeavouring for the dozenth time to puzzle out the reason for the very odd behaviour of the young couple she was harbouring beneath her roof—one of them closeted upstairs in a private parlour, the other lounging gloomily in the coffee-room, consuming far more French brandy than was good for him—cast a harassed glance at this new element in the picture. She saw a tall, fair young man, obviously a member of the Quality, upon whose face was an expression of the keenest impatience. It seemed that the gentleman was in the greatest anxiety to come up with her young guest.

She said doubtfully, "Why, yes, sir, she *is* here—but I misdoubt she'd be wishful to see company."

"Is she badly injured, then?"

"Oh no, sir, not at all! It was only the shock, as you might say. I'm sure she was feeling quite recovered when I looked in on her half an hour ago."

"And the gentleman with her?"

Mrs. Yarden shook her head disapprovingly. "No, sir, there's nothing the matter with *him*," she said, "except that he'll be as drunk as a wheelbarrow before the cat can lick her ear if he don't leave off calling for more of my best brandy! He's in the coffee-room; I'm sure you can see *him* if you like."

This suggestion, however, appeared to find little favour with the newcomer. He was looking very thoughtful and not at all ill pleased, and for a moment seemed quite oblivious of Mrs. Yarden's presence, his pale-blue eyes wearing a considering look, as if he were rapidly formulating some plan in his mind.

After a few moments he said abruptly, "I must see the young lady. Will you direct me to her?"

Mrs. Yarden's honest face creased in a perplexed frown. "Why, to tell you the truth, sir," she said, "she is laid down upon the sofa, resting, and may not wish for visitors. Unless it might be a relation—"

"But, you see, I *am* a relation!" the gentleman said, a sterner look appearing upon his face. "In point of fact, I am her husband! And now, ma'am, if you will be good enough to show me to my wife's apartment—"

"Well, surely to goodness!" Mrs. Yarden breathed, the truth of the matter suddenly breaking upon her like a thunderbolt. "And she was running away from you with that young villain in the coffee-room! Why, I never in all my born days—! Such a nice young man as he looks, too, without rumgumption enough to say 'Boh!' to a goose!"

"Yes, yes!" said the gentleman, even more impatiently. "But my wife—?"

"Upstairs, sir, in my very best parlour," Mrs. Yarden said, glancing down at the handsome *douceur* that was being pressed into her hand. "But you won't go to be hard upon her, now, will you?—for I'm sure she's that sorry already that she ran off, and I can give you my word as a Christian woman that she's not been alone with the young gentleman for five minutes together as long as they've been in my house. He's been sulking down here in the coffee-room the whole time since the *other* gentleman and lady left—and why *they* didn't take her off with them I'm sure I don't

230

know, if she *was* the young lady's grandmother, as she claimed to be—"

She had been leading the way up the narrow staircase as she spoke, but at this point the gentleman halted her with a sharply spoken, "Wait!" She turned her head in surprise, to find him regarding her frowningly.

"Yes, sir?"

"An elderly lady?" he enquired abruptly. "Dark, aquiline-featured? And escorted by a younger gentleman, also very dark?"

"Yes, sir. That's them to the life! Do you know them, sir?"

"I know them," the gentleman said. "Where are they now?"

"Oh, sir, truly, I couldn't tell you!" said the harassed landlady. "All I can say is that they went off again in the gentleman's curricle. There was a good deal of excitement, you see, what with the young lady crying and saying she wished to be left alone, and all of them at loggerheads, it seemed, like a bag full of cats—"

The gentleman, still frowning thoughtfully, appeared to abandon the hope of extracting any more information from her and bade her lead the way on up the stairs. He was still looking preoccupied when she halted before a closed door at the head of the staircase, but at this point shook off his abstraction and informed her that she might go.

"Yes, sir—but I—you—you won't go to offering violence to the young gentleman in my house?" she enquired, with renewed anxiety. "Being a female myself, I know the young lady is apt to lay all the blame upon *him*—but, to tell you the truth, he seemed to me as cast down to find himself in this case of pickles as she did, and I'm bound to say he's never made the least push to see her since the other lady and gentleman left, besides being clean raddled by this time with all the brandy he's drunk—"

The newcomer assured her that he had no intention of calling the young man to account within her house, his only concern being to remove his wife from the compromising

231

situation in which she found herself; and, this point having been settled between them, Mrs. Yarden departed down the stairs, leaving the newcomer to rap upon the door she had indicated to him.

His knock was answered so immediately that it seemed obvious that Miss Leyland had been expecting it. That she had not been expecting to see *him*, however, was equally obvious from the look of total astonishment that crossed her face the instant her eyes fell upon him.

"Michael Pentony!" she exclaimed. "How in the world did *you* come here?"

"As it happens, by post-chaise, my dear Lydia," Mr. Pentony said composedly. "May I come in?"

He stepped past her, as he spoke, into the room, closing the door behind him. Lydia, still overcome by astonishment, demanded, "But how did you know I was here? It isn't *possible—*"

"On the contrary, it is quite possible," Mr. Pentony said, stripping off his gloves and laying down his curly-brimmed beaver with the air of a man who had every intention of remaining where he was for some time. "Fatiguing, yes—but perfectly possible, my dear. And a trifle expensive as well, I might add, for information is not to be come by gratis, you know."

Lydia, who had attended to this speech with growing indignation, which she felt quite capable now of expressing in her much improved state of strength and spirits, interrupted at this point to say rather ominously, "I daresay by *that* you mean that you have been bribing servants again! What did Sidwell tell you?—for I am sure you got nothing out of Winch!"

Mr. Pentony smiled his calm, narrow smile. "Really, you do me an injustice!" he said. "What could I do, on arriving in Green Street to find your household all in a turmoil—you and your grandmother apparently having gone out of town in the greatest haste, your brother absent too—but to attempt to learn if there was something I could do to assist you? And, as you see, I have spared no pains in this

232

praiseworthy endeavour, which has involved really a tiresome number of enquiries at toll-gates and posting-houses, but which fortunately has at last been crowned with success."

"Oh! Would you say 'fortunately'?" Lydia, who had by this time overcome her first surprise and discomfiture, enquired with a sweetness that might have warned Mr. Pentony of danger. "I definitely would *not*—but then some people may *enjoy* jauntering about the countryside to no purpose."

"Ah, but I do not think it has been to no purpose," Mr. Pentony said. "May I sit down?"

"No!" said Lydia.

"But I think I shall," Mr. Pentony said, coolly suiting the action to the words, "and I should advise you to do likewise, my dear, for I have something to say to you that you would be well advised to attend to. And if," he added, as she stood looking furiously down at him, "you have any notion of calling upon Harlbury to assist you, let me inform you that he is at this present, in the landlady's words, as—er—drunk as a wheelbarrow on her best French brandy."

"*Harlbury!*" exclaimed Lydia, momentarily diverted. "I don't believe it!"

"Nevertheless, it is true," said Mr. Pentony. "I do not know what means you employed to embroil him in this business, but I can assure you that if you expected to use this affair to entrap him into matrimony, you have little chance of success. It must be quite as clear to you as it is to me, after observing him last night at Vauxhall, that he has not the smallest *tendre* for you, and, though I believe he must at present be suffering a considerable degree of remorse over the situation in which you have landed him, I do not believe it to be sufficient to cause him to lead you to the altar—especially since his mother would be so very greatly adverse to his taking such a step."

Lydia, seeing that her visitor had no idea of leaving, sat down in a chair opposite him and regarded him with marked contempt.

"I have not the smallest intention of marrying Lord

Harlbury," she said. "And now, if you have anything more to say to me, Mr. Pentony, I wish that you will say it and go. I am *not* in the mood to be civil to you, you know!"

"Yes, I do know," Mr. Pentony said composedly, "but *that*, my dear, is an attitude I should advise you to amend. You are in no position to reject an offer of help from any quarter just now, with your brother having gone off in this most reprehensible way with Miss Beaudoin and your own reputation in the greatest danger of being compromised beyond repair. You had much better come to realise at once that you need me quite as much as I need you."

Lydia looked at him, her brows drawing together in a sudden frown. "As you need me?" she repeated. "Why should you—?"

"Come come," interrupted Mr. Pentony, with a slightly impatient shrug, "pray don't trouble to pretend that you don't understand me! You would not have been at such pains to prevent this elopement if you had not been persuaded that there is more at stake than the social blight that would be cast upon your brother and Miss Beaudoin by the manner of their marriage! I know, as a matter of fact, that you have been doing your best to promote the match; but the situation took a different turn—did it not?—when you learned that I had fallen from favour with Sir Basil and that there was now a chance that your brother might inherit a fortune!"

Lydia looked at him resignedly. "Is there anything that you *don't* know?" she enquired. "Really, you are the most utterly devious person! I imagine you must have a network of spies that would put the Bow Street Runners to shame!"

"Let us say, at any rate, that you would be obliged to get up very early in the morning indeed to best me on any suit," said Mr. Pentony, not at all discomposed by this thrust.

"Yes, but you are not *quite* so clever as you like to think," Lydia was goaded to retort, "or Sir Basil would not have found you out. He is furious with you—"

"He *was* furious," Mr. Pentony corrected her smoothly. He reached into his pocket and, drawing out a pretty

234

enamelled snuff-box, refreshed himself unhurriedly with a pinch of its contents. "When he was informed, however, of how small the odds now are that Mr. Bayard Leyland will ever be able to take that place in the *haut ton* to which he—Sir Basil, that is—aspires for him—"

He broke off, satisfied that his shaft had found its mark. Lydia was looking perfectly white, and said after a moment, in a small, gritty voice, "Do you mean that you have already told him—?"

"My dear, only think a moment—would you have expected me to keep such a piece of news to myself? I am not *quite* so altruistic; as I have told you before, there is a fortune at stake, and I have no idea of seeing it slip out of my hands if I am able to prevent it."

He was watching her intently as he spoke; but if he had expected her to give way to despair he was disappointed. She did, indeed, jump up from her chair and walk away from him to the window, as if to conceal her agitation from him; but when she turned again her face, though still pale, wore a look of resolution.

"Well, it does not signify!" she said. "Northover and Grandmama are sure to have come up with Bayard by this time, and if he and Minna return to town in *their* company we shall be able to keep the tattle-boxes quiet, after all, and persuade Sir Basil that no harm has been done."

"Do you think so?" Mr. Pentony was engaged in dusting from his sleeve with his handkerchief a few grains of snuff that had fallen upon it, and gave his response in rather a negligent tone. "Dear me, what a trusting creature you are! To believe it would be in my power, that is, to restrain myself from letting fall to at least two or three of my mother's friends—ladies with such valuable connexions in the *ton*, and so anxious to be able to spread the newest *on-dit* amongst them—the diverting tale of this day's adventures—"

Lydia looked at him with frank loathing. "Yes, I might have known that you would do so!" she said. "Very well, then—you may succeed in ruining Bayard's chances with Sir

Basil, I suppose! But if I were you, I should not be *quite* so certain of benefitting by it. Sir Basil has no liking for tale-pitchers, you know!"

Mr. Pentony raised his eyes to her face. "I am aware of that," he said, rising deliberately and bridging the few steps between them to possess himself of her hand. She snatched it away. "No, don't repulse me, Lydia," he said, taking it again and clasping it so tightly that she could not have withdrawn it without an undignified struggle. "Let us face facts. Alone, neither of us can be assured of winning the prize of Sir Basil's fortune, for your brother has scotched his chances forever by this scandal and I too am no longer in his good graces, owing—as you doubtless know!—to the curst tattling tongue of that butler of his. But together—if you were to marry me—"

"Well, I shall not marry you! I have told you that before!" Lydia said, again endeavouring to draw her hand from his.

This time he let her go, but she saw from the look on his face that this was far from the end of the matter.

"My dear—pray listen to me!" he said, in a slightly quickened voice. "What have you to gain by refusing me? I promise you, if I am able to go to Sir Basil and tell him that you will be my wife, I shall be able to bring him around. He has taken a liking to you, and his displeasure with me is not so deep-rooted that the knowledge that you have agreed to be my wife will not weigh the scales in my favour once more. And I can promise you that on my side, at least, it will not be a loveless marriage, and that I shall do my best to bring you to feel the same! You are—exceedingly attractive to me, Lydia!"

"Thank you very much, but *you* are not exceedingly attractive to me, Mr. Pentony, and I do not at all wish to marry you!" Lydia said rather distractedly, wondering what new trials to her composure this luckless day could bring. "And now will you *please* go away? I really have no more to say to you."

She had turned away, so that she did not observe the rather odd expression that came upon his face at these words, but it might have astonished her if she had. She had never seen him when caution and composure had not blended in his manner, and, if she had thought of the matter at all, would certainly have said that he was a man in whom emotion would never overcome calculation.

She was soon to learn how mistaken she had been. Apparently the events of the day, raising, as they had, both great anxieties and even greater hopes in Mr. Pentony's breast, had shaken his usual careful control, and the result was that she found herself the next instant enveloped in a greedy and importunate embrace, and heard his voice saying urgently in her ear, "Lydia! Only listen to me for a moment! You *must* marry me—"

"If you do not let me go this instant, I shall scream!" Lydia said, struggling furiously to free herself, but finding that coping with the determined advances of a well-muscled young man was quite a different matter from repulsing Sir Carsbie's dandified attempts to snatch a kiss. Her struggles had the effect only of causing Michael Pentony to tighten his embrace, as he said quickly in her ear, "No, no—it will not do, Lydia! You *must* have me; this has gone too far! I have told the landlady I am your husband, come to seek my runaway wife—"

"You have told her *what!*"

Even Mr. Pentony, involved as he was in the twin turmoils of passion and ambition, was momentarily shaken by the absolutely incredulous fury he saw at that moment in Miss Leyland's face, and only the fact that her voice had risen to a somewhat undignified squeak on the last word enabled him to retain his poise. He did not, therefore, relax the close embrace in which he still held her, and was hurriedly going further into his explanations of the reasons why it behooved her to receive his addresses with more complaisance—somewhat disjointed ones, it was true, for she had never ceased in her determined efforts to free herself —when the door suddenly opened behind him and a third actor burst upon the scene. Unfortunately for Mr. Pentony, he had his back to the door, so that the first intimation he had of this new turn of events was the feel oɩ a heavy hand falling upon his shoulder, tearing him away from Lydia and swinging him violently around to face his attacker, but Lydia, facing the door, recognised her rescuer at once, and shrieked, "Northover!" at almost the same instant.

WHAT HAPPENED NEXT LYDIA would have been hard put to it to describe, though, flung back by Mr. Pentony's abrupt release of her against a stout oak table, she had an excellent view of the proceedings. Furniture went flying as Mr. Pentony, going down under a well-directed blow to the point of his jaw, crashed in his fall into a pair of chairs and a tall whatnot stand. Lydia, flying to rescue the lamp perilously tottering at the edge of the table, missed the next few moments, during which Mr. Pentony evidently succeeded in getting to his feet, for when she saw him next he was staggering across the room toward Northover with red fury in his eyes. There was a confused interval during which the two men, with Mr. Pentony doggedly clinging to Northover in a fierce attempt to wrestle him down, went careering about the room with sundry crashes and the sound of splintering furniture punctuating their progress—and then suddenly, to Lydia's amazed admiration, Mr. Pentony was hurled decisively to the floor in a manoeuvre too quick even for her to follow. In a moment he was up again, but only for an instant; a blow from Northover's left dropped him decisively this time and he lay prone, his head resting almost at Lydia's feet.

Northover came over quickly and took Lydia's hands in a hard grasp.

"He hasn't hurt you?"

"No! Oh, no! But—thank you!" Lydia gasped. She looked down, awed, at Mr. Pentony's recumbent form. "Is he dead?"

"No—only stunned. Damned impudent dog! What the *devil* is he doing here, Lydia?"

"He—he found out somehow from Sidwell what had happened and—and managed to trace me here, I expect. But—oh dear, Northover, I am in the most dreadful coil! He has told the landlady I am his runaway wife—and, what is even worse, he says he has already told Sir Basil of Bayard's elopement with Minna! And now you have come back without them—!"

She got no further, for at that moment a shriek from the doorway brought her to a sudden halt. Her eyes and Northover's flew to the door, to light upon the petrified figure of Mrs. Yarden, her hands clasped to her plump, palpitating bosom as she surveyed the wreckage of her best parlour.

"Mercy upon us!" she gasped. "What's to do here? Jem! Jem!" She turned to a small boy of about ten who had come up behind her and was peeping around the corner of the door, trying to see what was going forward inside the room. "Go and fetch the Constable as fast as you can run," she implored, "and tell him there's a gentleman murdered in my best parlour, and the furniture all broke to pieces—"

"Nonsense!" Northover cut in, coming across to the doorway in two swift strides and collaring Jem—not a difficult matter, as Jem showed no disposition to remove himself from the scene of these fascinating crimes, and had remained rooted to the spot, goggling at Mr. Pentony's peaceful form on the floor. "There is no need for the Constable; the gentleman and I have merely had a slight disagreement. And as for the furniture—" The Viscount cast a rapid glance about the room and, releasing Jem to draw out his purse, thrust several gold coins into Mrs. Yarden's automatically extended hand. "This will make all right, I believe," he said soothingly. "And now, if you and Jem will leave us alone—"

"Miss Leyland!" a new voice suddenly broke into the conversation from the doorway. Mrs. Yarden and Jem were thrust aside and Lord Harlbury, looking extremely dishevelled but highly resolute, strode somewhat uncertainly into the room, where he halted and stood staring about him with an uncomprehending gaze. His eyes lighting upon the Viscount, a guilty but obstinate expression settled upon his face. "Know you don't like it—told me to stay in the coffee-room," he said, "but—heard a noise—devilish sort of commotion—came to see if—be of assistance to Miss Leyland—"

240

"Very commendable of you," Northover said approvingly. "But, as you see, no assistance is required, Harlbury. I suggest that you return to the coffee-room."

"No!" said Harlbury with unexpected spirit, speaking so loudly as to make Mrs. Yarden jump. He added more mildly, "Been thinking it over. Thinking for hours. Got it all clear now. Must marry Miss Leyland. Go back to town tonight—uncle a bishop—special licence—no delay—"

"Harlbury, for heaven's sake, *do* stop talking fustian and go downstairs as Northover bids you!" Lydia broke in indignantly. "There is nothing for you to do here!"

But his lordship's eyes had by this time taken in Mr. Pentony upon the floor and, quite disregarding Lydia's words, he said rather darkly to Northover, "That—that's Miss Pentony's brother. Friend of mine. Had a turn-up with him?"

The Viscount acknowledged that he had, but again suggested the propriety of his lordship's leaving the matter to him. By this time, however, both Lydia and Mrs. Yarden had recollected their duty, as females, to succour any gentleman stretched unconscious at their feet, and were bending together over Mr. Pentony, one lady loudly bidding Jem to run to her chamber and fetch the hartshorn, and the other wetting her handkerchief from the pitcher upon the table to apply it to his forehead.

Their attentions proved unnecessary, however, for Mr. Pentony, sitting up abruptly, and regarding the scene somewhat dazedly but quite sapiently out of one unmarked eye and another rapidly turning a horrid purple-red colour, uttered something that sounded remarkably like an oath. Lydia instantly rose from her knees beside him and resumed an expression of loathing, directed to his notice.

"Come, come, sir," Mrs. Yarden said soothingly, taking up the handkerchief that Lydia had dropped and dabbing professionally with it at the blood trickling from the corner of her patient's mouth, "you'll be feeling better in a moment now, I'll be bound. And if you'll be good enough to tell me if you'd like to charge either of these gentlemen before a magistrate, I'll see it done—for running off with other men's

241

wives," she said, directing a quelling glance at Harlbury, "is what I can't abide, nor what business it is of the *other* gentleman's" (this to Northover's address) "if you choose to come to take back your lady wife, I can't imagine—"

"I am *not* his lady wife!" Lydia said violently, drawing a look from Mrs. Yarden's offended female sensibilities as much wounded as it was astonished.

"Not his, neither! Lawks, ma'am—*miss*!—but he said—"

"I don't care what he said! I am *not* his wife!"

"No," Harlbury corroborated her words, with a gloomy air. "Not *his* wife. Mine. Affianced, that is." He turned his harassed gaze upon Northover and repeated stubbornly, "Thought it all out. *Must* marry her. Good God, even my mother will see *that*!"

"I doubt it," Northover said equably. "But, at all events, this is hardly the time or the place to discuss your matrimonial plans."

Lord Harlbury, however, was paying him no heed; his eyes were fixed upon Lydia in a kind of detached and fascinated resignation.

"I shall probably murder her if I am obliged to live with her," he stated with unexpected clarity, after a moment. "*Not* a gudgeon. Can see that myself. But bound in honour—"

Northover, making a praiseworthy attempt to command his countenance, told his lordship that he doubted such a sacrifice would be required of him, and again directed him to take himself off downstairs.

But Harlbury stood his ground. "Not," he announced firmly, "until I know what's going on here!" He looked at Mr. Pentony, who had by this time, with Mrs. Yarden's help, managed to get to his feet and had collapsed into a chair beside the table, and enquired with some interest, "Is your sister here, too?"

"No, she is *not* here!" Lydia said, goaded quite beyond endurance. "*Do* go away, Harlbury! You are only making matters worse! And I am *not* going to marry you, so you may put that idea quite out of your head!"

"Not—?" His lordship looked at her hopefully.

"No! Under no circumstances!" Her eyes chanced to meet the Viscount's, and she saw the irrepressible quiver of a telltale muscle at the corner of his mouth. The colour flamed into her cheeks. "Northover, I warn you," she said, "I shall do you an injury if you laugh at me!"

"No, no, Lydia—not at you! At all of us!" said the Viscount, the gleam still in his dark eyes.

But he controlled himself sufficiently to guide Harlbury to the door, assuring him that supper and a pot of strong coffee were all that was necessary to set him on his legs again, and promising him that he need feel no further responsibility upon Miss Leyland's account. He followed this action with a firm representation to Mrs. Yarden and Jem that their presence was no longer required, and, in spite of Mrs. Yarden's protests against leaving a gentleman upon whom the Viscount had already wrought such horrid violence alone in the room with him, except for Lydia's dubious protection, she was inexorably swept outside and the door closed behind her.

"And now," said Northover, turning at once to Mr. Pentony with a somewhat grimmer expression upon his face, "we'll have this out to the finish, my buck." Mr. Pentony, turning a ghastly white under the purplish swellings that disfigured his countenance, cast a rather wild look at Lydia, as to the only person available who might shield him from further immediate mayhem committed upon his person—an action that drew an impatient shrug from the Viscount. "You must be a clothhead if you think I should attack a man in your state!" he said. "But I want an explanation from you, Pentony, and I intend to have one, so you had best make up your mind to give me the truth without any roundaboutation. How did you come here, and for what purpose?"

Mr. Pentony, mustering up what dignity he could under the handicap of a swelling eye, a cut lip, and what he was horribly convinced were several loose teeth, muttered a somewhat expurgated repetition of the explanation he had previously given Lydia—that, having discovered by a chance

243

call in Green Street something of what had occurred there that morning, he had come in search of Miss Leyland to offer her any aid that lay in his power.

"Even," he added, with a somewhat vindictive look in that young lady's direction, "the protection of my name, my lord —which can scarcely be construed as a dishonourable offer!"

"On the contrary—a most honourable one," Northover said coolly, "if it had not been made in such a way as to place her under compulsion to accept it. Informing the landlady that she was already your wife, and then forcing your attentions upon Miss Leyland, scarcely go down with me as the actions of an honourable man." He saw Mr. Pentony open his mouth to utter a protest and added, with an impatient gesture, "No, don't try to justify yourself. You had much better cut line and tell me the truth, for I warn you that I have little time to waste upon you. You told Miss Leyland you had already informed Sir Basil Rowthorn that young Bayard has run off with Miss Beaudoin. Is that true?"

"Yes," muttered Mr. Pentony, with a glance, in spite of his injuries, of such malevolent triumph upon his face that Lydia could not forbear breaking in to say indignantly, "Of course it is true, for it is utterly what one might have expected of him! And now, if you please, he thinks that *I* will help him to chouse Bayard out of a fortune by marrying him. Well, I shan't! I daresay we shall all end in the Fleet, but I don't care: I had as soon marry a—a snake!"

The muscle quivered again at the corner of Northover's mouth, but he only said quite gravely, "I honour your principles, Lydia, but I scarcely think you need look forward to their dooming you to such a dismal future. You see, in the first place I do not believe that Mr. Pentony has yet seen Sir Basil."

"Not seen Sir Basil?" Lydia's eyes followed Northover's in swift incredulity to Mr. Pentony's face, but what she saw there made her exclaim suddenly, "Oh! I do believe you are right."

"I am quite sure that I am," the Viscount said dryly. "You were a widgeon to have swallowed *that* fling, my love. Is it likely, do you think, that your—er—ardent suitor here would have wasted his time in running to Sir Basil with what he could not yet dignify as anything more than a piece of steward's-room gossip, when every moment he delayed in setting out after you made it less likely that he would reach you in time to prevent Harlbury's becoming so entangled in the business as to feel that he must offer you marriage? *I* don't think it!"

"No—nor do I, now you put it to me so!" agreed Lydia, looking accusingly at Mr. Pentony. "So *that* was a lie, too! I might have known it! Only"—her voice faltered suddenly as she turned again to Northover, "even if he has not already done so, there is nothing to prevent him from telling Sir Basil *now*. Indeed, it must become known, since you were not able to find Bayard—"

"What makes you think I have not found him?" said the Viscount. "Or that I should have come back here if I had not? You need have no further worries on *that* score, Lydia. Your brother and Miss Beaudoin—well chaperoned, I may add, by your grandmother—are at this moment on their way to Great Hayland, where they have been so kind as to agree to pay me a visit—"

"On their way to Great Hayland!" Lydia looked utterly astounded. "But I don't understand—"

"Come, come!" said the Viscount reprovingly. "Surely you cannot have forgotten so soon that Great Hayland lies particularly convenient to the road from Bristol to London! I daresay they may even have reached it by this time, as it is a matter of only five miles or so to the south of here. And when you and I have joined them there, together with Lord and Lady Gilmour, to whom I have sent a most urgent invitation to be my guests as well, I have no doubt that we shall make up a very agreeable party—"

"Lord and Lady Gilmour!"

"Why, yes! I rather flatter myself that they will be on their way before first light tomorrow, so that the notice I am about to send to the *Morning Post* announcing their presence at Great Hayland—along with that of their daughter and your family—can scarcely be considered as premature. I fancy," he added, "that Sir Basil will be immensely pleased to read it there—for I understand that, even though he does not go into Society himself, he is addicted to perusing the columns devoted to the activities of the *ton* quite carefully each day."

"Oh!" gasped Lydia, gazing at him almost in awe. "You really have been frightfully *tortuous*, Northover! I should never have guessed it of you; it is *quite* as good as anything I might have contrived myself!"

"Thank you!" said Northover, overcome. "A notable tribute—but you must not be too generous, Lydia! I am quite sure *you* would not have compounded for anything so commonplace and respectable as a mere house-party if you had been given *my* opportunities." He turned his attention to Mr. Pentony once more, his face altering slightly, in a way that made that gentleman stir uncomfortably in his chair. "And now," he said, "since I shall take it upon myself to escort Miss Leyland to Great Hayland, may I suggest that I find your company quite unnecessary, Mr. Pentony? You will find the landlady eager to attend to your comfort, I have no doubt, if you wish to remain here for the night—which," he added, with a critical glance at Mr. Pentony's marred countenance, "I strongly advise you to do."

But Mr. Pentony, though he rose from his chair, made no immediate move to leave the room.

"Ay," he said, in a low, shaking voice that Lydia, with her customary flair for the dramatic, could only describe to herself as murderous, "you have contrived well, Northover—but you are bacon-brained if you think that I will keep silent about this day's work to old Rowthorn! I shall return to town at once—and when he hears of it—"

There was an odd gleam in the Viscount's dark eyes, but his pleasant drawl was, if anything, only the more marked as he said coolly, "No, no—it is you who have windmills in your head, Pentony, if you think you can carry *that* face to Rowthorn without his putting you through such a shrewd catechism on the head of it that *your* part in this business

246

will not come out! He has a way of getting to the heart of a matter without ceremony, you know! And, at any rate," he added, "what makes you believe that he will care a rush for your tales? If you do not know him well enough by this time to realise that he is interested in results, not words, you have wasted the years you have spent in cultivating him. You may take my word for it that, while the world is treated to the sight of a young man of the highest expectations marrying a young lady of unimpeachable birth and breeding against a background of family approval, *ton* parties, and a fashionable wedding, he will have no fault to find with young Bayard."

The rather ghastly sneer upon Mr. Pentony's face became even more pronounced.

"And Miss Leyland?" he enquired. "Will she too find that her reputation is able to survive the test she has put it to today? I think not! When it becomes known that I found her here alone in this inn in Lord Harlbury's company—"

The odd light—almost phosphorescent, it seemed, to Lydia's fascinated gaze—leapt again in Northover's eyes, and this time there was something in the level composure of his voice that penetrated even Mr. Pentony's fury.

"As to that," said the Viscount very gently, "it may be as well for me to warn you that if I ever chance to hear of your having spoken of Miss Leyland in terms other than of respect, it will give me the greatest pleasure to call you to account for your words. It may enlighten you further, I believe, if I tell you that I intend to make Miss Leyland my wife."

If the Viscount had been in a mood to be amused at that moment, the astonished, even thunderstruck, expressions upon the two faces before him might have appealed irresistibly to his risibilities, never under stern control. But he was not in that mood, and neither pair of widened eyes directed now upon his face found the slightest trace there of anything to give them the idea that he was not entirely in earnest in what he said.

It was Mr. Pentony who recovered his voice first. He said,

247

"Your wife! This is indeed news to me!"—with a profound chagrin that again the Viscount, in another mood, could not but have found comical.

Now, however, he merely remarked, "Yes, I rather fancy it is. All the same, I should advise you to believe me when I tell you that I should feel not the slightest compunction in putting a bullet through you if it were to come to my ears that you had been so indiscreet as to spread malicious gossip concerning Miss Leyland—and I must warn you that I am held to be an excellent shot. And now," he said again, this time in tones of marked impatience, "I am beginning to find you a dead bore, Pentony, and if you don't relieve us of your company at once I really think I shall be obliged to *encourage* you to leave."

Mr. Pentony, however, was in need of no more encouragement. With a crestfallen air that he tried in vain to conceal behind the tatters of his composure, he informed the Viscount that threats had no power to move him—adding hastily, however, as he saw that gentleman's hands double into a pair of purposeful fists, that he was no tattle-monger and his lordship need have no fear that any unwary gossip on his part would reveal the events of that day to the world.

This was more satisfactory, and Northover allowed him to depart in peace, observing cheerfully to Lydia as the door closed behind him that he would probably go and make himself agreeable to Harlbury—"for, though everything else has failed, he has still the hope, I daresay, that his sister's charms will bring him into Parson's mouse-trap with her one of these days," he said.

Lydia regarded him severely, but with a look of some shyness in her eyes—a very unusual look, which the Viscount had never seen there before.

"Yes, I expect you are right," she said, "but that is not to the point, Northover! I wish you will tell me what can have possessed you to pitch him such an outrageous Banbury tale! Of course I am much obliged to you for trying to stop his tongue—as well as for finding Bayard, and all the rest," she added conscientiously, "but, since he is certain to find out the truth—"

"Ah, yes! The truth!" said the Viscount pensively, regarding her with very steady dark eyes in which, she felt, there was an odd, intent warmth. "And what if I have already told him the truth, Lydia *mia*?"

"That you—wish to—intend to—?" Lydia's heart began abruptly to beat unaccountably fast, and she turned away from him, saying hurriedly, "I wish you will not talk flummery to me, Northover! I am not in the mood. And now, if you don't mind—I am rather tired, and I should like to go on to join Grandmama and Bayard at once—"

"Yes, I know," Northover said. He moved closer and, before she knew what he was about, had both her hands firmly clasped in his own. "You have had a trying day, haven't you, my little love?" he said. "But if you can spare me another ten minutes of your conversation before we go—"

Lydia looked at the closed door behind him, and into her mind there stole the lowering thought that his lordship was about to take advantage of her present unchaperoned state to make an improper proposal to her. She managed to say in a rather suffocated voice, "No—please!"—and attempted to draw her hands away, but she discovered that, without an unbecoming struggle, this was quite impossible to accomplish. She also found it impossible, for some reason, to look up into his lordship's face.

After a moment she heard his voice asking abruptly, with what appeared to her a deceptive mildness, over her head, "Tell me, Lydia—why did you refuse Harlbury?"

The colour flew into her cheeks. She flung up her head, meeting his eyes.

"*That*," she said, "is none of your affair!"—adding inconsistently, "If you *still* think I was abominable enough to lure him to take me off with him so that he would feel obliged to make me an offer—"

"I don't," Northover interrupted reassuringly. "But does

it not seem a trifle odd to you, in view of what I have heard you say on the subject of matrimony, that you should be so very *determined* to have none of his suit?"

She gave him a darkling glance. "I know very well what I have said! But I am *not* a—a man-trap, Northover, whatever you may think!"

"Oh, no!" he agreed gravely. "I came to that conclusion myself last night at Vauxhall, when I heard you so cavalierly reject Sir Carsbie's very obliging offer—though I must admit that my faith in you suffered a slight set-back when I learned you had gone off with Harlbury—"

"Well, you *must* have known the reason I went off with him," said Lydia with asperity, again endeavouring vainly to draw her hands free of his firm grasp, "and that it had nothing to do with anyone's marriage except Bayard's. Which puts me in mind that you have not told me where you found him—"

"Oh, at an inn at Theale. I told you Minna would not travel in a storm."

"And you explained it all to him—about the inheritance, I mean?" Lydia enquired, a little anxiously. "Because he must have been very much surprised and—and put about to see you."

"He was," said Northover, grinning slightly. "In fact, your grandmother and I had quite a Cheltenham tragedy enacted for us, with Minna swooning away and your young brother ranting a great deal of fustian about thwarted lovers, before we could succeed in convincing him that not even Lady Gilmour's marble heart was likely to remain unsoftened before the affecting thought of her daughter's marrying a fortune to rival Golden Ball's. In fact, it is exactly my conviction that it will not, that makes me so certain that we shall see her and Ned at Great Hayland as fast as horses can bring them, once Trix has learned how the situation stands."

The mention of Lady Gilmour's name appeared to be an unfortunate one. Lydia, whose interest in her brother's affairs had caused her momentarily to forget that Northover still held her hands imprisoned in his, said, "Oh! I see!" in a determinedly cool voice, and then, more pettishly, as she again attempted to wrest her hands free, "*Do* let me go, Northover! What point is there in holding me here like this?"

"None at all," said the Viscount promptly, and thereupon swept her into his arms. "Shall I convince you that I am in earnest, Lydia *mia*?" his voice came in her ear as his lips brushed her hair—an oddly thickened voice, she noted, with a new, more urgent tone in it that she had never heard before.

Miss Leyland, firmly convinced by this time that she was experiencing in person the methods by which the Viscount had notoriously succeeded in making conquests of so many of her sex, found herself struggling against an ignoble desire to burst into tears. Perhaps, she thought, in not very logical confusion, it had been the offers made to her by Mr. Pentony and Lord Harlbury that had inspired him to use this particular manoeuvre to bring her into his net—but she was *not*, she told herself firmly, such a green girl as to be deceived by such lures! Spiritedly fending off Northover's attempts to turn his mouth from her hair to her lips, she managed to surprise him sufficiently by the violence of her resistance to free herself from his embrace, and, when he attempted to renew it, astonished both him and herself by dealing him a resounding slap, with the full force of her arm behind it.

"Now *that*," said the Viscount, recovering himself first and speaking with a wounded air, "is unjust, my girl! The first and only honourable proposal of marriage I have ever made in my life, and to be received in such a fashion—!"

"If you do not stop making game of me, I shall do it again!" Lydia threatened, her voice breaking in spite of her furious efforts to control it. "I am *not* one of your lady-birds, Northover!"

251

The Viscount's brows rose in genuine surprise. "Good God, I should think not!" he said. "What can have put *that* idea into your head?"

Lydia swallowed a very hard lump in her throat. "You sent me f-five thousand pounds," she said. "And you s-said I could have m-more if I liked—"

"So that is it!" said the Viscount, taking her averted face in his hands and obliging her at least to turn it in his direction, although she refused to raise her eyes to his face. "A misunderstood gesture of the purest philanthropy if ever I saw one! Lydia, you absurd little vixen, will you *look* at me? I want to marry you, my girl!"

She glanced up at him suspiciously, quite unconvinced, and still on the edge of tears. "You are not a marrying man," she said accusingly, after a moment. "You told me so yourself, Northover. You know you did."

"I wasn't then. I am now," his lordship said, changing his ground in an entirely conscienceless manner.

"Oh!" said Lydia, shaken quite off her balance by these unfair tactics. She looked down again, appearing to become very much absorbed in contemplating one of the buttons on his lordship's waistcoat. "Well, I—I daresay a person *might* change his mind," she conceded presently, in a rather small voice.

"Especially," Northover said, "when he is given such irresistible temptation to do so. Oh yes," he went on, with a rueful smile, "it goes sorely against the pluck with me, Lydia *mia*, to be obliged to admit that I have met a woman I cannot live without, but, believe me, you have turned the trick!" His voice was suddenly serious again—that new, changed, vibrant voice. "I need you, by God I do!" he said, and the next instant—she did not quite know how—she was in his arms again, and his mouth came down on her parted lips almost fiercely, in a kiss that sent the blood racing through her body. "*Will* you marry me, you enchanting— exasperating—abominable little rogue?" he demanded, and then prevented her entirely from answering this urgent question by kissing her again so very roughly that she had

252

an unaccountable sensation of being swept quite away from all safe past moorings on a flood of new and entirely uncharted emotions.

She came out of the darkness of his embrace to the sound of an insistent tapping upon the door.

"Kit!" she gasped, endeavouring to regain her lost poise. "Let me go! There is someone at the door!"

"Let there be," said his lordship, ruthlessly kissing her once more. "Will you marry me, Lydia?"

"Yes—oh, yes! But *do* let me go now! We *must* open the door or I shan't have a shred of reputation left!"

They were spared the trouble of doing so, however, by the door's being opened from the outside at that moment; Mrs. Yarden's round, anxious face peered into the aperture.

"Oh, madam—that is, miss—" she began, and then, catching sight of the Viscount, who still, most improperly, had his arm around Lydia's waist, exclaimed in scandalised astonishment, "Lawks a-mussy! Lunnon folks! And not married to this one, neither, I'll be bound!"

Lydia, casting a reproving look, somewhat marred by the fact that her eyes were brimful of laughter, at Northover, disengaged herself from his embrace and said soothingly, "No, but I am going to be, Mrs. Yarden. You may be the first to wish me happy, if you please!"

"Well, I'm sure I do, madam—*miss*!" said Mrs. Yarden, looking dubiously at the Viscount, whose attack upon Mr. Pentony, with its concomitant destructive effects upon the furnishings of her best parlour, apparently caused her to feel considerable doubt as to the future felicity of any young lady so unwise as to set up housekeeping with him. "Only it *does* seem odd, with *three* gentlemen to choose from, that—"

"That she's taken the worst bargain?" Northover finished it for her irrepressibly, as she broke off in some confusion at the path down which her unwary tongue was leading her. "Never mind; I have a fondness for her, you see, and if she conducts herself properly from this time out, I shall probably not feel obliged to break up the furniture more than once in a quarter. And now," he added, receiving with full

253

appreciation the speaking look of reproof cast at him by his promised bride, "if you will be good enough to tell us why you have interrupted us—"

"Yes—to be sure, sir!" Mrs. Yarden collected her flustered thoughts. "It's about the post-chaise you said when you came in you was wishful to have at once—and ready at the door it is this minute—"

"Thank you!" said Northover. "We shall be down directly."

His tone did not encourage her to linger, and she was therefore obliged to curtsey herself out, with one last reluctant glance of curiosity at the very improper couple she was leaving behind her. Lydia turned laughing, self-conscious eyes upon Northover.

"Kit, we are abominable!" she said. "The poor woman! What on earth must she think of us?"

"On the whole," the Viscount said, considering, "I believe she thinks you a foolhardy young woman to undertake to share bed and board with a brute like me. But, on the other hand, I have Harlbury on *my* side, for he *did* say, you will recall, when he offered for you, that he was afraid he would be driven to murder if he were obliged to live with you."

Miss Leyland favoured him with a glance of great severity. "Yes, I *saw* the look in your eye when he said that," she accused him. "And you *are* a brute to laugh at me, for, after all, I only did what was necessary to bring Bayard back. How was I to know that Harlbury would be so nonsensical as to feel himself obliged to offer for me?"

"How indeed?" agreed Northover, his eyes alight. "It is only what any young woman of sense would have known. How happy I am that I have never been tempted to marry a young woman of sense!"

"But I *am*—" Lydia began indignantly; but her words were stopped very rudely indeed by the Viscount, who pulled her into his arms and kissed her with such ardour that it seemed, after a few moments, quite redundant to continue the argument.

"And now," he said presently, releasing her at last and

gazing down at her with the regretful look of a man resolutely deciding to place duty above inclination, "we must really be off to Great Hayland, if my plan to lend respectability to this day's work is to succeed. I have even hired a post-chaise for you, you see, so that you will not be obliged to ride in an open carriage at this hour." He picked up the Italian straw confection that had begun the day so charmingly, but was now in a somewhat bedraggled condition, owing to the rough treatment it had sustained, and looked at it unfavourably. "Is this your bonnet? I cannot feel that Cupitt will approve of my bringing home a bride with such a dispirited creation upon her head," he was going on—but he was interrupted at that moment by a horrified exclamation from Lydia.

"Cupitt!" she ejaculated. "Good heavens, Kit, you *cannot* be bringing this houseful of people down on him and Mrs. Cupitt without warning! And not only *us*—I mean Bayard and Grandmama and me—but Lord and Lady Gilmour, as well! He will go mad, and I shall not blame him in the least!"

"Nor I," said Northover, looking at his love with his eyes again alight. "But it may be as well, after all, for him to accustom himself to such things if he intends to remain in my employ, for I have a decided presentiment that, once you are Lady Northover, he will be under the necessity of steeling himself to sustain even more disconcerting events. I know *I* am already endeavouring to do so myself."

"Wretch!" said Miss Leyland, blushing.

It was an appellation, however, which the Viscount scarcely seemed to resent, for his only response to it was to kiss her once more.